A World of TROUBLE

DON'T MISS OUT ON ANY OF THE MISCHIEF!

THE BAD APPLE

A WORLD OF TROUBLE

Merits of Mischief

#2

A World of TROUBLE

T. R. BURNS

ALADDIN

NEW YORK LONDON TORONTO SYDNEY NEW DELHI

ALADDIN
An imprint of Simon & Schuster Children's Publishing Division
1230 Avenue of the Americas, New York, NY 10020
First Aladdin hardcover edition May 2013

For information about special discounts for bulk purchases, please contact Simon & Schuster Special Sales at 1-866-506-1949 or business@simonandschuster.com.
The Simon & Schuster Speakers Bureau can bring authors to your live event. For more information or to book an event contact the Simon & Schuster Speakers Bureau at 1-866-248-3049 or visit our website at www.simonspeakers.com.
Designed by Karina Granda
The text of this book was set in Bembo.
Manufactured in the United States of America 0713 FFG
2 4 6 8 10 9 7 5 3 1
Library of Congress Cataloging-in-Publication Data
Burns, T. R., 1978–
A world of trouble / by T.R. Burns. — First Aladdin hardcover edition.
p. cm. — (Merits of mischief ; book 2)
Summary: More mischief and trouble abound during Seamus Hinkle's second semester at Kilter Academy, where the students earn credit for behaving badly and the adults are keeping huge secrets.
ISBN 978-1-4424-4032-6 (hc)
[1. Behavior—Fiction. 2. Boarding schools—Fiction. 3. Schools—Fiction. 4. Tricks—Fiction. 5. Humorous stories.] I. Title.
PZ7.B937455Wo 2013
[Fic]—dc23
2012031542
ISBN 978-1-4424-4034-0 (eBook)

For Sean E. Boy

ACKNOWLEDGMENTS

Many talented Troublemakers earned many demerits bringing this story to readers. At the top of the class are Rebecca Sherman and the crafty crew at Writers House; Liesa Abrams, Mara Anastas, Lucille Rettino, Carolyn Swerdloff, Lydia Finn, Matt Pantoliano, and the other Aladdin rabble rousers; and my extremely mischievous and supremely supportive family and friends.

Thank you all. Now stop reading and start acting up.

Chapter 1

My face is melting. The goopy blob that was my forehead is slipping south, its molten heat softening everything in its path. I'm literally liquefying, right here, in the back parking lot of Shell's Belles.

Okay, maybe not literally. That'd leave a pretty big mess, which is what I'm trying to avoid. That's why I'm still wearing this helmet when all I really want to do is rip off what's left of my head and chuck it in the Dumpster I'm hiding behind.

"Soft as silk! How *do* you do it?"

Merits of Mischief

A familiar voice crackles in my ear. I sit up straight, swipe one hand across the helmet's tinted face shield. My view's still fuzzy, so I flip up the plastic, rub my thumb over the damp interior, and lower it again. Through the small window I watch the teenager lounging in the purple salon chair. He holds a gossip magazine in one hand and pets his hair with the other. Grins at the young woman who stands over him with a comb and scissors, then at his reflection in the mirrored wall. Raises his palm for a high five, and gets one.

A good Troublemaker is an invisible Troublemaker. That was the first thing Houdini, my math teacher, told me when he found me standing on a bench in baggage claim and waving both arms three days ago. Apparently, he missed his own memo.

"What do you think about upping the cool factor?" Houdini asks.

"The cool factor?" the stylist repeats.

"Like with a blue streak. Or a lightning bolt. Or a blue lightning bolt."

"You mean . . . in your hair?"

Houdini laughs. The stylist laughs. I roll my eyes, settle back in my seat, and wonder why I'm surprised. After all, like most of my new teachers, Houdini's only a few years older than I am.

He might have a grown-up job, but he's a kid. Kids break rules. Even their own, I guess.

Still, if I'd known he was going to get a makeover before doing what we'd come here to do, I would've asked to stay at the hotel. Where there's air-conditioning. A mini fridge. Bottomless buckets of ice.

I'm considering dunking my head in the dirty snowbank next to the Dumpster, ostrich-style, when the bell above the back door jingles. A woman walks out. She wears a white velvet coat with a black fur collar. Her blond hair, newly done, forms a stiff half-moon around her head. She pinches a cell phone between her thumb and pointer finger. Against the parking lot's gray backdrop, her red nails glitter like rubies.

Or maybe even apples. Perfect, shiny . . . *powerful* apples.

For a split second I picture the woman falling, her body slamming into the frozen pavement, her face twisting in pain. The image is so vivid I start to stand, to go toward her. But then I remember where I am. Why we're here. And I stop.

"She's leaving," I hiss into the helmet's small microphone.

I listen for a response. None comes. All I hear in the earpiece is muffled chitchat and country music.

The woman pauses by a shiny SUV. I tear my eyes away and scan the salon's windows. They're cloudy—but I can still see that Houdini's chair is empty.

"Target's on the move," I say, louder this time. "Do you copy?"

I hear guitars strumming. Fiddles plucking. Ladies giggling. I glance back and hold my breath as the woman unlocks her car. My responsibility for this leg of the mission is not to let her out of my sight—even if that means leaving Houdini behind. So I slide forward. I take the silver handles in both hands and place one foot on the kick-start lever. I relax slightly when her cell phone rings, thinking I've won more time, but right after she answers it and gets in her car, the engine hums and brake lights illuminate.

"Um, hello? Houdini? I know you're busy, but the lady? The one we're following? I think she's about to leave."

The warmth of my breath combined with the heat radiating from my face creates a new, wet coating inside my helmet shield. As quickly as I wipe it away, a fresh one forms.

I can't see. I can't see, and I'm supposed to drive this scooter, which resembles a fighter jet on wheels, through a strange town. Across ice and snow. Without drawing attention to myself or losing my target, who, given the way her tires are currently sending dirt and pebbles spiraling through the air, is in a hurry. Worrying about this only makes my heart thump faster, which makes me hotter, which makes it even harder to see.

I'm here because I'm the best of the best. Because I can do things other kids my age can't—or so I've been told.

But it's clear a mistake has been made. Again.

"I'm so sorry," I say, watching the gray film before me thicken, "but you've got the wrong guy. I can't—"

The scooter dips suddenly. I drop both feet to the ground and squeeze the handles. Houdini's voice sounds behind me and echoes in my ear.

"I don't. You can. And winners never apologize."

The scooter bolts forward. My boots skid across pavement. I really hope this thing can be steered from the backseat, because if not, we're about to become Kentucky roadkill.

"So I think I get it!" Houdini calls out.

The scooter jerks to the left, then the right. Fighting wind and gravity, I pull up my boots, find the footrests.

"Get what?" I call back.

"The high maintenance! My hair's never looked this good!"

"Well, I *don't* get it! I thought we were supposed to stay invisible!"

"We are!"

"But you followed her inside! And sat right next to her!"

The scooter hits a rock. We sail through the air. Eventually the scooter drops to the ground and speeds up again.

"Sometimes being seen is the best way not to be seen!"

This makes no sense. I might point that out, but then we round a curve and tilt sharply. My body's pulled down and to the right. I hug the bike with both legs. Release my fingers, lean forward, and wrap my arms around the handles. Close my eyes, even though it's as dark as night inside my helmet.

"I was one of the girls!" Houdini continues. "I had to be—the supply closet was in full view of the rest of the salon. It was safer to do that and win their trust than it was to sneak around. We can't get into trouble before we've made any ourselves!"

I'm not sure how to respond, so I don't. We cruise along for several minutes. I don't ask where we're going or what we'll do when we get there, and Houdini doesn't tell me. All I know is what he shared when I woke up this morning: Today we finish what we started three days ago. And as soon as we're done, I can go home . . . where a very different sort of trouble waits for me.

"You're up."

I blink. A mental picture of Mom biting into a fat cheeseburger disappears.

"So I am." I note that we're no longer moving—and that I'm still vertical on the bike and not horizontal on the side of the road. "Nice driving."

"Phenomenal, actually. But that's not what I meant."

I slide off my helmet and find Houdini standing next to me. I peer past him to the small red house with white shutters. I've spent fifty of the last seventy-two hours monitoring live video feed of the property's occupants and activity, so I know the home almost as well as I know my own. That, however, doesn't make it any less strange to be parked behind a bush at the end of its driveway.

"Everything looks okay," I say. "Sounds it too."

At which point a door slams. A familiar voice yells. High heels hit the floor like bullets to a concrete wall.

Houdini holds a purple purse toward me. "Don't worry. I emptied it for its owner before filling it up again."

I take the bag. Unzip it. "You said you were getting weapons."

"I did. You're welcome."

I pull out a short, plastic tube. Thanks to Mom's endless pursuit of fuller, bouncier hair, I actually know what it is. "A roller? What am I supposed to do with this?"

"You're the marksman. You'll figure it out."

Snow flurries drift around us, but a fresh layer of sweat spreads across my face anyway. Houdini must notice because he steps toward me and offers more explanation.

"Bows and arrows? Paintball rifles? Water grenades? They're great, but generic. They can do damage to anyone, anywhere. If you want to make a lasting impact, it's always better to personalize." He shrugs. "Plus, try getting a metal Frisbee through airport security."

"Boomaree," I mumble.

"What?"

I drop the roller back in the purse. "Frisbees are for kids." This is something Ike, my tutor, told me back at Kilter. "Boomarees are part Frisbee, part boomerang. They're for Troublemakers."

Houdini grins. "You can rock this, Hinkle."

Can I? Maybe. In the past few months I've definitely done things I never thought I would.

But do I *want* to?

A scream shatters the snowy stillness. And just like that, I stop thinking and start moving.

I put on the helmet, throw the purse over one shoulder. I stoop, then shoot forward. As I run, I keep one eye on the ground and the other on the shadowy figures hurrying behind pulled curtains.

"IV in Q3." Inside my helmet, Houdini's voice is steady yet urgent. "ML in Q2—scratch that. ML backtracking to Q1."

He must be watching the live feed on his K-Pak. I translate quickly. IV is Innocent Victim, also known as Molly, an eleven-year-old only child. Q3 is Quadrant 3, or the bedrooms in the rear of the house. ML is Mother Lubbard, our target. Q2 is Quadrant 2, the combined living and dining room, and Q1 is Quadrant 1, the kitchen.

I'm so busy decoding Houdini's locations I don't think about what they mean until I'm in the backyard, crouched beneath the living room window. Through the lace curtains I watch Mrs. Lubbard storm from the kitchen. Then I glance behind me to confirm that Mr. Lubbard is in his usual spot: the small woodshed, where he pretends to build bookcases while actually playing poker online.

"D2 washed the white sweater," Houdini says.

I turn back. "Wasn't she supposed to?"

"The cotton cardigan, not the cashmere V-neck. ML's freaking because the sweater shrunk ten sizes."

"Then maybe she should give it to her daughter. As a thank-you for everything else Molly—IV—has done right."

"A good mother probably would."

But this, we know, isn't Mrs. Lubbard. After all, a good mother doesn't treat her daughter like an overworked, under-paid employee. She doesn't demand that her indentured servant vacuum, dust, mop, and scrub every window in the house every single day, before the young girl's even done her homework—and then punish her when she finds a rolled oat on the floor or a smudge on the glass. And she definitely doesn't do all this when her real priorities are spending hours at the salon, soaking in bubble baths, and recovering from the exertion with daily two-hour naps.

Mr. Lubbard, of course, is no prize himself. But he hides out mostly to get away from the missus, so if we fix her, there's a good chance we fix him, too.

"ML and IV en route to Q4."

Houdini sounds even more serious now. Once I translate, I know why.

Quadrant 4 is the basement.

"Copy," I say. And then I run.

I reach the back door outside just as Mrs. Lubbard and Molly reach the basement door inside. Mrs. Lubbard flings open the entrance to her daughter's worst nightmare. Molly's back hits the opposite wall. Her head shakes back and forth.

I reach into the purse.

Two shots. One to break the door's small window, and one to teach this mother a lesson she'll never forget. That's all it'll take.

My fingers find what feels like a thick rubber band. They keep digging until they hit the purse's hardest, heaviest item, which turns out to be a jar of lime-green goop. On the way out, they snag something long and prickly.

An elastic hair tie. Pauline's Pear Pomade. A metal comb. These are my weapons.

"IV WW about to commence," Houdini says.

Waterworks. Molly's about to cry.

I slip the hair tie around the jar. Hook my left thumb on the elastic and pull back the jar with my right hand. Raise both arms. Close one eye. Aim.

"*ML* WW about to commence?"

Mrs. Lubbard's about to cry?

I lower my weapon and lean toward the door. Houdini's right. Our target's face crumples as she holds out one hand, examines her fingers, and fans her eyes. Molly steps toward her, concerned.

"Now, Hinkle," Houdini urges. "Her defenses are down. Take your shot."

I start to aim again—and then stop. Because what am I doing? Who am I to try to teach anyone—but especially an adult I've never even met—anything? What do I really know about this family? I know what I saw on video, but what about everything our cameras didn't catch? What if Molly was a total terror last week? What if all that we've seen the past three days, all the yelling and fighting and demanding, is simply one desperate mother's way of dealing with her out-of-control daughter?

Parent-kid relationships can be complicated. I get that. I've *lived* that. And I don't want to make this one any worse.

"Start the scooter," I tell Houdini, already running. "It's not happening."

"What do you mean it's not—?" He pauses. "You've got to be kidding."

"Nope. Sorry. I tried to tell you I wasn't cut out for—"

"Fingernails."

My earpiece must be malfunctioning. I tap the side of my helmet. "What?"

"ML's fingernails. She pretended to give a flashlight to IV, and when she yanked it away, her nails brushed against the wall. Her manicure's ruined. That's why she's crying."

Houdini's voice sounds different. Not just serious. Nervous, too. It makes my feet slow beneath me.

"Now she's yelling," he continues. "She's got IV by the elbow. She's pushing her toward the stairs."

My feet come to a stop. I stand there and listen—to Houdini's play-by-play. Molly's whimpers. Soon a door slams. The deck shakes.

Molly falls silent.

"She's in the basement," I say.

"Yes," Houdini confirms.

"Where she can't reach the overhead light."

"Correct."

"And she's so scared of the dark she needs three lamps on just to fall asleep at night."

"Right."

I take a deep breath. "Get her out through the storm door. I'll take care of Mom."

When Houdini informed me earlier that I'd be the one teaching Mrs. Lubbard the ultimate lesson, and I asked how I was supposed to do that, all he said was that I'd know once the moment was right. I didn't believe him.

Until now.

For the next ninety seconds, I don't think about what I'm doing. I just do it. I follow along the side of the house, peeking in windows to monitor ML's progress. By the time she reaches the marble vanity in the bathroom, I'm in position, locked and loaded. As she sits on the velvet-cushioned stool, I slide open the window and take aim.

The elastic hair tie makes for a stellar slingshot. I use it to fire everything Houdini swiped from the salon, including Pauline's Pear Pomade. Nail files. Curlers. Cans of hair spray. Combs. Brushes. I'm careful not to hit my target directly, but I don't mind when the weapons fly around Mrs. Lubbard so fast she twists and turns and falls off the stool. And while she's not struck, the same can't be said about her precious beauty supplies. Jars of lotion break. Perfume bottles shatter. Tubs of powder shoot up and fall back down, releasing thick white clouds. I discover a clump of bobby pins near the bottom of the purse and fire them at the small lightbulbs framing the mirror. I break all but one so that Mrs. Lubbard can see what happens next.

A bottle of nail polish slams into the middle of the mirror. Red liquid drips down the cracked glass. A note, scribbled in lipstick on a piece of hair foil, stays in place with fake-eyelash glue.

Mrs. Lubbard is curled in a ball on the floor. Her arms cover her head. Her shoulders tremble. She stays like that for a few seconds, then gets up slowly, tiptoes to the mirror, and leans forward to read the message.

It's pretty good, if I do say so myself.

> Think you pay a price to look nice?
> Not BEING nice can put you in the poorhouse.
> Make it up to Molly. Or lose everything.

Mrs. Lubbard stands up straight. Presses the fingers of one hand to her lips. Looks around.

By the time her gaze turns toward the window, I'm gone.

Chapter 2

DEMERITS: 200
GOLD STARS: 0

TO: shinkle@kilteracademy.org
FROM: kommissary@kilteracademy.org
SUBJECT: *Très chic! Magnifique!*

Bonjour, Monsieur Seamus!

Once upon a time, Beauty and the Beast met, fell in love, and lived happily ever after.

That was then. This is now. And you, Seamus Hinkle, are a million times scarier than the oversize

> fur ball that held Belle captive. The only thing your Beauty—otherwise known as one Mrs. Lubbard of Hoyt, Kentucky—could ever love about you is the fact that you're gone. Way to go!

I stop reading. Lower my K-Pak to my chest. Look at the ceiling.

I'm a million times scarier than the Beast? A tall, terrifying monster that could rip his pretty prey to shreds if he wanted to? Really?

The thought's so confusing I want another one to push it aside. So I pick up my handheld computer and finish the note.

> Every demerit and gold star you earn is recorded and stored forever in Kilter's virtual filing cabinet, but to give all students a fair shake at a fresh start, your tallies return to zero at the end of each semester. Now, with an agonizing week and a half to go before school resumes, you already have a solid lead on your classmates! For successfully completing your first real-world combat

> mission—and teaching one power-hungry mother a lesson she won't soon forget—you received 200 demerits. With no gold stars to subtract, you have 200 credits.
>
> If only all equations were this simple, right? Well, just take Marla off speed dial next semester, and they can be!

I think of Marla, Kilter's phone operator. I haven't spoken to her in days. I kind of miss her. Does she have K-Mail? Maybe I should send her a quick note.

My K-Pak screen flashes. I look down and see a small camera icon. When I press it, a photo of a hair dryer appears.

I keep reading.

> Given your recent activity, we thought you might want to expand your troublemaking arsenal. Which is why we're superstoked to recommend the Kilter Koiffurator! You can load it with the ammo of your choice (we prefer peanut butter) or leave it empty and fire hot air. Either way, with an

impressive fifteen-foot range, it's guaranteed to give your target a whole new look—Seamus-style! And at 195 credits, it's practically free.

Consider it a gift. 'Tis the season, after all!

At Your Service,

The Kommissary Krew

Before I can decide whether to save or delete the e-mail, my K-Pak buzzes with a new message.

TO: shinkle@kilteracademy.org

FROM: loliver@kilteracademy.org

SUBJECT: hey

S—

My flames of combat have been successfully extinguished.

Yours?

—L

I smile as I respond.

TO: loliver@kilteracademy.org
FROM: shinkle@kilteracademy.org
SUBJECT: RE: hey

Hi, Lemon!

How are you?? What was your mission? Where'd Fern take you? I can't wait to hear all about it!

Mine was good. Accomplished. And pretty fun, actually. I'll tell you everything when we get back to school.

Happy holidays!

—Your Favorite Roommate

I reread the note, check for typos. My eyes stop at "when we get back to school," and stay there. This hesitation reminds me of another e-mail I've been meaning to write. So I send Lemon's and start a new one.

TO: parsippany@cloudviewschools.net
FROM: shinkle@kilteracademy.org
SUBJECT: Hi!

Dear Miss Parsippany,

Thank you so much for writing me back. After what I did, I'd understand if you never wanted to talk to me again.

I stop typing. What I did was the worst possible thing anyone could ever do to someone else. For months I felt terrible about it. And guilty. And lonely. Now, five days after learning the truth, I'm still getting used to the fact that it's something I only *thought* I did. And that I don't have to feel terrible, guilty, or lonely anymore.

Grinning, I delete the last sentence. I'm still thinking about what to replace it with when the coffeemaker downstairs starts beeping. I look up and check the window across the darkened room. The pulled shade is glowing.

It's time.

This is one message I don't want to rush. So I save it and put my K-Pak on the nightstand. I get up and make the bed. I put on my bathrobe and swing by the dresser mirror, lingering long enough to wipe the crusties from my eyes and comb my hair.

"You can do this," my reflection and I tell each other.

My only other option is to hide out in my room forever, so I do it. I cross the room. Open the door. Go downstairs.

And see my parents for the first time since the last time. When I wondered if I'd ever want to see them again.

"A little to the left," Mom says.

"Got it," Dad says.

"Too far. Back to the right."

"Okeydoke."

My heart thumps faster. Mom's sitting on the couch in the living room, coffee cup in hand. Dad's standing on a step stool, straightening the crocheted angel on top of the tree. The fireplace is lit. Stuffed stockings hang from the mantel. The ancient record player spins scratchy carols. Shiny presents wait to be opened.

Somehow, it looks like nothing's changed.

"For heaven's sake, Eliot." Mom starts to stand. "Let me do it. It has to be absolutely perfect in case—"

"Merry Christmas."

Mom falls back on the couch. Dad teeters on the step stool. "Jingle Bells" skips on the record player. I walk down the remaining stairs and into the room.

"Seamus?" Mom's eyes are wide. Her mouth is open. I'm

pretty sure she thinks I'm the Ghost of Christmas Past.

"Son?" Dad grins and hugs the tree for balance.

"When did you . . . ?" Mom asks. "How did you . . . ?"

"Last night," I say. "Kilter car service. It was really late and I didn't want to wake you, so I just let myself in and went to bed."

This is followed by a long pause. I'm about to apologize for sneaking in when they both come at me like they're the twelve-year-olds and I'm the pony they've been begging Santa for. There are hugs. Kisses. Claps on the back. It's like a cheesy scene out of *It's a Wonderful Life*, one of Mom's favorite black-and-white holiday movies.

And you know something? I kind of like it.

"Would you like some hot chocolate?" Mom asks.

"Sure."

"How about some gifts?" Dad asks.

"Okay."

I have to admit, it feels a little weird diving into our regular Christmas morning routine without referring to where I've been, what I've been doing, and why. My parents and I have things to talk about, so much to figure out . . . But what's a few minutes more? No matter what, we have to move forward. And maybe the best way to do that is to ignore how we got to the present. At least for a little while.

The morning's so merry I start to think this really might be true. But then I open my last gift: a fancy label maker Dad ordered from his favorite office supply website. The box flaps are sealed in five layers of tape, like he was so excited he worried he might rip them open and keep the gadget for himself. Neither of us can tear through the security shield, so I hurry to the kitchen for a pair of scissors.

They're not in their usual spot in the ceramic utensil jar. Thinking she might've misplaced them after a tiring clipping session, I check Mom's coupon drawer. They're there—but I have to dig through more than coupons to find them.

"Hey, sport!" Dad exclaims. "Your pops really did a number on this box. You might want to bring a knife, too!"

I don't bring a knife. I don't bring scissors either.

I bring something I was obviously never supposed to see.

"You knew?"

Mom's stuffing ripped wrapping paper into a garbage bag. Dad's fiddling with the label maker box. Both stop and look at me when I speak.

I hold up my discovery. "Why didn't you say anything?"

Dad's bushy brows lower. His narrowed eyes shift from me, to Mom, and back to me. "What are you talking about, son? What do you have there?"

"The *Cloudview Chronicle*."

"But it's Christmas," Dad says. "The paper doesn't come today."

"It didn't." I look at Mom, who's stuffing the garbage bag again. "It's from October."

"October!" Dad claps his hands to his thighs and tilts back in his chair. "And I'm usually so on top of the recycling."

"Mom put it in a place no one but her ever checks."

"The coupon drawer?" Dad asks. "But that's only for—"

"Coupons. Right." Mom bends down and yanks a shiny green ball from the floor. "The paper had a special section that day. Lots of deals with no expiration dates. So rather than clip each one, I decided to—"

She's cut off by the sharp smack of the *Chronicle* hitting the coffee table. The newspaper's folded in thirds. One article's circled in red marker. Two red exclamation points follow the headline.

"'Local Substitute Breaks Up Brawl, Praised for Bravery,'" Dad reads. He leans forward and squints at the photo. "Huh. She looks familiar."

“She should,” I say. “She’s Miss Parsippany.”

Dad’s eyes meet mine. He waits for me to correct myself. When I don’t, he presses his palms to the sides of his head, like he wants to keep his brain intact. He skims the article, flips to the front page, and returns to the circled story. I watch Mom, who’s now sorting through albums by the record player.

“Bing?” she asks. “Frank? What do you think?”

“I think I’d like to know what’s going on,” I say.

It takes Mom a long time to answer. First she examines the back of each record cover. Then she puts Crosby in the cabinet, slides Sinatra from the paper sleeve, and dusts the vinyl with the hem of her bathrobe. After that she places the record on the turntable, lowers the needle to the spinning disc, and sways side to side as “I’ll Be Home for Christmas” fills the room. It’s only when Sinatra starts repeating the same note that she seems to snap out of her trance. She adjusts the needle and finally turns around.

“It’s no biggie,” she says.

“But Miss Parsippany’s alive. And she shouldn’t be. That’s why you sent me away, because I . . .” My voice fades. It’s still so hard to say, even though I’ve had five days to wrap my head around the truth. I try again, forcing the words from my mouth before they can shoot back down my throat. "Because I supposedly killed her."

Mom crosses the room and sits in the armchair by the fireplace. "Principal Gubbins called the night of the cafeteria incident to tell us that Miss Parsippany was still unconscious. Chances of her waking up were slim. Annika was making a special, rare exception in accepting a student after the semester had already started, and she needed a decision right away. I didn't want you to miss the chance to attend the best reform school in the country, so I enrolled you without waiting to hear that your substitute teacher had officially passed."

If Kilter's a reform school, I'm Frosty the Snowman. But unlike this one, that conversation can wait.

"But once you knew she was okay," I say, "why didn't you come get me?"

Mom shrugs. "Because you threw the apple."

"Because I saw Miss Parsippany heading for the fight. She was small. The kids were big. I wanted to break it up before anyone got hurt."

"You could've run for other teachers."

"There was no time."

"You could've yelled across the cafeteria."

"It was too noisy."

Sinatra starts hiccupping again. As Dad jumps up and hurries to the record player, I consider what Mom's implying. She knows I didn't kill anyone, but she doesn't know everything I did at Kilter—intentionally or otherwise. Which means . . .

"You think I'm a bad kid. Still."

Her head tilts to one side. The corners of her eyes soften. "I think no one's perfect. And a little self-improvement, whatever its motivation, is never a bad thing."

"What about Parents' Day?"

"What about it?"

I take a deep breath. Here it comes: the question I've been struggling to guess the answer to for weeks. It's a million times more perplexing now.

"Why did you tell everyone I was a murderer?"

She sips her coffee. Rolls it around her mouth. Swallows. "I didn't know you hadn't told your classmates."

"Still. Parents' Day was in November. You knew then that it wasn't true, and you said it anyway."

"I was nervous. Excited. It just came out."

She says this lightly, easily, like it was a silly joke people laughed at, then forgot. But they didn't forget. Lemon, Abe, Gabby, Elinor . . . They didn't talk to me after that. They barely looked at me.

Mom stands up. She comes over to me, puts her arms around my shoulders, and kisses the top of my head. "I'm sorry. It was an accident."

An accident. I can relate, can't I?

I'm still trying to decide, when the doorbell rings. Down the hall, the front door opens and closes. Heavy footsteps thump toward us. A low voice calls out, "Ho, ho, ho!"

And my worst nightmare comes to life. Again.

"Bartholomew John?"

He freezes just outside the living room, his face hidden behind the bright red petals of the poinsettia plant he's holding.

"What are you doing here?" I look up at Mom. "What is he doing here?"

Her face is white. Still around my shoulders, her arm is tense.

"BJ works part-time at Cloudview Cards and Carnations." Dad hurries past us. "He meets all our houseplant needs—at half price."

It's a good thing Mom has me in a vise grip, because I can't feel my legs. My head swirls with images. I barely make out soggy fish sticks. A mouthful of braces behind a lopsided sneer. Fists flailing and apples flying.

"But it's Christmas," I say, fighting to keep my voice—and legs—steady.

"Cards and Carnations is open three hundred and sixty-five days a year." Dad's voice is bright. Happy. Without the slightest hint of surprise or confusion.

"Is that why he was here on Thanksgiving?"

Mom's arm falls from my shoulders. She steps back. "How do you—?"

"I heard him. In the background. When I called."

"You called on Thanksgiving?" Now Dad sounds confused. He looks at Mom. "I thought Kilter didn't permit phone privileges."

"They made an exception for the holiday," I lie. Considering the situation, it seems necessary. "But service is pretty bad up there. You probably couldn't hear me before I got cut off completely."

This is followed by a long pause. Even the record player, in between songs, is silent.

"I'm sorry."

I really am sleeping. That has to be it. I'm sleeping, and all of this—the newspaper, Mom leaving me at Kilter for no reason, my arch-nemesis standing in our living room—is a dream. It's the only possible explanation.

"That's why I came over on Thanksgiving," Bartholomew John continues. "I know that apple was meant for me, not Miss Parsippany. I shouldn't have been fighting with those other kids, and you were just trying to stop us."

He hands the poinsettia to Dad, revealing his face. It looks different. Longer. Straighter. Maybe because it's not laughing or scowling. He clasps his hands behind his back, and for a split second, seems to peer past me. I glance over my shoulder and wonder if Mom really nods at him, or if I imagine that, too.

"It's my fault you were sent away," Bartholomew John says as I turn back. "And I wanted to apologize to your parents in person. And now I want to apologize to you."

My arms hang at my sides. Moving slowly, carefully, so no one notices, I press one palm to one leg. I take a small piece of flesh between the tips of my thumb and pointer finger, and squeeze.

It hurts.

"How'd you know I'd be home today?" I ask.

"I didn't. I just stopped by to deliver the plant. But I figured you'd come home eventually, and whenever you did, I'd tell you how sorry I am."

"Have you been here since Thanksgiving? And before today?"

"A few times. Your parents are good customers."

"Do you always let yourself in?"

"He rang the bell," Mom offers. "But he probably thought we didn't hear it over the music. So rather than let our pretty poinsettia freeze to death on the front stoop, he tried the door himself. Isn't that right, Bartholomew John?"

She smiles. He smiles.

"Best customer service in town," Dad says, placing the plant on the coffee table.

"I'm going to make breakfast." Mom heads for the kitchen. "Why don't you boys sit? You have a lot to chat about over the next ten days."

The next ten days? If our visit has a time limit . . . that means Mom thinks we'll be parting ways when school starts again.

Ignoring Bartholomew John, who snatches a candy cane from the Christmas tree before flopping onto the couch, I look at Dad. His eyes are lowered to the newspaper next to the poinsettia. I hope he'll say that nothing's set in stone. That since I didn't kill anyone I shouldn't have been sent away in the first place and so definitely don't need to be sent away again.

But he doesn't say this. He doesn't say anything.

"Be right back," I say. "Just want to take a shower."

As I start upstairs, I think about my parents. Bartholomew John. Lemon, Abe, and Gabby. Annika, Ike, and Houdini. Elinor. I'm so distracted, when I reach my bedroom door I almost trip over the brown package on the floor.

My palm hits the wall for balance. I bend down for a closer look. A small card rests on top of the package. My name's on it. I look up and down the hallway, like a mischievous elf is hiding nearby waiting to see my reaction. Not spotting any pointy ears or shoes, I take the card and read it.

Dear Seamus,

Please accept this as a small token of our great appreciation. We can't wait to see what you achieve next semester!

Fondly,

Your Kilter Family

The handwriting's familiar, but I can't place it. I slide the card into my bathrobe pocket, bring the package into my room, and close the door.

The token, I soon find out, isn't small at all. It's the Kilter Icickler, a long, skinny device that turns water into frozen daggers with the push of one button and launches them with the push of another. I picked up a display model in the Kommissary once and put it right back when I saw that it cost two thousand credits.

If weapons can be considered gifts, this one's great. Part of me is even tempted to try it out in the backyard. Maybe with Bartholomew John as my target.

But I don't. I put the Icickler back in the box, slide the box under my bed, and head for the shower.

Chapter 3

DEMERITS: 200
GOLD STARS: 0

You know those lists Santa Claus has? That separate naughty kids from nice ones so there's no confusion about who gets what when December 25 rolls around? Well, I think the big guy finally went digital and experienced a major computer malfunction that jumbled everything up. Because, given all the trouble I've made, there's no question which list I should be on—or that I don't even deserve the lump of coal normal bad kids get. Yet somehow, the presents keep coming.

First there's the Icickler. Then there's the Flake Kompressor, a large contraption that can pack an entire snowdrift into a single snowball. Next comes a set of Kringle Stars, which look like they belong on top of Christmas trees but have tips sharp enough to pin heavy stockings to marble fireplace mantels. After that are K-Puffs, marshmallows that morph into pellets suitable for BB gun or slingshot use when dunked in hot liquid. Every day a new package wrapped in plain brown paper appears by my bedroom door. And every day I shove another tempting trouble-making item under my bed or into my closet. I don't mention them and neither do my parents, which makes how they arrive just as puzzling as who they're from.

This goes on for a week. Then, on New Year's Eve, I run out of hiding spots.

"Come on," I mumble, leaning all my weight into the latest delivery.

But it's no use. The package is too big. My closet's too full. Giving up, I flop on my bed, take my K-Pak from the nightstand, and start a new message.

TO: ike@kilteracademy.org
FROM: shinkle@kilteracademy.org
SUBJECT: Thanks, and . . .

Hi, Ike!

I don't want to interrupt your vacation, but I just had to thank you for all the sniper supplies you've been sending. They're awesome!

I also wanted to ask a favor. I don't know if you plan to send anything else, but if you do, would it be too much trouble to ship it to school instead of my house? Kilter's cover will definitely be blown if my mom finds any of this stuff, and that's a real possibility because her preferred hobbies are cleaning and organizing.

Thanks again!

From,

Seamus

I send the message. Almost instantly, my K-Pak buzzes with a response.

TO: shinkle@kilteracademy.org

FROM: ike@kilteracademy.org

SUBJECT: RE: Thanks, and . . .

Hey, Seamus!

Sounds like someone has a secret Santa! Would love to take credit, but I've been skiing with the fam and haven't thought about Kilter since we left. (No offense.)

BTW, can't wait to hear about the mission. I expect details our first day back!

—Ike

Huh. The packages have been unmarked, with no addresses or other hints of origin. I'd assumed that Ike, who introduced me to bows and arrows, paintball rifles, and the Boomaree back at Kilter, was sending them in hopes that I'd get a jumpstart on next semester. Apparently I was wrong.

I try again.

TO: houdini@kilteracademy.org
FROM: shinkle@kilteracademy.org
SUBJECT: Rewards?

Hi, Houdini!

Thanks again for taking me on my first combat mission. It was awesome!

Along those lines, do we get, like, prizes for completing missions? Just wondering because I've gotten a ton of troublemaking stuff since I've been home. If so, and if you have anything to do with it, thank you!! Also, is it possible to change the shipping address? My room's getting pretty crowded.

Happy New Year!

Seamus

I hit send. My K-Pak buzzes.

TO: shinkle@kilteracademy.org
FROM: houdini@kilteracademy.org
SUBJECT: RE: Rewards?

If we got prizes, I'd quit the teaching gig and only go on missions. Then I'd start a black market, hock supplies to the highest bidders, and buy a tropical island in the middle of the Pacific Ocean.

—H

Okay. I guess that's a no.

Next I try my friends.

TO: loliver@kilteracademy.org;
ahansen@kilteracademy.org;
gryan@kilteracademy.org
FROM: shinkle@kilteracademy.org
SUBJECT: Quick Question

Hi, guys!

Have you been getting mysterious brown packages? Filled with the kind of stuff the Kommissary sells?

Just wondering!

—Seamus

They must carry their K-Paks everywhere because I get replies immediately.

TO: shinkle@kilteracademy.org
FROM: loliver@kilteracademy.org
SUBJECT: RE: Quick Question

S—

Negative.

—L

TO: shinkle@kilteracademy.org;
loliver@kilteracademy.org;
gryan@kilteracademy.org
FROM: ahansen@kilteracademy.org
SUBJECT: WHAT DO YOU MEAN?

You've gotten mysterious brown packages? How many? When? What do they look like? What's inside?

This sounds serious. Also unfair.

—Abe

TO: shinkle@kilteracademy.org;
loliver@kilteracademy.org;
ahansen@kilteracademy.org
FROM: gryan@kilteracademy.org
SUBJECT: RE: Quick Question

OMG!!! Seamus, it's sooooo great to hear from you! How are you?? How was the mission??

I miss you all—yes, Abe, even you—sooooo much and can't WAIT for school to start! Three short days to go, yay!!

xoxo,

Gabby

It's just me. Again. There's only one person who's singled me out like this before, but after what she did—or didn't do—on my last day at Kilter, I'm not really in the mood to send that note.

But thinking of her does inspire me to send another.

TO: enorris@kilteracademy.org
FROM: shinkle@kilteracademy.org
SUBJECT: Hi!

Dear Elinor,

How are you? Are you having a nice vacation?

I just wanted to say hi. Also, I've been thinking about you all break and—

I stop typing. Delete the last sentence. Start again.

> Also, I've been wondering if you're okay. You were pretty badly hurt the last time I saw you, so I just want to make sure you're all better now.
>
> I hope you are! See you soon.
>
> From,
>
> Seamus

I reread the note and consider deleting "See you soon." I don't want to make promises I can't keep, and I'm still not sure about this one. But then I leave it and hit send. Because no matter what or where, I hope I do see Elinor. And sooner would be better than later.

I wait one minute. Two. Five. Unlike my other Kilter contacts, she must not be attached to her K-Pak. Or maybe she thinks it's weird that I wrote to her. Or that I waited so long to check in. In any case, my in-box stays silent.

At the seven-minute mark, I consider continuing Miss Parsippany's note, which I still haven't finished, for distraction. Before I can, there's a knock on my door.

"Dinner's almost ready!" Mom calls out.

"Be right there!" I call back.

Her footsteps head down the hall. I get up, retrieve my latest gift, a K-Plow, from the floor, and survey the room for a good hiding spot. I'm about to rearrange the weapons under my bed when my thumb hits a button on the K-Plow's handle. The large metal scoop, which looks exactly like the one at the end of Dad's snow shovel, shoots out and up. I fly back from the force.

"Whoa," I whisper.

I've been on my best behavior at home, so haven't tried out any of the Kilter gifts. Even though part of me has wanted to. But what harm can one little experiment do? Especially in my room with nobody around?

I dart to the door and crack it open. The hallway's empty. I can barely hear my parents' muffled voices. Satisfied, I close the door, dart to my bed, and grab a pillow. I stand in the middle of the room, place the pillow in the metal scoop, and dig my heels into the floor. Gripping the handle with both hands, I hold my breath and press the launch button.

I'm prepared this time, so the force only nudges back. Unfortunately, the same can't be said for the ceiling—which the feather-filled ammunition breaks through. Plaster flakes rain down. The pillow stays up.

In the dresser mirror, my reflection smiles.

Mom yells that dinner's on the table. I toss the K-Plow on my bed and cover it with blankets. I check my K-Pak once more and try not to care when there are no new messages.

And then I go downstairs. Where my disappointment is replaced with confusion.

"What's all this?" I ask.

Dad winks at Mom. She winks back. They're in the living room, which is decorated with balloons and streamers. The coffee table is set with plates and silverware. The fireplace and Christmas tree are lit. The television screen glows blue.

"Hinkles' Rockin' New Year's Eve!" my parents declare.

I blink. "What?"

"Like on TV," Dad explains. "With Times Square and the falling ball."

"You mean the show we tape and watch the next day because it's on too late?"

"Exactly," Mom says.

"I don't get it," I say.

"There's nothing to get." Mom takes a tray from the armchair ottoman. "We just thought it'd be fun to switch things up."

But what about tofu-and-broccoli casserole? Old Maid? One cup each of hot apple cider? All of which we enjoy in the dining room before going to bed at a reasonable hour, the way we do the last night of every year?

"Are those fish sticks?" I forget those questions as my eyes lock on the platter of orange rectangles.

"You like, yes?" Mom asks.

"Um, yes."

I drop to the floor by the coffee table. Dad sits across from me and Mom sits on the couch. Dad holds up silver party hats and noisemakers.

"Essential party wear," he says.

"And entertainment," Mom adds, reaching for the TV remote.

I look over my shoulder. Gasp.

"*Lord of the Rings*?" I ask.

"*The Two Towers*," Mom clarifies.

"But you think these movies glorify silly, violent fantasy worlds that give good kids bad ideas."

She shrugs. Smiles. "So?"

So nothing, I guess. If it's all right with her, I'm not about to complain.

For the next three hours, we eat, cheer on Frodo, and blow our noisemakers whenever Gollum hisses "my precious." It's fun. Probably the most fun my parents and I have ever had together. Which is why I don't wait for the end of the movie to stop the DVD.

"Bathroom break?" The question bursts from Dad's lips like he's been holding his breath. "Thank goodness!"

"Wait," I say as he starts to stand. "Please."

He perches on the edge of the couch. Mom leans forward. They look at me, a combination of curious and concerned.

"I want to stay," I say.

"It's late," Mom says. "No one's going anywhere."

"No, I mean . . . in three days. When school starts again. I want to stay here and go back to Cloudview."

Dad starts to smile. Then he glances at Mom, whose lips press so tightly together they practically disappear, and stops. I understand the mixed reactions. We haven't talked about school since Christmas morning. They didn't know I was having second thoughts—or any thoughts, for that matter.

"But you did so well at Kilter," Mom says.

"I did well at Cloudview, too."

"You said you liked your new classes and teachers."

"My old ones were fine."

"I already told Annika you'd be back."

"I'll tell her I changed my mind."

"Your friends will miss you."

A sharp pain pierces my chest. I almost look down to check for a Kringle Star.

"I'll miss them, too," I say.

Mom frowns. Dad crosses his arms over his lower abdomen. I try to explain.

"Kilter was great. Really. But the thing is, I was never supposed to go there. Since I didn't really kill Miss Parsippany." I smile and let that sink in. "And I'm not a bad kid. Sometimes I forget to put away my clean clothes or roll down the cereal bag inside the box. . . . But that doesn't make me bad. It just makes me a kid. Right?"

"Right." Dad nods.

I look at Mom. When her eyes stay lowered to her lap, I add one last thing.

"And as much as I'll miss my friends, I'd miss you guys more."

Mom smooths her skirt. Picks an invisible piece of lint from her sweater. Straightens the plastic HAPPY NEW YEAR! tiara on her head and says, "It's almost midnight. I better get the confetti ready."

She stands and goes to the kitchen. Dad slides down the couch and leans toward me.

"It's nine o'clock," I say.

"Your mother doesn't like going back on her word," he says.

"She'd rather not see me for five months?"

"I'm sure there will be more Parents' Days."

The corners of my mouth grow heavy. My chin puckers.

"Now, now." Dad pats my shoulder. "Kilter has a sterling reputation. Its alumni have gone on to the country's best universities. They've become doctors and lawyers and CEOs. You were a great kid when you got in, but who knows what you might become when you get out?"

I know. After all, Kilter trains every student to become one thing and one thing only.

And just like that, I know what I have to do.

"How about that bathroom break?" I ask. "Meet back here in five?"

I don't wait for his answer. I jump up and dash to the kitchen. It's empty, so I try the dining room and den. They're also empty, so I charge upstairs and down the hallway, glancing into every room I pass.

Mom's not in any of them. After following a series of mysterious thuds and thumps, I finally find her in the attic. Crouched in a crawl space. Hidden behind a mountain of dusty trunks and boxes. This seems like a pretty strange place to store confetti, but then, I don't really get her love of Brillo pads and color-coded sweater stacks, either.

A thick curtain of cobwebs hangs across the entrance. I push them aside with an abandoned clothes hanger.

"Mom, there's something I need to—"

Tell you. That's what I planned to say. Then I would've revealed all Kilter's best-kept secrets in hopes of making her see that it's not the place she thinks it is, that I really don't belong there.

But I don't say anything. I look around instead. At the scissors and tape. The rolls of brown wrapping paper. The dozens of unopened cartons all bearing the familiar silver KA logo.

Mom, kneeling before a pair of superstealth Kilter Knight-Vision Goggles, retail price: ten thousand credits.

"Seamus." She climbs to her feet, hits her head against the low slanted ceiling. "I can explain."

Maybe so. But I can run.

Which I do. And in a move that'd make Houdini proud, I take the goggles with me.

Chapter 4

DEMERITS: 200
GOLD STARS: 40

Are you sure you have everything?" Dad asks.

"I think so," I say.

"Toothbrush? Underwear? Anti-fungal foot spray?"

I look at him.

"Fungus is a fact of life. You don't want to be caught unprepared. Whenever we go away, your mother always packs an economy-size can of . . ."

His voice fades. My gaze turns up and away, toward the chain-link fence topped with barbed wire. On the other side is an ice-covered lawn. A large gray building with no windows. My home for the next five months.

"She wanted to be here," Dad says quietly.

Given my discovery three days ago, this is an understatement. "I know."

"It's just so hard to keep your foot elevated in a car for eight hours."

It's actually pretty easy if you stretch out in the backseat. But this, of course, isn't really the issue. Mom's ankle swelled to the size of a small watermelon after she tripped chasing me across the attic, prompting her to wrap it in ice packs and gauze, lie on the couch with her foot on a pile of pillows, and moan for days. But before sunrise this morning, on my way to the kitchen for a glass of orange juice, I caught her doing jumping jacks to her favorite workout video.

Her ankle's fine. She was just trying—and failing—to win sympathy points. And she definitely would've come to Kilter if I'd let her. But after recovering from the initial shock of finding her in the attic, and telling myself I would've appreciated the opportunity to explain my bad behavior a few months ago, I gave Mom a chance to do exactly that. It was after dinner the next day. We were alone in the kitchen, washing the dishes. I asked her about the weapons. She said they just started arriving one day, and she assumed they were some kind of test as part of Kilter's unconventional yet highly successful reformation program. Like they were sent to me so that, as a recovering bad kid, I could practice resisting temptation.

I might've believed her. But as she spoke, her voice shook. Her hands trembled. She dropped not one, not two, but *three* plates. Plus two forks and a butter knife. After we cleaned up the mess, she excused herself to take a hot bath. And went to the attic instead.

There was no way I could sit in the car with her for eight hours and not demand to know what was really going on. But Dad was obviously clueless about what his wife was up to, and I didn't want him to think anything was any more wrong than usual. So this morning, I told Mom she should probably stay home to take care of her foot. Her eyes bugged and her chin dropped at the request, cracking her wrinkle-cream mask, but she didn't argue. Probably because that was easier than trying to dodge the questions she knew would follow. By the time Dad came downstairs for coffee, her ankle was wrapped and elevated. And when she asked him to drive me to Kilter himself, she moaned for good measure.

"Ready?" I ask now.

Dad takes a deep breath. Squares his shoulders. Nods once.

I lift the gate's latch. The metal's so cold I feel it through my gloves. The bottom of the gate is frozen to the ground, and it takes both of us yanking to crack the ice. When we finally do, the entrance shrieks open. We fly backward. I grab Dad's arm to steady him on the slick sidewalk.

"Check-in lasts all morning." His voice is shaky, like his legs. "We passed a diner a few miles back. Maybe we should grab a bite to eat before—"

"It's okay," I say. "This is a great opportunity, remember?"

He doesn't look half as convinced as he sounded when he told me the same thing on New Year's Eve, but he follows me anyway. As we start up the slippery front path, I think about the last time we made this trip. Mom had practically sprinted toward the building, leaving me in her dust and Dad straggling even farther behind. Minutes later, she couldn't seem to leave fast enough. I'd assumed then it was because she wanted my reformation to begin ASAP.

In a way, I guess I was right.

"Waiting for spring?" a low voice explodes from hidden speakers.

I quicken my pace, glance over my shoulder to make sure Dad's not flat on his back.

"If you think it's treacherous out there, just wait till you see what's in *here*."

We reach the front steps. The thick steel door inches open, howling like an injured animal. I take Dad's arm again, and this time, I don't let go.

A figure appears. From previous experience—and only from previous experience—I know it's female. She wears dark green pants and tall black boots. A shiny, dark green coat that puffs out not from feathers, but from bulbous biceps and ripped abs. A black wool scarf wound tightly around her neck and past her chin. A bomber hat with furry ear and forehead flaps. Aviator sunglasses, even though it's overcast—and she's indoors. In the glasses' mirrored lenses I see my unblinking eyes, Dad's open mouth.

"Hello, Ms. Kilter." My breath forms a dense white cloud.

"Seamus." Her head turns ever so slightly to the left. "Mr. Hinkle."

"Hi," Dad says. Then, apparently remembering he's the temporary parental leader, he stands up straighter and looks Annika square in the sunglasses. "Good morning. It's so nice to see you again."

"Nice?" The corners of Annika's lips twitch. "Good one. No Mrs. Hinkle today?"

"No." Dad pulls me closer. "Seamus's mother wanted to come but was detained by an injury. Nothing too serious, mind you. She'll make a full—"

He's cut off by crackling. As Annika adjusts the volume on the walkie-talkie attached to her belt, the hem of her coat lifts, revealing a loaded gun holster. Handcuffs. Pepper spray.

"Know what I say about injuries?" she asks.

In her mirrored lenses, I see Dad's Adam's apple rise and fall.

"They're the body's way of saying we need to take it easy?" he guesses.

The corners of her mouth lift higher. "We should book you for the entertainment portion of Parents' Weekend." The corners drop. "But no. Injuries are physical manifestations of mental weakness. And nothing irritates me more."

I picture Elinor lying on the snow-covered ground, her skin red and blistered.

"Shall we?" Annika looks at me.

I look at Dad. He hesitates, then grabs me in a hug. His belly trembles against my cheek, and I know he's fighting tears.

"I'll be okay," I whisper, doing the same. "Promise."

"Still haven't shaken that word, huh?"

Dad and I pull apart. Annika stands with her back to the open door, one arm extended toward the lobby.

"Don't worry," she says. "If we do nothing else this semester, we'll make sure your son learns to stop making guarantees he doesn't know he can keep."

I feel Dad's eyes on me. I avoid them as I adjust my duffel bag strap on my shoulder and step inside.

"We'll be back!" Dad cries after me. "For Parents' Weekend! Never forget that your mother and I love—"

The door slams shut. My heart shoots toward my throat.

Annika's boots clomp against the floor as she crosses the room. It takes several seconds for my eyes to adjust to the darkness. When they do, I see that the room looks just as it did the first and only other time I was here. Besides a small wooden desk and an empty coat hanger, it's empty. The walls are bare. Maybe nothing changes at Kilter—except for its fearless leader.

Just like my last first day last semester, Annika ditches her military-esque uniform as soon as Dad leaves. She must wear real clothes under the fake ones, because in the time it took my eyes to get used to the room's dim lighting, her pants, coat, scarf, and boots have been replaced with jeans, a long white sweater covered in silver flowers, and shiny gray shoes that look like a cross between ballet and bedroom slippers. She's still wearing the bomber hat and sunglasses, although the hat's flaps are now folded up and the sunglasses are perched on top of her head. The weapons are gone from her waist; a K-Pak is in their place.

"Am I late?" I ask.

"You're right on time." Even her voice is different. Lighter. Sweeter.

"Am I the last one?"

"Not even close."

"But you changed your clothes. Don't you need to wear the uniform for the other families?"

"I'm not very big on small talk. The faculty and staff handle most of the meet-and-greets."

I look around the empty room without moving my head.

Annika explains.

"All new students enter Kilter for the first time through his building. When they arrive, they have no idea what to expect.

They're scared. Confused. Some of them cling to their parents and bawl like babies."

My cheeks warm. This part is familiar.

"I introduce myself to them and their parents, as I did with you and yours, so that everyone understands the severity of the situation. I make sure to leave an unforgettable impression so that I don't have to remind them on drop-off days of subsequent semesters. It helps that parents like to believe that the director of the best reform school in the country is too busy devising ways to turn their bad kids into good ones to waste time with idle chitchat. Plus, the faculty members really dig the chance to don fake threads—and up the intimidation factor. They're excellent Kilter representatives."

"But if I'm not late or the last one here . . . ?"

"Where are these excellent representatives?" She shrugs. "In a barren field. A deep ditch. The middle of a frozen lake. New students are terrified to come to Kilter, but returning students are always thrilled. On the first day of each semester, in order to keep the school's true purpose a secret from parents, who would at the very least remove their kids and at most blow our cover for good, returning students must feel the same kind of trepidation they felt on their first day ever."

"So you have them dropped off in the middle of nowhere?"

"Sometimes. Wherever it is has to be completely different from wherever they were left the time before so as to keep them guessing—and nervous. This makes their parents nervous and reassures them that Kilter's doing what it should."

Anywhere else, this would make absolutely no sense. Here, it seems perfectly logical. Still, "This is my second semester. How come I wasn't dropped off in the middle of a frozen lake? How come you met me, and not Houdini or Wyatt or Fern?"

She pauses. Her blue eyes narrow slightly. Her lips press together. "Because I couldn't tell."

"Couldn't tell . . . what?"

"Whether you wanted to come back."

"Of course I wanted to come back. I went on the real-world combat mission. I e-mailed my friends. I even tried to get here—"

"Early. I know."

I frown. "Ike and Houdini told you I tried to hitch a ride?"

"No. The Kommissary Krew did when you earned forty gold stars before the semester had even started." She clucks her tongue. "Regardless of intention, soliciting your tutor and instructor for advance arrival is akin to brownnosing. And no one gets a head start at Kilter—unless he steals it."

I open my mouth to explain that I wasn't trying to get a head start, at least not on troublemaking, but before I can, Annika spins around.

"In any case, based on other observations and sources, I wanted to be the one to greet you today. You've had great success up until now, but the past is pointless without the present. I wanted to see for myself if you came here committed. Focused. Ready to do whatever it takes to continue down the right path."

I've been at Kilter five minutes, tops, so I don't know how she could tell anything besides the fact that I'm still here. But something must've satisfied her because she opens the door, turns toward me, and beams.

I peer past her, through the door. Even from ten feet away I can see green grass. Flowers. Blue sky.

"Still think you're in the wrong place?" Annika asks.

My heart pounds as I force my eyes to hers. "No, ma'am."

She winks. "Good boy."

I start to follow through the doorway, then stop and spin around. I dart down the length of one wall, then another and another. I scan the base of each, looking for a large gray box.

"See a mouse?"

"I'm looking for the bin," I say. "To put my stuff in for screening."

Annika laughs. "Did you think we really checked your bags last time?"

I did. But then, why would they? Belongings that might be confiscated from a normal bad kid, like matches, scissors, and nail clippers, are as useful in the Kilter classroom as pencils, erasers, and rulers are in non-Kilter classrooms.

Which means I taped the Kilter Knight-Vision Goggles to my torso for no good reason.

"You've been given a new room this semester," Annika says. "Why don't we check it out?"

As I hoist my duffel bag onto my shoulder and follow her outside, I feel a little foolish—and nervous. Between checking for the bin and earning forty gold stars, I'm not off to a good start. And since being here keeps me far away from home, where I can't be while I try to figure out why Mom did what she did, I need to stay on Annika's good side. I need her to believe I'm a real Troublemaker. Especially since, as far as I can tell, she doesn't know the one thing that would get me immediate and permanent expulsion.

Annika heads for a stone fountain shaped like a globe. At the top, a silver *K* and *A* rotate slowly, sending water streaming down the round sculpture. A turbo golf cart is parked next to the fountain. She hops in the cart and nods to the passenger seat. I climb in. Clear plastic straps slide around my waist and chest and tighten instantly, locking me in place a millisecond before the vehicle jolts forward.

We drive to a section of campus I've never seen before. Several buildings are scattered among small hills and valleys. A narrow gravel path weaves between the trunks of towering evergreen trees. When we slow down, I see that the buildings are actually rustic log cabins with modern accents, like stainless steel porches and motion-sensor doors. I recognize a few of my classmates walking, talking, and laughing. In a large central clearing, four Troublemakers throw a football around.

It's just like summer camp. Only it's winter. And one high-tech cabin could fit two of my family's houses.

"We like to give students as much freedom as possible as soon as possible." Annika returns waves and smiles to a trio of passing

Troublemakers. "So whoever successfully passes the first semester moves here the second semester."

"Did everyone in my class pass?" I ask.

The golf cart jerks to a stop.

"Almost," Annika says.

Before I can wonder who didn't make the cut, she hops out. I hurry after her. We head for a two-story log cabin with a large front yard, a tree-lined walkway, and not one but two stainless steel balconies. It's by far the biggest, fanciest house on the farm, so must belong to a teacher or some other adult in charge.

But then Annika jogs up the front steps. Reaches for the door. Says, "Welcome home, Seamus."

And is swallowed whole by a burning black cloud.

Chapter 5

DEMERITS: 200
GOLD STARS: 40

Annika!"

I drop my bags. Charge up the steps. Clamp one hand over my mouth and nose and thrust my free arm into the darkness. My throat burns. My skin itches and aches at the same time. Tears spill from my eyes, but I won't close them. I can't. I've done some pretty questionable stuff the past few months, but abandoning Annika now, letting her go up in flames . . . That would be no different from killing her myself.

I open my mouth to yell her name again, but the heat's too

intense. I start choking. My lungs tighten. My chest pulsates. I drop to my knees, hoping for clearer air, but it's just as dark by the floor. I crawl and squint, trying to see something, anything through the blackness.

It's no use. It's too hot. Too dark. I can hear crackling, so the fire must be nearby, but I can't see it. And now my throat's closing, my eyelids are drooping . . .

Annika!

Her name shoots through my head as my body sinks to the floor. My arms and legs hold out the longest, letting my chest hit last. When it does, the pain's so great, I picture my heart melting, oozing through my ribs, dripping to the floor, forming a purple molten puddle.

That's the last thing I see.

Until I see Lemon.

His face is softened by a gray haze, but I can still make out his fuzzy eyebrows and shaggy brown hair. The downward slope of his eyes. The cluster of pimples at the tip of his nose. A silver mask over his mouth.

"Breathe," he says.

I shake my head.

"Do it. Now."

"I can't."

He reaches forward. His fist shoots toward my head and his fingers pop open, like he's going to give my face a high five. I close my eyes and brace for impact. . . . But it doesn't come. There's only a slight pinch as Lemon grabs my mask, tugs it away from my mouth, and gently releases it.

"Okay," I say. "I'm breathing."

He jumps to his feet and disappears. Sitting up, I inhale, exhale, and take in my surroundings. A silver oxygen canister sits on the floor next to me; it's connected to my face mask by a thin, clear tube. A coatrack stands next to the canister. A table holding a blackened fruit bouquet and a digital WELCOME, TROUBLEMAKERS! card stands next to that. Across the foyer, an open doorway leads to a living room. Through the lingering gray smoke I see overstuffed couches and chairs. A floor-to-ceiling flat-screen TV. A pinball machine and foosball table.

"Where did you get those?"

My head snaps to the left. The front door's open. A figure stands there. It's lighter outside than it is inside, so I can't tell whose it is.

"Seamus, you shouldn't have!" A second, smaller figure appears. It scoots around the first.

"Gabby?" I ask. "Is that you?"

A pair of blue eyes near mine. They open until lash meets brow, and hold. I want to slide back, but the stare's intensity locks me in place.

"It's you," I say.

"And *that* is an amazing belated Christmas present," she says, still staring. "You're so sweet to try it out for me! It's always such a bummer when you've been dreaming about something for, like, ever, and then when you finally get it it's broken or needs batteries or something. This one time—"

"Ten thousand credits."

The blue eyes blink. Instantly freed, I scramble to my feet. Once upright I see that the first figure belongs to Abe.

And that my reflection in the mirror on the opposite wall is wearing the Kilter Knight-Vision Goggles.

"I got five hundred demerits for making Annika cry," Abe continues. "That wouldn't buy half a lens."

Annika. I've been so distracted about my own near-death experience I forgot about hers. Ignoring Abe, I dart down the hall. I'm slowed by the oxygen tank I'm still connected to, so I yank the mask from my mouth and over my head. The mask's elastic strap catches on the goggles. They slide off—and drop into Lemon's hands.

"Sorry," he says. "I know you were pretty attached."

I look at him. The feeling leaves my face. "Did she . . . ? She didn't . . . ?"

Lemon's two eyebrows become one as he tries to fill in the blanks. A second later his forehead relaxes and they part again. He shuffles past Abe and Gabby and stands in the front doorway. Knowing Lemon well enough to know this is his way of telling me something without actually telling me something, I follow. Together, we watch Annika sprint across the main field, spin, and catch a football thrown by one of our classmates. She spikes the ball and curtsies as the gathered crowd cheers.

"I guess she's okay," I say.

"Of course she is. I was talking about these." He holds the goggles toward me. "I grabbed them because I thought the bump under your coat was your K-Pak, and I didn't want you to sound the alarm before I had a chance to get the situation under control. I didn't expect you to scream instead."

Remembering the searing pain I felt only moments earlier, which was apparently caused not by fire but by fire starter tearing duct tape from skin, I take the goggles.

"Um, hello?" Abe asks. "Can we please get back to more important matters?"

Lemon's eyes slowly roll up and to the left, meeting mine. I smile. We both turn around, and seeing neither smoke nor flames, I close the door.

"Such as, Abraham?"

Abe's neck juts forward. His head drops to one side. His gaze and both pointer fingers shoot toward the goggles still in my hands. "Ten. *Thousand.* Credits. Even if Gabby had a red braid and no friends, Hinkle still wouldn't have blown that much bank on her. Because no one in our class has that kind of coin—or at least, they shouldn't."

One of several responses would be appropriate right now. Like the fact that I didn't buy the goggles. And that the red-braided girl he's referring to does have friends, although his point is pointless since that's all she and I are. And that he has no idea how many credits I've earned. And that even if I did buy the goggles, for Elinor, with my own Kilter currency, it's really none of his business.

Unfortunately, not one of these responses makes it from my head to my mouth. Fortunately, Lemon answers on my behalf.

"Two things." He leans back against the door, slides his hands into his jeans pockets. "First, it's way too early to start power-tripping. And second, Houdini probably gave Seamus the goggles on his mission, for his mission."

"Three things," Abe retorts. "First, this isn't about me. It's about playing fair. Second, the so-called real-world combat missions were like normal assignments done at home. All I got from Wyatt for completing mine was a box of watercolors. And third, Seamus is a big boy. He can speak for himself."

Abe looks at me. Lemon looks at the floor. Gabby, apparently convinced that no matter what, the goggles aren't for her, picks up her suitcase and heads down the hall.

I didn't do it.

Suddenly this is the most tempting response. Abe's been suspicious of me from my very first day at Kilter, which came several weeks after everyone else's, and that feeling was multiplied by millions when Mom announced my crime on Parents' Day. He seemed to come around a bit after the Ultimate Troublemaking Task, when we all worked—and succeeded—together, but his reservations clearly run deep. If I tell him the truth, that it was all a big misunderstanding because I didn't actually kill Miss Parsippany, so I can't be the supertalented Troublemaker every Kilter faculty and staff member thinks I am, maybe he'll back off. Maybe we can even be friends.

"Help!"

I'm so focused I don't know if Gabby actually cries out or if I'm still suffering from an acute case of damsel-in-distress savior syndrome.

"Somebody? *Anybody?*"

I glance at Lemon. "You put out the fire, right?"

His lips settle into a straight line as he steps, then sprints, down the hall. Abe and I follow close behind. We find Gabby in the kitchen. She faces a long wall of stainless steel cabinets, her back to us.

"Where is it?" Lemon asks.

"Are you okay?" I ask.

"Are you kidding?" Abe asks.

Gabby groans. Her body rocks back and forth. A quick scan of the room shows it's free of flames, and besides the stuff spewing from the open suitcase on the kitchen table, nothing seems out of place.

And then a thought occurs to me. Our class is divided into six groups by troublemaking talent. I'm in the Sniper Squad. Lemon's in the Fire Starters. Abe's in Les Artistes. Gabby's in the Biohazards, which uses both real and fake bodily functions to startle unsuspecting targets. Is this some kind of trick? To give her a head start while the rest of us waste time arguing?

If it is, she's just warming up. Because she raises her shoulders sharply, lets them drop, and spins around with a sigh before one of us gets too close to spook.

"It's broken," she announces.

"What is?" Lemon asks.

"This drawer. And this drawer and this drawer and this drawer." She taps the glistening silver counter as she walks alongside it. "None of them open."

Abe strides across the room. He grabs the handle of the first drawer with one hand and pulls. When it doesn't give, he takes the handles with both hands and tries again. The third time he plants his feet before the bottom cabinet and leans back until his arms straighten and his body stands at a forty-five-degree angle.

"Yup." He pulls himself up, releases the handle. "Broken."

"Maybe they're locked," I offer.

"There are no keyholes," Lemon says, investigating.

"Maybe they're computer-controlled," I say. "Or voice-operated."

Lemon steps back. Lowers his head. Thinks. Several seconds later he reaches into his sweatshirt pocket and returns to the drawer. He crouches down and bends forward. His torso blocks my view, but I know what he's doing as soon as I hear the soft, familiar click . . . of his lighter.

"Know what?" Gabby says. "It's okay. I'm sure Kilter has a fabulous handyman. I'll just shoot him an e-mail."

Lemon doesn't say anything. He doesn't move, either. Soon thin, gray wisps appear. They float toward the ceiling.

"Dude," Abe says. "Melting the thing isn't going to—"

There's a sharp pop, like a firecracker going off. Gabby cries out. Abe bolts for the kitchen door. I leap up and lunge for the sink. Lemon steps back. The gray wisps floating before him thicken, darken to black. Red flames shoot up from the drawer. Before I can figure out what just happened—or how to work the faucet—ice-cold water sprays down from the ceiling. I smile, relieved that our somewhat faulty state-of-the-art house is equipped with a perfectly functioning sprinkler system. . . . But then I realize the liquid doesn't look like water. It's not clear. It's not white, either, like the foam from a fire extinguisher. It's pink. Blue. Yellow. Purple. Green. It smells funny too. Kind of like Mrs. Lubbard's bathroom. And rather than put out the fire, it makes it grow.

"Paint!" Abe wipes his lips as colorful streaks run down his face.

"Good Samaritans!" Gabby rummages through her open suitcase.

"Don't!" Lemon spins around.

I turn back to the sink. Yank both knobs to the right and left. Not one drop of water falls from the faucet, so I check the wall for some sort of power switch. Maybe everything in the kitchen was turned off for vacation and just needs to be turned back on.

And then I see it. Not a power switch. A digital silver arrow. It's sparkly but faint and pulsates weakly, like an old neon sign. It starts where the countertop meets the wall, right behind the faucet, and aims up, toward the top of the upper cabinets—and a glass cookie jar. The jar glows softly with the light of a digital silver bull's-eye.

I run to the other side of the room, dodging my frantic friends and slipping across the slick tile floor. I rip the goggles back over my head and start spinning them around one finger like a lasso.

I've barely turned back around when I let them fly. Holding my breath, I watch them soar through the air.

"Duck!" I shout when they near the cookie jar, shielding my face with my arms.

Only shards of glass don't rain down on us. The goggles hit the bull's-eye, but the jar doesn't break. It simply tilts back, then pops forward, like a carnival game target. Guessing I didn't hit it hard enough, I look around for something else to throw—just as the sink explodes.

"On it!" Gabby yells. She empties the contents of her suitcase onto the table and runs to the sink, which is actually intact despite the water bursting from the faucet with the force of a fire hose.

"Move!" I call out to Lemon and Abe as I slip and slide across the room again.

The flames grow taller. Paint falls faster. By the time the four of us carry the heavy suitcase to the drawer, heave it up, and dump out the water, I think the chances are good that we'll still need backup.

But I'm wrong. It works. The fire fizzles out immediately. The sprinkler system shuts down. Ceiling and floor tiles shift like puzzle pieces, sucking out smoke and draining paint.

The drawer opens.

Gabby squeals and claps. She reaches into the drawer, removes a pair of scissors, and skips to the kitchen table.

"That's it?" Abe scoffs, shoving wet hair from his forehead. "That's what was so important?"

Unfazed, Gabby takes a ball of fabric from the mountain on the table and wrings it out over the sink. "You'll thank me every time you see these pretty gingham curtains hanging in our living room."

"No, I definitely will *not*—" Abe stops. Looks at her. "What did you just say?"

Gabby grins. Lemon leans against the counter. I retrieve the Kilter Knight-Vision Goggles from the floor.

"She said *our* living room," I say.

"As in ours . . . *and* hers?" Abe shakes his head.

I nod.

"But she's a girl."

"She's also one of us." I hold the goggles toward him. After he takes them, confused, I remind him of our alliance. "And we're a team. With a Capital *T*."

Chapter 6

DEMERITS: 230
GOLD STARS: 40

TO: parsippany@cloudviewschools.net
FROM: shinkle@kilteracademy.org
SUBJECT: Happy New Year!

Dear Miss Parsippany,

Hi! How are you? Did you have a nice vacation? How are you feeling?

Thank you very much for answering my e-mail. Given what happened, I would've understood if you'd deleted my message without ever opening it. And I know I've said it before, but I really am sorry about all that. (Note to self: If you're going to throw an apple at a moving target . . . STOP. Eat apple instead.) ☺

I'm also sorry it's taken me so long to get back to you. I got your note during finals last semester, and then I went home, and you know how crazy the holidays are. Besides being busy, I also wasn't sure if you really wanted me to write back. I know you said I could in your note, but the fact that you answered mine shows how nice you are. And I didn't know if you were just being extra nice by inviting me to write again.

But it's a new year. I'm not big on resolutions, but I do like the idea of starting over. With a clean slate. And I thought maybe that's what we could do. So I decided to take you up on the offer and see what happens. If you want to write back, I'd love to hear from you. If you don't, I totally understand. Either way, I'm really, really happy you're okay. And

I hope your new year blows the old one out of the water.

Sincerely,

Seamus Hinkle

I reread the note twice, then hit send and watch the digital envelope swish around the K-Pak screen. When the envelope disappears, I wait for an error message to pop up and remind me that Kilter e-mails can't be delivered to non-Kilter addresses. That's what happened when I tried writing Dad last semester. And this school's so big on keeping its secret I wouldn't be surprised if the IT department blocked Miss Parsippany's external e-mail address after discovering our accidental exchange.

But the screen stays blank. So I get up, even though I still have an hour before class, and head to the bathroom to get ready.

As cool as it is to have our own house, Lemon, Abe, Gabby, and I learned last night that nothing in it works the way it should. Just like the faucet stayed dry until I hit the cookie jar, the TV didn't turn on until Abe made a wall mural using fireplace ash. Gabby's bedroom door only opened when she did three cartwheels down the hallway. We played foosball when the game table's knobs finally unlocked after Lemon raced around the living room, lighting a dozen tall candles with the flame of a much smaller one before the smaller one melted away. And I couldn't pull back the blankets on my bed until I first hit every glowing star in the constellation of stickers on my ceiling with a pair of balled-up socks.

It's fun, but time-consuming. Fortunately, the bathroom isn't too complicated this morning. The showerhead turns on with one flick of my towel. Toothpaste dispenses when I toss my pajamas into the hamper. Moisture automatically evaporates from the mirror over the sink after I fire five Q-tips into the trash can under the counter.

I dress quickly and check my K-Pak for new messages. There aren't any. I consider e-mailing Dad again, just in case the no-outside-e-mail policy changed, but decide against it. I've been meaning to write Miss Parsippany for a while, but part of the reason I finally did this morning was because I started feeling homesick. Mom always makes a big production on the first day of each new semester, complete with pancakes and pictures, and despite everything, I wouldn't mind the fuss. Miss Parsippany's not my mother, but she's still an adult. Who seems to care. I thought if she wrote back right away, that might help fill the emptiness in my stomach.

But she didn't. And if my e-mail reaches Dad, he'll tell Mom, who will probably think I miss them. Which, even if that's true—*especially* if it's true—she doesn't really need to know.

So I fill my stomach with breakfast instead.

"Holy home fries," I say when I reach the kitchen.

Lemon's sitting at the table. He looks up from a magazine, then back down again. "Our resident artist works in many mediums," he says.

Including food. Potatoes, waffles, and scrambled eggs have been arranged in a towering "KA" sculpture. Melon, berries, and banana slices circle the structure's base. Juice waits to be sipped from cups made of braided orange peels.

"Did Abe have to make all this in order to eat?" I ask.

"Don't know. He and Gabby were gone by the time I got up."

"Are we sure he did it? Maybe the Kanteen made a special first-day delivery."

Lemon's eyes stay fixed on the magazine as his head, then chin, tilt forward.

"Got it," I say, seeing the *A. HANSEN CREATIONS* signature scrawled in maple syrup on the glass platter. I take a plate from the stack next to the sculpture, serve myself a helping of each breakfast item, and sit across from him.

We don't speak for several minutes. Lemon's not exactly a chatterbox, but still. We haven't seen each other in weeks and were never alone to catch up last night. I want to know how his real-world mission was, what else he did over vacation, if he's happy to be back. I've learned it's best not to ask too much too soon, though, so I start carefully.

"Your eggs are way better."

"My room's a death trap."

I stop chewing. "Sorry?"

He sighs. Sits back. "My furniture's made of twigs. My mattress is stuffed with tissues. My walls are covered in paper, not paint. And everything must be coated in kerosene or hair spray, because each time I light a match, sparks fly in every corner of the room. That's why I almost burned the place down ten minutes after getting here yesterday. I wasn't prepared."

I swallow. "But you didn't burn the place down. Everyone's fine. And now you know."

"It doesn't matter. I'm good at starting fires—not putting them out."

"You're great at both. Our dorm room was still standing when we moved out, wasn't it?"

"Yes. Because of the Kilter Pocket Extinguisher. And Smoke Detector with Automatic Flame Eliminator. Both of which you bought."

I'd disagree, but he has a point.

"I can stay with you," I offer. "In your room, at night. It'll be just like last semester, except I'll sleep on the floor—which, according to my mom's health magazines, is great for the back. I can even wait until Gabby and Abe go to bed and then make sure I'm in my room again before they get up. They'll never know."

This gets a half smile. And though he doesn't accept the offer, he doesn't shoot it down, either.

"We should probably get going," he says, standing.

He's right. I don't know how long it'll take to get from the Freshman Farm to class, and I don't want to be late. I clear my plate, fling my fork at the dishwasher handle to open it, and quickly clean up. Then I dash to the bathroom to brush my teeth and check my appearance one last time.

"Hey, Lemon?" I ask as he shuffles by the open doorway.

"Do you think this shirt looks okay? Should I wear the blue one instead? Or maybe—"

The front door opens and closes. Grinning, since this is normal Lemon behavior, I stick with what I'm wearing, grab my jacket and backpack, and hurry outside.

It snowed during the night, and the ground and trees glisten. The air's cool but the sun's warm. Laughter and excited conversation surround us as we pass other students. The pleasant experience is a far cry from being stuck in the front of an old yellow school bus between our ancient driver, Wheezing Willy, and Bartholomew John, who always found the back of my seat a stellar sparring partner.

It also almost makes me forget why I'm here—and that I shouldn't be.

According to the e-mail Annika sent last night, our schedules haven't changed. Which means our first class is math. When we reach the classroom building twenty minutes after leaving the Farm, we're five minutes early. Lemon shuffles to the couch at the back of the room and collapses like we just walked a hundred miles instead of one. I stop just outside the doorway. The front row of desks is empty, but Annika didn't say anything about keeping the same seats. So I survey my other options.

"Dodge the draft," a low voice says near my ear.

I jump. Houdini steps back.

"It's toasty in here." He taps the digital thermostat on the wall next to the doorway, which is set to seventy degrees. "But by the windows? And her Royal Ice Queen? You'll never be warm, no matter how fast your heart beats." He places one palm to his chest. Shivers. Smiles.

"Maybe I should've worn slippers instead of shoes."

Houdini's eyebrows lift above the tops of his sunglasses. He glances down at his feet, which are enclosed by fluffy gray squares beneath the hems of flannel pajama pants, then up at me.

"Hinkle the quick-comeback kid. Who'd have thunk it?" He holds out a fist. "I'd give you ten demerits, but your current lead doesn't need them."

I bump his fist with mine. He yawns, stretches, and goes inside. More classmates arrive. I say hi, wave. Most return the greeting without hesitating. This is different from the end of last semester, when they were still wary of their killer classmate. It makes me hopeful that a new start really is possible.

Thirty seconds before class begins, I scan the empty hallway. Listen for footsteps. And finally enter the room.

I find a seat near the windows. As I remove a notebook and pen from my backpack, I try not to stare at the chair next to mine. Because for the first time since I started taking this class a few months ago, it's empty. And I know it's silly, but I'm afraid if I look too closely or give it too much attention, it might stay that way.

"Behold!" Houdini lifts one leg, lets his heel drop onto the desk at the front of the room, and sweeps one hand toward his foot. "Your challenge this semester."

"Ugly shoes?" Abe guesses. He's sitting a few chairs away in the middle of the room.

"Bad personal hygiene?" a girl named Jill adds, eyeing Houdini's stained sock.

"Cement blocks," he says. "Granted, these are filled with cotton, but you get the idea."

It takes some stretching of the imagination, but soon I see that his slippers are shaped like gray concrete cubes.

"To pass last semester," he continues, "you had to 'get' each one of your teachers with the skills they taught. To get me, you had to steal something of mine without my knowing. At the time, that probably seemed impossible."

A few kids nod. No one disagrees.

"It was actually a walk in the park." He lifts his other leg, crosses his ankles on top of the desk. "And get ready to run. Because now we're coming after you."

"What does that mean?" Gabby asks.

"In order to pass this semester, you must avoid attacks by all of your teachers. Just like you stole my stuff, I'm going to steal yours."

"You did that last semester," Lemon says. "When you took my favorite lighter."

"And my stuffed unicorn," Gabby says.

And my robot cuff links.

"I did that to teach you how to do it yourselves. And I gave everything back. This semester, no such luck. If I steal it, I keep it."

"And we fail?" Abe asks. "Like, automatically?"

"You get three shots. If you avoid the first attempt, you're done. You earn a hundred demerits and are free to focus on normal class assignments. If you fail the first attempt, you earn a hundred gold stars and have to earn a second chance."

"How?" a kid named Austin asks.

"By getting one of your classmates."

"So in order to get another chance with you," Abe says slowly, "I'd have to steal something of, say, Hinkle's?"

"Without him knowing," Houdini says. "Exactly."

"That sounds complicated," Jill says.

"It is. Successful Troublemakers don't just make trouble. They thwart it. That's how they stay sharp and keep their edge. It's hard to be bad when you're constantly looking over one shoulder." Houdini wiggles his slippers. "Hence the running. In concrete. With what feels like the weight of the world dragging you down."

Some kids exchange looks. Others move their backpacks from the floor to their laps, then scoot forward so their stuff is safely locked in place between their legs and desks.

I open my notebook and start writing.

"Questions?" Houdini asks.

I raise my hand.

"Shout it out, Seamus," he says.

"Could you please go over the demerits again?" My hand moves faster across the page as he does. After he's done, I ask, "Will there be opportunities for extra credit?"

"Why would you need extra credit?"

"Like if we get a late start. And need to catch up." My hand stops as I realize how this sounds to everyone in the room. We're all here, so we're all starting at the same time. "Or if we want to buy something really expensive at the Kommissary."

"If you want to buy something really expensive at the Kommissary, don't blow your credits on cheap—" Houdini pauses. When he speaks again, I hear a smile in his voice. "Oh. I get it. You're taking notes for little miss—"

He's cut off again, this time by a sharp buzzing. Feeling the burn of twenty-eight curious gazes, I keep mine fixed on the page before me. A long minute later, Houdini continues.

"Save the ink, Hinkle. Your entire class is present and accounted for."

I raise my eyes. Slowly. He's holding up his K-Pak, which apparently just received a new message. I don't have to read it to know what it says.

My heart sinks as my eyes shift left, to the empty chair. Which is going to stay that way.

Because Elinor's not coming back.

Chapter 7

DEMERITS: 230
GOLD STARS: 40

"Armpit toots," Gabby says.

"Armpit farts," Abe says.

"Toots."

"Farts."

"I'm a girl. We toot. Only when absolutely necessary, and in total privacy. What you Neanderthals do is very different." Gabby leans forward and looks past him. "Just thinking about it makes Seamus turn red."

She says this fondly, like me blushing is as cute as a kitten purring. I'd change the subject, but we're talking about our real-world combat missions as we walk back from dinner, and I'm curious to know the outcome of hers.

"So you were at the convenience store," I prompt.

"At the *gas* station," Abe reminds us with a chuckle.

"And the employee was cleaning the slushie machine," I say.

"Right." Gabby nods. "He was taking forever because he kept sneaking sips of Arctic Berry Blast and Turbo Choco when his boss wasn't looking. I was in the next aisle, pretending to check out the gum. Hiding in full view, just like Samara said."

Samara's our biology teacher. She takes her job more seriously than Houdini does, so I'm happy to hear her instructions were the same as his.

"I watched him for a minute or two, waiting for my moment," Gabby continues. "Then, when his face disappeared into a plastic cup, I let one rip. From my pit. Which is kind of hard to do underneath a turtleneck and down coat."

"What happened?" Lemon asks.

"Total freak-out. The guy jumped so high I checked the ceiling for dents. And not only did he drop the cup, sending slushie flying everywhere, he bumped into the machine levers.

By the time he realized the machine was on, the counter and floor were covered in blue and brown liquid." Gabby talks fast, her voice excited. "His hands shook as he cleaned up. I think he thought the sound came from him."

"What'd you do after that?" I ask.

"I bought some Bubble Tape like nothing happened. And I got out of there."

"No, I mean later. Where did you and Samara go next?"

She shoots me a look. "What do you mean?"

I start to rephrase the question, then consider why she might be confused. I must take too long to answer because Abe takes over.

"I made my mom's knees give out. My dad had to catch her so she wouldn't hit the floor. That's how good my living room redesign was."

"Your what?" Lemon asks.

"Living room redesign. Wyatt said I had to use 'non-habitual' art skills to shock my parents. That ruled out spray-painting walls, appliances, and hardwood floors, so I had to think outside the box. While my parents were getting ready for bed one night, I reupholstered and rearranged the living room furniture, hung up new curtains, and added unique accents throughout the room."

"So your real-world combat mission . . . was to redecorate?" Gabby asks.

"Redesign," Abe corrects.

"And your parents didn't think you had anything to do with it?" I ask.

"I'd left hours earlier to spend the night at a friend's house. Or so they thought. Plus, it was a lot of heavy stuff for one kid to move in five minutes." He stands up straighter, lifts his head. "And it really was pretty."

I'm about to ask if his mission consisted of anything else when we come upon a group of older Troublemakers. They're crowded around the gazebo in the campus's main garden, clapping and bobbing in place. Every few seconds one of them whoops and cheers, and the others laugh.

"Must be a concert," Lemon says.

"Let's check it out," Gabby says.

I don't hear any music, but we head for the gazebo anyway. I'm shorter than the next-shortest student by five inches and can't see inside, so I try to sneak peeks whenever shoulders separate. It's still quiet except for the applauding and cheering, which grow louder every second. I expect to catch a glimpse of a sword swallower, human pretzel, or some other silent circus performer.

But the structure's empty.

"Look." I nudge Lemon and nod at the older Troublemaker standing before me. Like everyone else (except me), she's wearing a silver ski parka. On her shoulder is a square patch. Two masquerade masks are sewn onto the patch. One's happy, the other sad.

"Ah," Lemon says.

These Troublemakers are Dramatists. They're the performers, and this fake appreciation for invisible entertainment is probably a homework assignment.

I'm about to alert Abe and Gabby to the fact so we can move on, when a loud pop sounds behind us. It's followed by a fizzle that seems to pass overhead. A few students break character to look up—and the rest follow when another pop sounds above the gazebo. A small dark cloud forms and rains shiny black drops. There's another mini explosion. And another and another. They seem to grow louder, come closer. More dark clouds appear, releasing a glittery downpour.

"Run!" someone shouts.

The group breaks. Troublemakers yank up their hoods, shield

their heads. They zigzag through the garden, trying to dodge drops. Soon Lemon and I are alone by the gazebo.

"It's dry." He lifts his arm. His jacket is untouched.

"Mine too."

He lowers his arm. "Home?"

"Meet you there?"

Not for the first time, I'm glad Lemon doesn't press. He slides his hands in his coat pockets and strolls away without another word.

I stay where I am, watching the outline of a dark red apple shimmer in the sky.

"I haven't seen hustle like that since the famous Kilter Painter incident last fall."

The red apple fades. I turn around.

"Hi, Ike."

I smile as my instructor steps out from behind a tree. His face is hidden by the brim of a Kilter Academy baseball cap, but I know it's him. And not just because of the impressive aerial call to attention he just launched.

Because he's wearing a black ski parka. Just like me.

"I usually see fireworks on the Fourth of July," I say as he comes closer. "Not the fourth of January."

"You didn't see fireworks." He stands before me and holds up a skinny silver baton. It looks like a magic wand, but with three buttons, a tiny screen, and a knob at its base. "You saw Direworks. Guaranteed to make those around you think the sky is falling and the apocalypse near."

"Cool. Where's the fuse?"

"No fuse. No fire. It's all electric."

"But the embers," I say. "That fell and fizzled out. They—"

"Weren't really there. The sparks, the smoke, the clouds. All digital images."

I must look skeptical because he presses buttons, spins the knob, and points the baton at the ground.

"Wait." I step back. "Maybe we should—"

The earth explodes between our feet. Or at least, it looks like it does. When the glowing fireball extinguishes and the dust settles, the small crater that just formed disappears. I bend down for a closer look and see blades of grass peeking through the thin layer of snow. They're standing upright, just like they were before Ike took aim.

"Want to try?" he asks.

I do. He steps into the gazebo. I follow. We crouch down

so those passing by can't see us behind the bushes encircling the gazebo's base.

"The buttons control the image," Ike explains. "You can set the type, color, and duration. The knob adjusts the direction. To fire, press down on the knob like you would a computer mouse."

He hands me the baton. I'm still trying to figure out which button does what when I hear voices approaching. One's male, the other female. They're quiet. Like they don't want to be heard by anyone else.

"Hand-holders at twelve o'clock." Ike stands on his knees to peer over the gazebo railing, then settles back down. "It's way too early for that. They deserve what's coming."

"Hand-holders?" I stand on my knees too. "You mean like a . . ."

Couple? That's what I try to say, but my mouth suddenly can't complete the question. Because as the older Troublemakers come closer, fingers entwined, heads tilted together, clearly en route to the romantic, dimly lit destination Ike and I are currently occupying, I remember the last time I was in said romantic destination. And who I was with. And how, even though we didn't exactly have the best time, since the time ended with one of us storming out in a huff, I still didn't want it to end.

I sit back down. "Why don't we find a teacher instead? Dinner's still being served. Some of them must be in the Kanteen. We can hide outside, wait for them to leave, and make them lose whatever they just ate."

Ike takes his baseball cap and spins it around so the brim's at the back of his head. "Seamus."

I pause. "Ike."

"Don't go soft on me."

"I'm not going soft. I want to go after a teacher. That's way harder."

He holds out one hand, palm up. I look at it, then him.

"Give it back," he says. "You're not ready. Your body's here, but your head's still on vacation."

I start to do as I'm told, which is what I always used to do before coming here. But then my eyes catch a flash of red on the other side of the gazebo. It looks like a flower petal, kind of like the ones on the poinsettia plant Bartholomew John hand-delivered Christmas morning.

I raise the Direworks baton. Press the buttons. Twist and hit the knob.

A laser beam shoots straight through the doorway, then up. It forms a fat white cloud. The cloud opens up, releasing a digital hailstorm so fast and furious I can't see the happy couple when I stand up. I can hear them, though. The girl cries out. The guy shouts her name. They try to run. Stumble. Fall. Even though they don't really feel a thing.

Ninety seconds later, the computerized ice chunks disappear. The couple's gone—most likely to the nearest building to wait out the weather. Ike smiles and holds up one hand.

"Ten demerits," he declares as I smack his palm with mine. "A good start—and a drop in the bucket of thousands you'll earn this semester."

I smile, then frown. I'm happy to earn more demerits, but hearing that girl cry out makes me think of Elinor getting hurt last semester. And what I learned in math class earlier.

"Ike, can I ask you a question?"

"Fire away."

"Is it weird when a kid doesn't come back to Kilter?"

"You mean after being home?"

I nod.

He shrugs. "Not really. Sometimes parents change their minds about their kid being here. Sometimes Annika does. It happens."

"Has anyone ever not come back for a different reason?"

"Like what? Being bored to death while waiting for the next semester to start?"

He chuckles. I don't. I've come up with lots of potential reasons for Elinor's absence, but anytime I picture her blistered skin and my thoughts head in the *D* direction, I think about *Lord of the Rings*, fish sticks, even Abe. Anything to keep the terrible idea out of my head. But Ike's joke brings it right back.

"Howdy-do, folks," a low voice says.

I leap to my feet. The Direworks baton falls from my lap. It rolls across the floor and stops before a gleaming brown penny loafer. Ike lunges for the device—but not fast enough.

"What do we have here?" The man stoops down. Picks up the baton. Shakes it by his ear. "George?"

A second man steps into the gazebo. He's older and rounder than the first, but they still look like twins. In addition to the same shoes, they're wearing identical khaki pants, red sweaters with embroidered snowflakes running down the sleeves, red earmuffs, and red fanny packs.

Because that's how the Good Samaritans roll.

"Huh." GS George takes the Direworks baton and holds it out at arm's length. "I can't say I've seen this one before."

"It's a conducting baton," Ike says. "For music class."

"Interesting." GS George gasps, turns to the first Good Samaritan, and taps him on the shoulder with the baton. "That reminds me. Know how I was dying to see the *Nutcracker* back home over break? Well you'll *never* guess what—"

"Um, excuse me?"

The Good Samaritans have already turned and started back down the gazebo steps. At the sound of Ike's voice, they stop and look over their shoulders.

"The baton?" Ike says. "We kind of need it for homework."

"Oh!" George's eyes widen as he holds the baton in front of his face, like he's surprised to see it still in his hand. "Of course. Good luck."

Ike takes the device. I join him in the gazebo doorway and watch the Good Samaritans hop on their two-person bicycle. They pedal off, rattling on about understudies, poor sound quality, and the perils of third-mezzanine seating.

"Do you think they saw the digital downpour?" I ask. "And came to check it out?"

"No."

"No?" I look at him, then follow his gaze to the sidewalk . . . where three more two-person bicycles, carrying six more Good Samaritans, roll by. Those in the front seats don't take their eyes off the pavement, but those in the back narrow theirs as they peer our way.

"I think they saw the digital downpour"—Ike claps me on the shoulder—"and came to check *you* out."

Chapter 8

DEMERITS: 245
GOLD STARS: 40

I see Mom. She's sitting at the kitchen table. The cordless phone's pressed to her ear. She talks, then laughs, the force throwing her head so far back I think it might snap off her neck. I smile, happy she's so happy, and walk toward her. Coming closer I notice a newspaper open on the table before her. There's a pair of scissors, too. And dozens of clippings. I scan them, hoping some of the coupons are for free fish sticks. . . . But they're not coupons. They're articles. About the Cloudview Cards and Carnations employee of the year. Cloudview Middle School's star student. Cloudview Nursing Home's most popular volunteer.

I stop next to Mom. Her head lifts. She looks at me and through me at the same time as she sings.

"You're the best son a mother could ever wish for . . . Bartholomew John!"

"*I'm* your son!" I grab the phone, bring the mouthpiece to my lips. "Do you hear me?"

"I think my great-great-great-grandfather heard you. And he choked and croaked on a chicken bone a hundred years ago."

I pull the phone away and look at Mom. When did she dye her hair orange? And why do her fingernails look like purple claws?

"Mr. Hinkle?"

I blink. The scene before me changes. The kitchen table's replaced by a bed. The stove by a dresser made of twigs. The refrigerator by a state-of-the-art portable ventilation system, retail price five thousand credits—or free if you swipe it from the Good Samaritan storage shed.

"Ms. Marla?" I ask.

"The one and only."

My fingers tighten around the phone. Now fully awake, I close my eyes and pull the pillow over my head.

"Are you calling to report an identity theft?"

"No," I mumble.

"Good to hear. If you were my son, Rodolfo would have some explaining to do."

Rodolfo. Her three-legged hairless Chihuahua.

"Would you like to report something else?"

I sigh. "No, ma'am."

"You know you get twenty gold stars just for picking up the phone, yes?"

I shove the pillow aside. "I thought it was ten."

"New semester, new stakes."

Of course. "Okay," I say. "Sorry to bother you. Have a nice night."

"Back atcha. Thanks for calling the Hoodlum Hotline!"

I hang up and toss the phone to the foot of my sleeping bag. I've been keeping it close by at night, in case of an emergency, and now I want it as far away as possible.

"Stop . . . drop . . . rollshhhhh . . ."

I crane my neck to look behind me. Lemon flops over onto his stomach, dangles one arm down the side of the bed, and resumes snoring. I take my K-Pak from the floor and check the time.

Four o'clock. And so far, only three minor incidents involving sleepwalking, hidden matches, and flammable furniture. This is a significant improvement over the first two nights I spent here. Because while some people dream of sugarplums, and while I apparently dream of Bartholomew John, Lemon dreams of flames—and then tries to bring them to life. I've been forfeiting sleep and using everything at my disposal—the Smoke Detector with Automatic Flame Eliminator, the Pocket Extinguisher, the portable ventilation system—to keep the situations under control, and successfully, too. Because I haven't had to call the Hoodlum Hotline for help.

Until tonight. When I called not because I needed to, but because Bartholomew John made me.

I try to go back to sleep, but like a nightmare you can't shake long after you've woken from it, I can't forget the image of Mom at the kitchen table talking and laughing with the son she wished she had. Eager for distraction, I turn on my K-Pak again and start a new K-Mail message.

TO: enorris@kilteracademy.org
FROM: shinkle@kilteracademy.org
SUBJECT: Me again!

Dear Elinor,

Hi! How are you?

I hope it's okay that I'm writing again. I know the general rule is to wait for an answer to your (my) first e-mail before sending another, but then I remembered this one time my dad entered a contest held by our local radio station.

The prize was a year's supply of No. 2 pencils donated by our local office supply store. To enter you had to submit an essay about what you'd do with the prize if you won. Dad spent hours on his, talking all about how he'd use the pencils for good, and donate half of them to writers in need, and spread the word about the importance of sometimes staying old-school in our super high-tech world. Then after he e-mailed the essay, he checked his account every five minutes for a response.

Only it never came. He thought it was because his essay wasn't good enough, but I knew better. Partially because it was amazing, but mostly because he had to be, like, one of two people who entered the contest. So after a few days, I asked if I could see his original note.

I found the problem right away. He was supposed to send the essay to djdusty@oldiesintheclouds.com. Instead he sent it to djrusty@oldiesintheclouds.com. DJ Rusty. Not Dusty. We sent it again, but by then it was too late. The winner was announced the next morning, and the other entrant won. Dad was so disappointed he used pens all year.

Anyway, I checked my last e-mail to you, and I got the address right. But computer glitches happen all the time. So I thought maybe it somehow vaporized in cyberspace instead of hitting your in-box. And just in case, I'd better try again.

Especially because Houdini said you weren't coming back to Kilter this semester. And I wanted to make sure everything is okay . . . ?

I hope it is. And that you are too.

From,

Seamus

P.S. If you did get my other note, sorry for this

one! And no pressure to write back right away. I'm sure you're really busy. Anytime's fine. Really.

I reread the message and send it before I can chicken out. The digital envelope is still swishing when my K-Pak buzzes.

Seeing the new e-mail at the top of my in-box, I bolt upright.

TO: shinkle@kilteracademy.org
FROM: parsippany@cloudviewschools.net
SUBJECT: Clean Slate

Dear Seamus,

Thank you for writing. It was so nice to hear from you. I had a lovely vacation and hope you did too.

I'm not big on New Year's resolutions either, mostly because I don't do well under pressure. (Case in point: trying—and failing, miserably—to break up a fight in the school cafeteria in hopes of making a good impression on my new employer.) Plus, the disappointment I feel when I don't meet whatever goal I set for myself twelve months after setting it is way worse than the general disappointment I feel for not achieving simple goals, like organizing my closet or vacuuming under the couch. Why invite such discomfort when you don't have to?

However, I'm with you on starting over. In fact, that's how I try to approach every day. Each morning I wake up and think about ways in which I can improve on the day before. For example, yesterday I had a chocolate doughnut for breakfast. Fried sugar rings aren't exactly nutritious get-up-and-go fuel, and I was reminded of that fact with a killer stomachache that lasted all day. So today I had a banana . . . and half a chocolate doughnut. It was a small improvement, but an improvement all the same.

How about you? Is there something you did today that you'd like to do differently tomorrow? If so, I'd love to hear about it.

With kind regards,

Miss Parsippany

P.S. How's your new school so far this semester? Are you enjoying yourself? Have Lemon, Abe, Gabby, and Elinor come around? I hope so!

Whoa. How does she know about . . . ?

Oh. Right. I e-mailed her when I didn't think she was alive to get the message, and told her all about Parents' Day, and Mom spilling the beans about what I did to get into Kilter, and my friends turning against me. For someone I met only once, she sure knows a lot about me.

I hit reply. Before I can start typing, my K-Pak buzzes with another message. I close Miss Parsippany's and read the new one.

TO: shinkle@kilteracademy.org
FROM: annika@kilteracademy.org
SUBJECT: Today

Dear Seamus,

I hope you're enjoying your first week back at Kilter.

I also hope you can join me for breakfast before first period this morning. I'll send a golf cart. Say around seven?

See you soon.

Annika

I look over my shoulder. Lemon's K-Pak is on his nightstand. I hold my breath and wait for it to buzz. . . . But it doesn't.

I'm being singled out. Again.

I don't want to be distracted when I write Miss Parsippany back, so I save her note for later. And there's no use trying to go back to sleep now since my head will only spin with thoughts of Mom and Bartholomew John, Annika and Elinor, so I stand, roll up my sleeping bag, and cross the room. I listen at the door before cracking it open, make sure Gabby and Abe are nowhere in sight, and tiptoe into the hallway. Leaving the door ajar in case there's another predawn bonfire, I head for my room.

As I shower and get dressed, I try to figure out why Annika wants to meet with me. The last time we ate a meal together, Lemon, Abe, and Gabby were there too. Dinner with Annika was our reward for getting Mr. Tempest, our notoriously hard-to-get history teacher. And though I've earned quite a few demerits already, I don't think I've earned enough to warrant high praise and some quality one-on-one time with the school director.

I'm brushing my teeth when it occurs to me.

Maybe this isn't a good meeting. Maybe it's a bad one. Like

a warning. After all, Annika's note came right after I called the Hoodlum Hotline. And in the administration building the other day, she said the reason she met me was because she wanted to see for herself if I really wanted to be here.

Is it possible I'm not making enough trouble?

Or, worse . . . did Annika find out I never made the trouble that got me into Kilter in the first place?

I'm still stressing about this two hours later when a horn honks outside. I jump up from the couch, grab my stuff, and run from the house. Annika's golf cart's parked at the end of our walkway, but it's empty.

Guessing Annika's talking to the Troublemakers next door, I hop into the passenger seat to wait. A clear seat belt zips across my torso and waist, yanking me in place. The gleaming white dashboard glows. A digital campus map appears. I have just enough time to make out the dotted line pulsating between a small square labeled FRESHMAN FARM 1 and a big one labeled A. KILTER HOME when the cart jolts forward. It picks up speed, shoots off the pavement, and zooms toward a fat tree trunk.

"Oh no." I try to reach for the computer screen, but my arms won't move. I try to close my eyes, but my lids are stuck. Locked in place by wind and gravity, I have no choice but to sit back and wait for collision.

The tree comes closer. My heart beats faster.

Dear Miss Parsippany. Yes, I did do something today that I'd like to do differently tomorrow. I got into an unmanned, malfunctioning death trap on wheels that—

The golf cart beeps and pulls back slightly. For a second, everything stills while I float forward, feeling like one of the bubbles in Dad's old lava lamp. A squirrel in the tree watches me. We're so close I can see its tiny nostrils flare and freeze.

The golf cart jerks right. Shoots forward again.

I have no idea how long the ride to Annika's lasts. It feels like hours, but given the way the entire campus passes by in a single fuzzy pink line, it's probably closer to seconds. What I do know is that once the cart finally stops, it takes great effort to pull myself out of the Seamus-shaped impression my body made in the seat.

Also, I can't feel my legs.

"Steady there, Gumbo."

I turn toward the house—or, more accurately, the wilderness palace Queen Kilter calls home. It has three floors. Five chimneys. Walls made of windows and held together by logs. A wide stone porch with matching pillars. Privacy bordering on invisibility, thanks to a sprawling forest of towering evergreen trees.

And standing before a tall arched door, Good Samaritan George.

Chapter 9

DEMERITS: 245
GOLD STARS: 60

Gumbo?" I ask.

"Weird green guy. Made of rubber. Slanted head. Talks like a girl."

Sometimes, when Mom goes to bed early and doesn't know how late we stay up, Dad and I watch the ancient-cartoons channel on TV. Because of this, I think I know who—or what, since that's unclear—GS George is talking about.

"You mean Gumby?" I ask.

He shrugs. "Carrot, carr-oat."

"You mean tomato, to-mah-toe?"

"Nope. I don't." He raises his palms and waves them from side to side. He steps one foot forward, lifts the toe of his penny loafer, brings his foot back, and repeats the mini kick on the other side. His shoulders bounce up and down as he smiles and sings some song about correct produce pronunciation.

The feeling begins to return to my legs. Before I can regain full function, GS George's K-Pak buzzes. He stops dancing, yanks the device from his fanny-pack belt, and reads.

"Come with me," he says, his voice flat and his face straight.

I look over one shoulder as I start up the wide stone steps. Not only is there no sign of the Kilter campus, there's no sign of a road or path that leads anywhere away from here. I can't even make out tire tracks in the snow or dirt. Does the golf cart actually take flight when it reaches a certain speed? Maybe it—

The door closes. The outside world disappears.

"This way," GS George says.

We walk down a long hallway, passing a conference room. Library. Den. Gym. I feel a little guilty peeking but tell myself that if there were something I wasn't supposed to see, I wouldn't see it. So there can't be, because all these doors are open.

All of them, that is, but one.

I stop by the last room on the left. The door's closed. Muffled voices talk on the other side. Whoever's speaking sounds hurried. Agitated. The white light shining out from the thin space between door and floor goes dark every other second, as if pacing feet keep passing by. As I listen, one voice grows louder. The feet stop. Annika yells.

"I don't care where, when, or how! We will *bury* that place. And be done with her, once and for all!"

"What place?" I whisper to GS George. "Who?"

"Gun it, Gumbo," he whispers back, taking me by the elbow.

My unofficial tour ends at the living room. There's an L-shaped couch. A coffee table. Bookshelves. The furniture's white, as are the floor and ceiling. The only color comes from the silver frames around the black-and-white nature photos on the walls and the ice-blue throw pillows on the oversize sectional. Everything, even the white logs in the fireplace, gleams.

If Annika ever kicks back and watches the ancient-cartoon channel with a bucket of greasy popcorn, she doesn't do so in here.

GS George motions to a white velvet armchair. I sit. He stands behind me, his hands on his hips. We face a wall of windows overlooking a turquoise lake and snow-capped mountains.

"What's that round thing?" I ask, squinting. "Is that Annika's A—?"

"Hello, Seamus."

I start to jump up just as GS George spins the velvet chair. When it stops, I'm facing the rest of the living room.

"Hello, Ms.—" I catch myself. "Hello, Annika."

She's sitting on the edge of the couch wearing dark jeans, an ivory turtleneck, and a fluffy vest made of silver peacock feathers. Her hair's pulled back in a tight ponytail.

"Sorry to keep you waiting. Hot chocolate?"

Without waiting for a response, she motions behind her. An older woman in a white skirt suit enters the room with a glass tray. On the tray a huge chunk of chocolate sits above a large candle with a hundred lit wicks. The heat melts the chocolate. The chocolate flows into a pitcher. The older woman stirs in milk and serves.

"Thank you," I say when she hands me mine.

"Still so polite." Annika sips from her mug, licks her lips. "You'll have to get over that."

A few months ago, I would've automatically apologized. But now I know Annika doesn't like that, either.

"I spoke with Houdini yesterday. He told me all about your real-world combat mission." She sits back. Folds her arms over her chest. "He was quite pleased with your performance. He said he's never seen a first-year student act with such . . . commitment."

I smile before I can wonder whether I should.

"And that pleased *me*," Annika says. "Did you enjoy yourself?"

"Totally." I nod. "I mean—yes. Thank you for the opportunity."

"You needn't thank others for what you've rightfully earned."

My mouth itches to apologize. I fill it with hot chocolate so it can't.

"Are you ready for another mission?"

I force the liquid down my throat. "What?"

She leans forward, rests her elbows on her knees. "Are. You. Ready. For. Another. Mission?"

I heard her, but, "We just got here. The Ultimate Trouble-making Task is still months away."

"True. And if you successfully complete the UTT, you'll receive another real-world assignment. In the meantime, I'm offering you an assignment to do here. On campus."

A sudden flash of light calls my attention to the other side of the room.

"Recognize him?" Annika asks.

I watch the moving image projected from her K-Pak onto the far wall. It's an elderly man staring, bug-eyed, into the camera. His eyes widen even more as the camera zooms closer. Then, when the lens is inches away, the man opens his mouth until I can see the silver filling his molars, and screams. That's what it looks like, anyway. Because this film's silent. It's short, too. As soon as the man yells, the footage rewinds and starts over.

"Of course," I say. "That's Mys—Mr. Tempest. Our history teacher."

"Correct." Annika shudders as the shriveled face zooms in, out, and in again. "Have you seen him lately?"

"No."

"Me neither. At least, not as often as I should."

I nod, remembering last semester. Wherever Annika was—at dinner, watching the Dramatists rehearse, trekking up mountains—Mystery was never far behind.

The image freezes. Mystery stares at us, his dried lips driven apart by a gaping black hole.

"As you can imagine," Annika continues, facing me, "as director of the country's most prestigious private academy, I'm very busy. Mr. Tempest is an asset to our educational community, but he is, shall we say, a bit of loose cannon."

"Aren't we all?"

Annika smiles. "Unlike most of us, Kilter's moody history teacher is known to run off, disappear, and ignore e-mails and phone calls for days on end. He needs to be monitored. Closely. Unfortunately, he's been even harder to keep track of than usual this semester, and I'm even busier than usual. I need someone to help me keep tabs on him. Someone talented. Trustworthy. *Committed.*"

I look back at GS George. He looks straight ahead.

"What do you say?"

I expect GS George to answer, but he doesn't. I turn back. My eyes lock on Annika's.

And it clicks.

"You want *me* to help?" I ask.

"Indeed. Based on your real-world combat mission performance and your success last semester, I'm confident you'd do an outstanding job."

"What about Houdini?" I ask. "Or one of the other teachers? Or an older Troublemaker?"

"No. No. No."

"What about Lemon, Abe, or Gabby? They were successful last semester too. And we all got Mr. Tempest—together."

She tilts her head, pretends to think about it, and straightens her head. "No."

"But . . . where do I look for him?"

"If I knew that, I wouldn't be enlisting backup."

"What do I do when I find him?"

"You notify me of his whereabouts and any odd behavior."

"What if he catches me?"

"You'll make sure he doesn't."

I sit back and lower my eyes to my hot chocolate.

"Do you have any other questions?" Annika asks.

"Yes." I look up again. "Do I have to?"

She stills, clearly thrown off. Then she throws her head back and laughs. "Bravo, Seamus. And no. You never have to do anything you don't want to."

I exhale. "Okay. Good. Because it's so nice of you to think of me, but I just don't know—"

"Silly me," she interrupts. "I left out the most important part: compensation. Since this is a job that would be performed in addition to your normal academic obligations, it would be rewarded accordingly."

"Like, with demerits?"

"Even better." She stands, strides to the fireplace, and rests one elbow on the mantel. "Do you remember what I gave you and your friends the last time you were here?"

"Amazing fish sticks?"

"And?"

I try to recall what the rest of Capital T ate. Then I remember food wasn't the only thing on the menu.

"Questions," I say. "One each. To you, about anything we wanted."

"Precisely. Should you accept this position, you'll earn one question per week. And unlike the last time you were here, this time I'll waive my right to refuse to answer." She faces me, smiles. "What do you think?"

I think I have a lot of questions. Like why my real-world combat mission was so different from everyone else's. And what it meant. And how Mom knew about Kilter's true purpose, and where she got all those weapons. I have to admit, it'd be nice to get some answers.

"Oh, one more thing," Annika adds. "This must stay between us. No one—not Lemon, Ike, Abe, Gabby, or any of your instructors—can know about our little project. If they find out, you and whoever was told will be expelled immediately and permanently."

Well, that settles it. I just got my friends back. There's no way I'm going to sign up for anything that could potentially make me lose them again.

I open my mouth to tell Annika this. But then she moves. And I notice a picture on the mantel that had been blocked by her elbow. It's the only one in the room that features a nature scene with people. There are four of them, on a beach. There's a beautiful woman with long dark hair. A man whose head has been ripped from the photo. A young girl with hair the same color as her mother's. Another young girl, with red hair . . .

. . . and eyes the color of worn copper pennies.

Heart thumping, I look at Annika.

"When do I start?"

Chapter 10

DEMERITS: 275
GOLD STARS: 60

Mission Monitor Mystery begins the second I agree to Annika's terms. And for the first six days, the assignment is as exciting as clipping my toenails. Because after not seeing Mr. Tempest anywhere for days, suddenly he's everywhere. Reading in the library. Doing laps in the indoor Adrenaline Pavilion pool. Painting a still-life of a bowl of fruit in the art studio. For someone so elusive, he's pretty easy to find.

Not that I'm complaining. As long as I uphold my end of the bargain, regardless of how difficult that may or may not be, I still earn the right to ask Annika questions. Which I need now more than ever since the Elinor sent-e-mail count is still me: 2, her: 0. Plus I don't want to be so distracted that I can't complete regular assignments or I fall behind in my classes, which are proving to be even harder this semester than they were last semester.

Take biology. A few days after my meeting with Annika, when Lemon, Abe, Gabby, and I get to class after lunch, we find Samara, our teacher, hugging a trash can and gagging like *her* lunch was still alive when she ate it and is now clawing its way out. Her hair hangs around her face, thankfully blocking our view, but the moaning and hacking is enough to make my own stomach turn.

"Oh no!" Gabby drops her backpack to the floor and dashes to our ailing instructor. "Are you okay?"

"Um, that might not be such a good—"

Abe's stopped by a loud, sloshy splat. Gabby freezes, her back to us and both hands in the air, like she's surrendering.

"Oops." Samara wheezes. "Sorry about that."

Gabby turns slowly. She looks at Abe, then Lemon, then me, trying to gauge the damage by our reactions rather than seeing it directly.

"It's not that bad," I manage.

"I've seen worse," Lemon adds.

"I'm sure it'll come out," Abe offers.

We're all lying. Because the damage is yellowish-green. Wet. Slimy. It covers the front of her silver ski parka and drips down her pants. I want to help her, to run to the paper towel dispenser on the other side of the room, but like a fight in the school cafeteria, I can't look away.

"Gotcha."

I peer past Gabby. Samara places the trash can on the floor, stands up, and brushes the hair away from her face. After what just shot out of her mouth I expect her skin to be white and sweaty, her eyes to be watery and bloodshot, her lips to tremble. But her skin's pink. Her eyes are clear. Her lips smile.

"That was a joke?" Abe asks.

"I'm not laughing," Gabby says.

"That was a lesson. And you'd be crying if it had happened outside classroom walls." Samara goes to the front of the room, where, I now notice, her desk has been replaced with a bed. She climbs in and pulls the blankets to her chin. "Because I'd have just gotten you like you've never been gotten before."

"Hey." Gabby tugs on the front of her coat. "It's gone."

She's right. The yellowish-green slime has disappeared. There's not even a stain to indicate it was ever there.

"Evapo-Goo," Samara says. "You're welcome."

We take our seats. Our teacher waits for everyone to arrive before pulling the blankets over her head, groaning, and coughing so hard the bed's legs scrape against the wooden floor. After a few minutes Marcus Cooper, a chubby Troublemaker sitting in the front row who came in after the fake hurling incident, stands and starts toward her, concerned. As he nears the bed and reaches out one arm, she flings off the covers and sits upright.

"Are you sick?" she demands.

Marcus stops, his arm still outstretched. "Should I be?"

"You don't look it."

"Then . . . I guess I'm not?"

"Wrong answer." Samara hops out of bed and faces us. "Feigning illness is one of the most powerful weapons in your troublemaking arsenal. Done correctly, you can not only get out of school—if you ever return to the normal kind—but you can also keep away your parents and other bothersome adults for extended periods of time."

"My mom takes me to the doctor when I get a hangnail," Eric Taylor says. "Even if I can convince her, I can't fool him."

"Of course you can. You have hundreds of ailments to choose from—headache, sore throat, upset stomach, dizziness, extreme fatigue, ear infection, sinus infection, chest congestion, food poisoning, heartburn, allergies, hay fever. The key is to exhibit the correct balance of measurable and immeasurable symptoms."

She aims her K-Pak at the wall behind us. Swiveling in my chair, I watch life-size digital images appear. They look like a bunch of random adults—until my eyes land on the couple at the far end. He's wearing a yellow sports jacket. She's wearing a red wool coat and matching high heels. Both are smiling like they're having the time of their lives.

Which, for most of Parents' Day, when this picture was taken, Mom and Dad were.

"We'll start with the basics," Samara says. "Flying fluids."

"Like lunch chunks?" Abe asks.

"Lunch chunks, boogers, saliva—whatever you can launch from your body to theirs. Adults claim such lofty maturity, but the truth is, they're grossed out by the same things we are. Probably even more so."

"So you want us to, like, hock loogies at our parents?" Eric asks, sounding much happier about this than I feel.

"Among other things, yes." Resting her K-Pak on the headboard, Samara flops onto the mattress and crosses her arms between her head and the pillow. "Five demerits for each hit below the belt, ten for belt to neck, and twenty for neck up. Bonus demerits for firing from a distance or while lying down, since in a real-world situation, you'd likely be giving this performance in bed."

I raise my hand.

"Yes, Seamus?"

"Um, I'm actually feeling a little dry today." I press one hand to my throat. "I think it's the cold outside combined with the heat inside. And I didn't eat much at lunch, so I'm not sure if—"

"Fake it."

"Sorry?"

Samara sits up. "You're not really going to be sick when you try to convince your parents you are. So fake the fluids. That's the point."

"But I don't have any Evapo-Goo."

"Neither do they."

I follow her nod to the back of the room, where my classmates are already sliming their respective adults. Some hock real loogies. Others fill up at the room's water fountain before firing. One kid squeezes a ketchup packet and a mustard packet into his mouth, swishes the contents together, and shoots the orange spray at his dad's forehead.

For the next thirty minutes, I try. I really do. But it's not as easy as it looks. For one thing, my throat *is* dry. For another, when I fill up at the fountain and try to spray water, most of the liquid ends up running down my chin and pooling on the floor by my feet rather than hitting my target.

And that's the biggest challenge. My target. Because despite everything, I can't seem to fire fluids, fake or not, at my parents. Call me crazy (and I do, silently), but something about it just feels wrong.

So I'm relieved when Samara finally gets up, turns off her K-Pak and the pictures of our parents, and says, "There is a shortcut."

We swallow. Wipe our mouths. Face her.

"By the end of this semester you'll all be projectile pros. But it never hurts to have backup, so with that in mind . . ." She raises one fist clutching what look like two short drinking straws. "Volunteer. Please."

Abe drops his cup of water, hurdles two desks, and joins her at the front of the room. Samara points one of the straws at his face, then sticks the tip in his open mouth. Five seconds later, she takes it out again and brings it in front of her eyes.

"Ninety-seven point eight degrees," she says, making me realize the straw is actually a thermometer. "A little chilly."

"Must be my cold heart." Abe grins, thumps his chest with one palm.

"Right. Try this one, Frosty."

Samara pops the second thermometer in Abe's mouth. He's barely pressed his lips together when the device starts beeping and squealing. Stunned, his lips part. The thermometer falls. Samara catches it.

"A hundred and *two*?" she gasps. "You poor thing! You'd better go to bed—but *not* the doctor, since you're clearly very sick but still two degrees shy of real physical danger—and sleep this off *immediately*!"

Her reaction's so sincere Abe nods and starts for the makeshift bed. He stops only when Samara taps him on the head with the second thermometer.

"The Foolproof Fever Reader," she announces, facing the rest of us. "Parental concern guaranteed or your credits back."

"Credits?" Lemon asks. "The Kommissary sells that?"

"Indeed. Except this is a superexclusive, limited-edition model. The Kommissary could only order two, which just came in last period. I got one, which means . . ."

There's one left. Given my inability to spew chunks on demand, the Foolproof Fever Reader is definitely something I want in my medicine cabinet.

Apparently, I'm not the only interested customer. Because when Samara checks the wall clock and nods to the door, giving us permission to leave two minutes early, every single Troublemaker charges across the room.

The Kommissary's on the other side of campus. Capital T starts out in a dead heat along with most of our classmates, but eventually Abe pulls ahead. Gabby gets distracted by a flock of Troublemakers making snow angels in the main garden, and drops out of the race to join them. Lemon and I keep pace for a while, but his legs are twice as long as mine, and I feel bad for slowing him down.

"Go ahead," I say. "Just don't let Abe get it. His ego doesn't need that boost."

Lemon nods and powers on. By the time I reach the Kommissary several minutes later, he and the rest of my classmates are already inside.

I stop at the entrance, pull off my mitten, and press one hand to the print pad just inside the door. The glass box glows as words scroll across its screen.

WELCOME, SEAMUS HINKLE! YOU HAVE . . . 215 CREDITS!

I wave to Martin the cashier, but he doesn't notice because he's busy trying to figure out how to break a four-way tie between Lemon, Abe, Jill, and Eric. Since I'm dead last, I head toward the marksman supplies at the back of the store.

I pick up a pack of Hydra-Bomb water balloons, which I've been meaning to try out with snow, and some batteries for the Kilter Smoke Detector with Automatic Flame Eliminator. I'm checking out the Koiffurator the Kommissary Krew e-mailed me about over vacation when I hear a series of strange sounds coming from the next aisle. There's a grunt. Sharp tapping. Whistling and humming. More tapping, then more whistling and humming.

"Good afternoon, Mr. Tempest," someone says.

Mr. Tempest. In the hair dryer's mirrored side, I see my eyes grow wide.

There's another grunt. Quick footsteps, like the Troublemaker who addressed our mysterious history teacher can't get away fast enough. More tapping.

Holding my breath, I replace the Koiffurator on the shelf. Tiptoe down the aisle. Round a display of steel snow sleds that double as protective body armor. Pick up a sled, hold it in front of my face, and peer over the top, careful to keep the rest of me behind the display.

He's halfway down the aisle, wearing a typical Mystery ensemble: corduroy pants, a turtleneck, a long wool coat, leather gloves, and a knit hat topped with a single pom-pom. All black, which makes his crinkled white skin practically glow. He looks up and around, like invisible hawks circle overhead, then back down at a glass box on the shelf before him. He leans forward, removes something from his coat pocket, holds it up to the case, and taps. He does this twice more, tapping a little harder each time.

"Can I help you, sir?"

Mystery jumps. As he does, I see a male Kommissary employee standing behind him.

"If I want help, I'll ask for it," Mystery grumbles. Then, perhaps recalling his New Year's resolution to be less cranky, he adds quickly, "Thank you for the offer."

The employee spins around and hurries back down the aisle. Mystery waits for him to disappear before looking up and around again. He waits a few more seconds, then returns his attention to the case.

Still holding the shield, I take one large step across the aisle for a better view and duck behind a display of assorted stink bombs. They come in a variety of shapes, sizes, and scents, like rotten egg, spoiled milk, and boiled cauliflower. Accidentally catching a whiff of the moldy cheese sample, I clamp one hand over my nose and mouth to keep from choking. The effort to stay quiet combined with the stench makes my eyes water—and me miss Mystery headed my way.

He brushes past in a black flash. Blinking back tears, I see glass shards on the floor where he just stood.

"Cleanup in aisle eight!" a voice declares from the store's speaker system.

There's a light whirring overhead. I look up and see a tiny silver orb with a square lens attached to the wall near the ceiling. It rotates toward aisle eight.

Security cameras. That's what Mystery was watching. Which means the glass on the floor was definitely no accident.

Not wanting to be mistaken for the thief, I step just close enough to read the display case's sign.

AX AND YE SHALL RECEIVE . . . THE SMALLEST, SHARPEST SLICER IN KILTER HISTORY! PRICE: 5,000 CREDITS.

An ax? Mystery's a history teacher. What does he need an ax for? And why couldn't he just buy it? Why go to the trouble of stealing it?

My pulse quickens as I picture Annika. Wait until she hears about this. Witnessing a Mystery crime—especially one involving a razor-sharp blade—has to earn me some sneaky-spy respect.

I start toward the front of the store, hoping Lemon's still there. I can tell him about this, right? Since anyone in the store could've seen what I just saw Mystery do?

Then it hits me. And I stop short.

Mystery *stole* an *ax*. Not borrowed or bought. Not a water balloon or battery pack. And then he fled like his life depended on it.

My heart thumps faster and sinks simultaneously. I turn and flee too, my feet moving like I'm the one being chased. I'm nearing the back door when my K-Pak buzzes inside my book bag. Thinking it might be Annika checking in after hearing about what just happened, I slow down to yank out the device.

And then I stop again.

TO: shinkle@kilteracademy.org
FROM: enorris@kilteracademy.org
SUBJECT: Hi

Dear Seamus,

Thank you for writing. It was nice to hear from you.

I know you're back at school and wondering where I am. My family had an emergency, so I'm still home. I hope to return to Kilter as soon as possible.

Talk soon.

Elinor

I don't know how long I stand there, staring at the message. What I do know is that by the time I look up from the K-Pak screen, the mess in aisle eight has been cleaned up . . .

. . . and Mystery's nowhere to be found.

Chapter 11

DEMERITS: 275
GOLD STARS: 60

TO: parsippany@cloudviewschools.net
FROM: shinkle@kilteracademy.org
SUBJECT: In Your Expert Opinion

Dear Miss Parsippany,

Hi! How are you? Did you kick your doughnut-for-breakfast habit yet? If not, I highly recommend dipping your fried sugar ring in warm cinnamon milk tomorrow morning. The cafeteria here served that for dessert recently, and it was AMAZING.

I've been thinking a lot about what you said about starting over each day. It's a great idea. Because whenever I do something I'm not proud of, I usually just feel bad and wish it had never happened. Sometimes I pretend like it never happened, unless it's so awful that pretending is impossible. So I love the idea of using the unfortunate incident as an opportunity to turn things around. And I'm going to try really hard to do that from now on.

Which brings me to a question—and a favor. You definitely don't owe me anything, especially not after what I did (even if what I did didn't kill you), but right now, I think you're the only one who might be able to help.

As a teacher, you know kids. You know parents, too. This must give you some great inside perspective.

So my question is: What do parents want? Like, REALLY want? Because up until a few weeks ago I thought they wanted their kids to make their beds, get good grades, be polite, respect adults, and generally stay out of trouble. But now? I'm not so sure.

And any insight would be greatly appreciated.

As for school, it's going well. My classmates don't run in the opposite direction when they see me, so that's an improvement. And Lemon, Abe, Gabby, and I are tighter than ever. I haven't seen Elinor yet because she's—

A sudden boom explodes near my ear. It's followed by a long, loud wail that sounds like a cross between a foghorn and a police car siren. It makes me drop my K-Pak, fall off the couch, and lunge for the coffee table—and phone.

"Hoodlum Hotline, how may I direct your call?"

That's what I hope Marla's saying on the other end, anyway, because I can't hear anything over the emergency drone.

"Bomb!" I gasp, trying to look out the windows and crawl under the coffee table at the same time. "Attack!"

"Crumb. Gobsmack."

I pause. That didn't sound like Marla.

The front door slams. I peer through the wooden legs of my fallout shelter. In the foyer, Abe shakes his head as he stoops down and picks up scattered papers from the floor.

"Mr. Hinkle? Would you mind repeating that?"

Now *that* was definitely Marla. I start to do as she asks when I realize I can hear again. The noise ended as abruptly as it began. The walls and ceiling are still intact. So are Lemon, Abe, Gabby, and, judging by a quick body scan, me.

"Sorry," I say. "False alarm."

"All righty then." There's a light clacking as Marla types her entry. "That'll be forty new additions to your starry sky."

I shoot up, smacking my head on the table. "What happened to twenty?"

"This semester, the more you call, the more you get."

Great.

"I'll add those to the hundred you just got for being gotten."

"What?" I ask, thinking the earsplitting noise must have compromised my hearing.

"You've got to be kidding," Lemon says.

"That's not fair!" Gabby declares.

"It's definitely a pickle," Abe says.

My alliance-mates are all looking at their K-Paks. Spotting mine where it landed three feet away, I shimmy out from under the table on my stomach.

"Oh, by the way," Marla says casually, "have you seen Good Samaritan George lately?"

I stop mid-shimmy and look around the room again, like I *should* see the ballet-loving Gumby fan somewhere. Maybe hiding behind a houseplant, monitoring us.

"Nope," I say.

"Okay." Marla sounds different. Almost disappointed. "I've updated your record. Thanks for calling the Hoodlum Hotline!"

I hang up, reach for my K-Pak, and climb to my feet.

"That was Devin?" I ask, reading my new K-Mail message. The note from our music teacher is blank, but the attached photo shows the mouth of a shiny brass instrument aimed toward our open living room window—and every single member of Capital T midair, hovering over furniture. It looks like a deleted scene from *Mission: Impossible.*

"And his merry music maker," Abe says. "I just saw him hot-trotting across the front expanse of grass, reaching said music maker toward the heavens like a triumphant pied piper."

"Can you *please* stop talking like my great-grandmother?" Gabby groans.

"Pardon me." Abe holds up both hands. "But if I'd like to acquire the most demerits for this week's Language Arts assignment by learning how to converse granny-style—and astound mumsie and daddy dearest in the future—that's my pejorative."

"Prerogative," I say.

"Huh?" Abe says.

"Never mind." I turn to Lemon. "Our music teacher snuck up on the house, opened a window, and wailed on his trumpet. To scare the you-know-what out of us."

"So it seems." Lemon slides down in the armchair. Clasps his hands loosely on his stomach. Closes his eyes. "And it worked. Unfortunately."

"Now we have to get a Troublemaker the same way," Gabby says. "For another chance *not* to be gotten by Devin. Which we need if we want to participate in the Ultimate Troublemaking Task, which I totally do."

"As do I. It is, as they say, a cannonplum."

"Conundrum," I say.

"Whatever." Abe flops onto the couch. "Let's flip the script."

"What do you mean?" I ask.

"I mean we should get Devin. And all our other teachers."

"That's what we did last semester," Gabby says.

"And we should do it again this semester. At the very least, we should go after whoever gets us. Bigger and better than ever before."

"But that's not what Houdini said we needed to—"

"I know," Abe says, interrupting Gabby. "But *we* are Capital T. And we go above and beyond the call of duty. That's what sets us apart from ordinary Troublemakers."

"So you want us to do what Houdini said . . . and get our teachers, too?" I ask.

"Exactly," Abe says.

I look at Lemon. His eyelids slide up slowly, indicating some interest.

"I can yodel," Gabby offers. "It's kind of a hidden talent. In fact, I've been the Washington State Fair Junior Warbler champion five years running."

"Congratulations!" Abe claps exaggeratedly.

"Thanks! I can teach you guys how to do it too. It's not on Devin's curriculum. He won't see—or hear—it coming."

Lemon's eyelids slide down. "I'm in."

"Me too," I say. Because with all these gold stars I'm earning,

I'll need more demerits if I'm going to keep Annika convinced that I want to be here.

"Fine," Abe says. "But let's start now. I don't want to waste time."

"Yay!" Gabby jumps up from her chair and dashes across the room. "I'll get my sheet music!"

I take her seat and return to my K-Mail. I finish my note to Miss Parsippany, check for typos, and send it. I've just clicked on Elinor's note for the bazillionth time since receiving it a few days ago when my K-Pak buzzes. I reluctantly close Elinor's message and open the new one.

TO: shinkle@kilteracademy.org
FROM: annika@kilteracademy.org
SUBJECT: Q&A

Dear Seamus,

You owe me an update and I owe you your first reward. Meet me at the helipad in fifteen minutes. A golf cart's waiting behind the snow-cone truck.

And remember: Don't. Tell. ANYONE.

Hugs!

Annika

The helipad? Snow-cone truck? Fifteen minutes? Hugs? Despite the reward, none of this sounds very appealing—and Gabby returns to the room with sheet music in hand before I can guess what it means. She drops to her knees on the other side of the coffee table and spreads out the pages.

"Okay, so, like most people, you've probably always thought the trick to a great yodel is in the throat."

"No, I haven't," Abe says. "Because like most people, I've never thought about yodeling. Ever."

Gabby doesn't bat an eye. "But really, it's in the stomach. Allow me to demonstrate."

She opens her mouth. I scoot forward.

"Wait," I say.

She closes her mouth.

"I'm so sorry. But I kind of have to go." Feeling my face warm, I hold my K-Pak in front of it. "Ike just wrote. He got some new weapon he wants me to try."

"Right now?" Gabby asks.

I nod.

"What's the rush?" Abe asks.

I shrug.

"Go," Lemon says. "We'll fill you in later."

"Oooh, our first group performance! I can't wait. Guys, you don't even know how much fun you're about to have. Let's warm up by taking our lips between our pointer fingers and thumbs and . . ."

Her voice fades as I leave and head down the hallway. I get my coat from the hall closet and hurry to the front door. I wave to Lemon as I pass the living room, but his eyes are closed again.

Outside, I spot the snow-cone truck right away. It's silver with frosty windows and an attendant who hands out paper cups to waiting Troublemakers. I find the golf cart right behind it. It's empty, just like last time. I climb in, wait for the seat belt, and brace for takeoff. I don't know where the helipad is so have no clue how long the ride will last, but I'm hoping less than twelve minutes. According to my K-Pak clock, which I manage to glimpse before the cart moves and the world blurs, that's how much time I have before Annika's fifteen-minute window closes.

For better or worse, the golf cart stops four minutes later. At first I think this is for better, since I have eleven minutes to kill—maybe by writing Elinor back. I still haven't done that yet, since I'm still trying to figure out what to say. She didn't exactly give me much to go on, and her note also gave me a strange feeling. I know it can be hard to tell what kind of mood someone was in when they wrote their e-mail (unless that someone's Gabby), but there wasn't a single exclamation point in Elinor's message. That has to mean something. . . . Doesn't it?

Unfortunately, the note will have to wait. Because when I get out of the golf cart, which has stopped in front of the Kommissary, Annika's already there.

"Good afternoon, Seamus!"

I follow the voice by looking up—and up and up and up—until my neck feels like it's bent back at a ninety-degree angle.

She's standing at the edge of the Kommissary roof. Her stride's wide, her fists are at her hips, and her long, ice-blue coat flaps around her like a cape.

"Shall we?" a male voice asks.

My chin lowers, bringing my head with it. A few feet away, GS George opens the Kommissary door.

I follow him inside. In addition to watching ballet, he must practice it himself, because he moves quickly, lightly, through the aisles. We reach the back of the store in no time. He leads me through an unmarked steel door, down one staircase, up another, and into a glass elevator. The door closes, GS George presses the UP button, and we shoot skyward.

This elevator ride's longer than any I've ever taken. Not one for being trapped inside a moving box, I try to distract myself with conversation.

"Ms. Marla was just asking about you," I say.

GS George doesn't look away from the silver lightning bolt moving in a wide arc above the elevator door, but he does smile.

"She wondered if I'd—"

I don't finish the sentence. I can't. Because we've left the building, literally, and are now rising high above the Kommissary roof. We're surrounded by blue sky. Fluffy white clouds swoop toward us. On the lawn far below, Troublemakers point and stare.

"Glass elevator chute," GS George says when we finally stop and the doors open. "Nifty, huh?"

He hops out onto what seems to be a large glass platform and jogs to the waiting black helicopter. I stand there, back and hands pressed to the clear elevator wall. I might stand there all day, frozen by a fear of heights I didn't know I had until this very second, but then I catch a flash of blue near one of the helicopter's windows.

Annika's already inside. Waiting for me.

I take a deep breath. Fix my eyes straight ahead. And step out of the elevator—just as the helicopter's blades start spinning. My fear of heights is nothing compared to my fear of being blown off the platform and falling ten stories, so I lower my head and pick up the pace.

When I climb into the helicopter, I freeze again. Mom hates to fly, so we never travel anywhere we can't drive to, which means I've never set foot in any gravity-defying vehicle—unless you count the Kilter golf cart. But I've watched enough movies to expect a few seats squished close together in a tiny tin bubble. What I find instead are two long, gray leather sofas. Plush white carpet. Black-and-white nature photos lining the curved walls. A small kitchen with real stainless steel appliances—and a server, preparing snacks.

Annika's typing on her K-Pak. She nods to the couch across from hers, so I sit. GS George hands me a set of white leather headphones, then disappears behind a sparkly silver curtain. I can't hear anything with the headphones on, so I don't know we're moving until I look out the window and see the tiny Trouble-makers disappear completely.

The flight is so smooth it feels like we're floating. I relax enough to watch the trees, fields, and mountains down below. Soon the helicopter picks up speed and the ground blurs. Eventually, my headphones beep. Annika's voice breaks the silence.

"Welcome aboard, Seamus."

I turn around. "Thank you."

She accepts a cup of tea from the server. "So. Tell me. What's happened since your last note?"

"Did you have a chance to read it?" I ask. It was a doozy, and she didn't write back, so I've been wondering.

"Of course. I'm very busy, but this is a priority."

"Well, that was the strangest thing I saw all week. Mr. Tempest . . . with the ax." I watch her sip her tea, wait for the shock to cross her face. But it doesn't.

"Did you follow him? And see where he went with it?"

"I tried." My eyes fall to my lap. I force them back up. "But no."

She shrugs. "He's an old man. He gets cold easily. He probably wanted to chop some wood for the faculty fireplace."

"But he stole the ax," I remind her. "He didn't buy it."

"He's not allowed to shop at the Kommissary. And he enjoys inviting suspicion—and freaking me out. As long as I know what he's really up to, I refuse to give him the satisfaction." Her K-Pak buzzes. She checks her messages. "What was he doing today?"

I review my thorough mental notes. "He had oatmeal and berries for breakfast, worked out at the Adrenaline Pavilion, and went to the library."

"Interesting," Annika says, although she only seems to be half listening. "Good job."

"Thanks." I breathe a silent sigh of relief.

"Have you thought about what you'd like to ask this week?"

I have. With so many questions it was hard to choose just one, but after careful consideration I decided to ask about Elinor. Now that I've heard from her I don't have to ask if she's alive, so I'll start with whether Annika knows when she'll be back at school. I want to ask about Mom, too, and how someone outside Kilter could get Kilter weapons, but the truth is, if I know Elinor's returning soon, that means she's really okay. And as long as I know she's really okay, I can stop worrying about that and focus on everything else.

This is called not putting the cart before the horse, as Mom would say. Or the equal sign before the multiplication symbol, as Dad would say.

But before I can answer, my headphones beep again. GS George speaks.

"Destination approaching. Ten o'clock."

If the helicopter's a timepiece, I must be sitting at noon, because Annika jumps up, leaps over the coffee table, and lands on the couch two feet away from me. Standing on her knees, she presses both palms to the window and looks down. I shift in my seat and peer through the clouds to the Earth below.

At first I don't know what we're looking at. There's a lot of flat, yellow land. A few houses lining one straight road. But then we tilt left, zoom over a beige hill, and shoot down before leveling off again. An enormous clear lake comes into view. In the center, far from the mainland, is an island. It has lots of rocks and no palm trees, but it's definitely an island. As we come closer I see what appears to be a series of crop circles, like the kind aliens tend to make in the middle of nowhere except not as round, drawn in the dirt. It's not until we're hovering directly above the island that I can see the circles are actually letters. Two, specifically.

A *K*. And an *A*.

"It's perfect," Annika breathes.

"What is it?" I ask.

"Not much now. But if all goes according to plan . . . soon it will be another Kilter Academy campus."

Something in her voice makes me look at her. She's smiling, but her eyes are watering.

"Are you okay?" I ask.

She doesn't shift her gaze as she answers.

"I told you, Seamus. One week, one question. That's all."

Chapter 12

DEMERITS: 310
GOLD STARS: 200

A week later I'm beginning to think the most mysterious thing about Mystery is Annika's interest in him. That, and his interest in brussels sprouts, which he eats with every meal, including dessert. But I keep following him, even when he goes places I'd rather not, like the Adrenaline Pavilion. That's where he spends an hour every afternoon, circling the outdoor track. I suppose I should be happy he no longer sprints through the gardens at midnight, the way he did last semester, but that just makes him less mysterious and me more confused.

At least I'm getting to work on my jump shot. As someone who's much better at throwing a digital basketball with a game controller than a real one with his own hands, that's something I never thought I'd say.

Now I keep my head lowered and dribble the ball as Mystery rounds the track near the court. When his footsteps continue in the opposite direction, I jog a few feet, raise my arms, and aim for the basket.

"You might want to watch out for that—"

I've just hopped. But instead of sailing through the air, my feet hit something hard. My torso shoots forward. The ball flies from my grip. I close my eyes and lower my arms, wondering as I drop toward the ground if a Kilter marksman has ever succeeded with four broken limbs.

I land on my side with a thud. Wiggle my fingers and toes, hands and feet. Open my eyes and see that everything works thanks to the large pile of snow that broke my fall.

I start to stand. I'm on my knees when a cold, wet blob hits my face. I fall back again, more from shock than force.

"Twenty demerits."

I bring one hand to my forehead and drag it down to my

chin. When I open my eyes this time, I see Ike standing over me.

"Five for feet to waist, ten for waist to neck, twenty for neck up." Ike grins and rests one elbow on what looks like a long silver handlebar. "You all right?"

"I'll live," I say, climbing to my feet. "What's that?"

"The Kilter Drifter. Guaranteed to create blizzards and snowbanks—and trip up unsuspecting passersby—even on the sunniest of days."

I check out the Drifter. The long handlebar leads to a silver box on wheels. It reminds me of Dad's old snowblower, except it's smaller, shinier, and, judging by the mini mountain that wasn't on the court seconds ago, faster.

"It's been pretty warm lately." I nod to the lawn, where yellowish-green patches outnumber white ones. "I don't think I'll be able to get many demerits."

"Think again." Ike stands up straight and pushes the Drifter, which hums as it comes to life. A thick white flume shoots out from a narrow chute at the machine's base, turning the asphalt on his left from black to white.

"It makes its own snow?" I ask.

"Would you expect anything less?"

I guess not. "But there's no one out here." Then, remembering why *I'm* here, I spin around and breathe a silent sigh of relief. Mystery's still trotting around the track.

Ike turns and pushes the Drifter back toward me. "If I didn't know better, I might think someone was in a very good mood today." Apparently seeing the confusion on my face, he adds, "As in . . . not bad."

Oh. He thinks I don't want to make trouble. That's definitely the last impression I want to be making.

"I'm ready," I say. "I just—"

I'm cut off by a new blizzard. Only this one's not made of snow; it's made of people. Twenty Troublemakers in white sweatpants, hooded sweatshirts, and knit caps sprint across the basketball court so fast, my visibility plummets to zero.

"Athlete hurdle practice," Ike says when they've passed. "Because your tutor would never steer you wrong."

As we head for the track, I try to distract Ike from any lingering suspicion he might have that I'm not up to his task, while working on Annika's at the same time.

"How much for the man in black?" I ask quietly.

Ike follows my nod. "Mr. Tempest?" He shrugs. "Same as everyone else."

"Really? Even though he's so . . . mysterious?"

"He's running in circles in plain sight."

"Right now," I say. "But not usually."

"Mr. Tempest's not that mysterious. He's quirky. That happens as you age." He glances at me. "Look at our parents."

He has a point, although I was hoping for some inside information from an older Troublemaker that I might somehow use to impress Annika. Before I can remind him that Mr. Tempest was the only teacher we didn't have to get last semester in order to advance, because he's supposedly so hard to get, *and* that Capital T succeeded in bringing him down only after thwarting his attacks on us, the Athletes take their positions.

"What's that bicycle doing there? And that garbage pail?" The track, which was totally clear a moment ago, is now covered in random items. "They're going to trip and fall before we've even started."

My questions are answered as soon as the Athletes take off. Because while normal track stars leap over hollow wooden squares, Kilter track stars leap over items you might find around your neighborhood.

"Start pushing," Ike says.

The first cluster races in our direction. I grip the Drifter's handlebar, turn, and walk. Snow flies from the chute. Unfortunately, it sails over the runners' heads and floats to the ground on the other side of the track. They sail over their next hurdle, a lawn chair, without breaking stride.

Hearing the next group coming up behind me, I look over my shoulder. I'm trying to pick a target when my right foot lands in a shallow hole. I squeeze the handlebar for balance, and freeze when it buzzes in my hands. Turning back, I see words scrolling across the silver metal. I touch ANGLE, then DOWN. The snow chute lowers.

The handlebar is a control panel. After some quick fiddling, I discover that in addition to its angle, I can adjust the snow's trajectory, speed, and volume. As the next group passes me, I focus on an easy target: the broad back of a large male Athlete. A wall of slush fires from the chute, makes a smooth arc six feet in the air, and slams between his shoulder blades. The force tips him forward and slows him down. Heart racing, I turn around as he scans his surroundings.

"Ten demerits," Ike says when I reach him. "Nice."

"Won't he know it's me?" I ask.

"Probably. But part of his training is learning how to avoid you. And if he tried to interfere with your lesson, he'd be slammed with gold stars—which would hurt way more than what you just did."

"Why not just use snowballs?" I ask as we wait for another group to approach.

"If a guy's hit with a snowball in the real world, he knows he's being attacked and will retaliate accordingly. If he's caught in snowblower crossfire, he'll likely assume it was an accident and go about his business. That's a million times more effective, especially when dealing with adults."

I want to point out that Dad's snowblower does what it says and nothing more. It doesn't create snow. Or control where it goes, or how fast it gets there. Practical application's nice, but you can't get fancy Kilter weapons in the real world.

Unless, of course, you're Mom.

I turn and walk. When the first cluster of runners comes around again, I aim for another male Troublemaker. I get both legs at once, making him stumble.

"Another five," Ike says. "Keep it up."

As the runners dash and hop along the far side of the track, I check on Mystery, who's still jogging in the outermost lane.

Then I ask Ike something I've been wondering, especially since seeing Kilter Academy's potential second campus the other day.

"What are you going to do?"

Ike looks up from his K-Pak. "What do you mean?"

"You're a fourth-year. This is your last semester. What will you do when you graduate?"

In other words, will he be going to regular college . . . or Kilter Kollege?

Something crosses Ike's face. His eyes darken. His mouth turns down. It's like a large cloud has formed directly above him. I'm tempted to look up and see if this is actually the case—but then the shadow lifts. And Ike looks past me.

"Now, that's a little strange," he says.

I follow his gaze to a group of runners. They're still running and jumping, so I'm not sure what he means. But then I glimpse a flash of black amid all the white.

Mystery's left his lane and joined the Athletes. He keeps pace in the middle of the group, which is packed so tightly together it's hard to see him. When they reach the southern end of the track a few seconds later, he scoots out between two Troublemakers, runs off the track, and keeps going across the lawn. His legs pump faster. Every few feet he glances behind him, like he's worried someone might follow.

I turn back. "Fern gave us a special assignment for gym class. I just remembered that I forgot to do it."

"No problem. As soon as you get fifty demerits, you're free to go."

I fight the urge to look back at Mystery. This effort makes fighting the urge to lie impossible. "It was due this morning. We get gold stars every hour we're late."

"Oh. Okay." Ike looks around. "Get five of them, from here, and you're a free man."

When I follow his gaze this time, I find it directed at a frozen pond a quarter mile away. Ten Troublemakers zip and spin in a heated game of ice hockey. Hitting five twirling targets at this distance seems like an impossible task, but the longer I try to talk my way out of it, the farther away Mystery gets.

So I stand up straight. Square my shoulders. Squeeze the Drifter handle. And aim.

My first shot misses. So does my second. And third and

fourth. The snow reaches the makeshift rink, but by the time it does, the Troublemaker's skated away and is nowhere near where he was when I first fired.

A quick check to the lawn shows Mystery approaching the far tree line. Heart thumping, I return to my task. As the skaters zigzag toward the net at one end of the pond, I have an idea.

I shift position, point, and shoot. The snowy stream makes a huge, rainbow-like arc toward the pond. Picking up speed as it descends, it nails the goalie's left shoulder. The goalie, who's three times bigger than every other player thanks to enormous silver padding, wipes out. He falls down and spins, face-first and spread-eagled, across the ice. Between his size and his hockey stick, which he still holds, he accidentally strikes one foot after the next until both teams are skating on their bottoms instead.

I turn around. Ike holds up one palm. I slap it with mine.

"Good luck with gym," he says.

"Thanks." I dart around the bench he's sitting on. "Where's my backpack?"

"Right where you left—" He stops when he sees that the

bench next to him, where I put my stuff before starting the task, is empty. "Well, that's too bad."

I'm on the verge of total panic paralysis when I hear something. Music. It's soft, but I can still make out the song, which is familiar. It plays during the *Return of the King* credits—and whenever I feel like listening to it on my K-Pak.

And then I see him. Houdini. Strolling toward the Adrenaline Pavilion gate—with my backpack hooked on one shoulder. My K-Pak, which he must've turned on, pokes out of the bag's front pocket.

I say good-bye to Ike, then run like I've never run before. Unfortunately, that's not fast enough. Houdini doesn't seem to be in a hurry, but his head start is so big I won't be able to catch up without losing sight of Mystery. I could grab a bunch of tennis balls from the indoor courts I'm about to pass, but throwing things would only stall him briefly before prompting him to book it across campus. I could just let him go . . . but he has my K-Pak. Which has my e-mail. No one's ever discussed Kilter's online personal privacy, but something tells me that, at a school for Troublemakers, if you can access another student's messages, you're a star and he had it coming.

So I do what I have to do. I swing by the ice rink, swipe a skateboard one of the hockey players left nearby, and silently vow to return it to the exact same place when I'm done so its owner can find it again.

And then I roll—and swish. Because this skateboard, like the Kilter Drifter, does things its normal counterpart can't. Like automatically shift from wheels to blades every time I hit a patch of snow or ice. And travel twice as fast with half the effort.

My foot's only hit the ground three times when I catch up to Houdini. I yank my backpack off his shoulder without slowing down.

"Way to hustle, Hinkle!" he shouts after me.

I throw the bag over my shoulder, change direction, and zoom across the lawn just as Mystery slips between two trees. I shoot into the woods thirty seconds later—and the skateboard immediately snags on dead leaves and fallen branches. I hop off, cram it into my backpack, and continue on foot.

Dear Miss Parsippany, I think. *Today I did another thing I probably should've done differently. I ventured into a dark forest, by myself, and trailed an ax-wielding loner to—*

My K-Pak buzzes inside my backpack. I pull it out and read while I walk.

TO: shinkle@kilteracademy.org
FROM: kommissary@kilteracademy.org
SUBJECT: Sizzling Cold Weather Accessories

Hi, Seamus!

The calendar might say it's winter, but it sure doesn't feel like it . . . because you're on FIRE! You just earned 75 demerits for tripping up the Athletes, swiping a fellow Troublemaker's skateboard, and stealing Houdini's backpack—which was yours first, of course, but became his the second he took it. That brings your total demerit count to 385. Take away the 300 gold stars you've earned for calling the Hoodlum Hotline, jumping at the sound of Devin's horn, and letting Houdini swipe your stuff, and that gives you 85 credits!

We realize things are probably just starting to heat up, but you'll still want to blend in. This in mind, we highly recommend the Kilter Knit Set!

I press the flashing camera icon. A photo of a teenager wearing gray earmuffs and a gray scarf appears. That photo blinks, so I press it, too. A second image loads. In this one, the kid flings the earmuffs like nunchucks and the scarf like a lasso.

I return to the message.

> Capable of reaching maximum speeds of 300 rpm (rotations per minute), this isn't your grandmother's handiwork! And while her priceless arts and crafts can take years to complete, the Kilter Knit Set can be yours today for 75 credits.
>
> Your classmates have no idea how much trouble a former ball of yarn can make. Stop by and start showing them!
>
> See you soon!
>
> At Your Service,
>
> The Kommissary Krew

Closing that message, I see a few more I missed while I skim them quickly.

TO: shinkle@kilteracademy.org;
loliver@kilteracademy.org;
gryan@kilteracademy.org
FROM: ahansen@kilteracademy.org
SUBJECT: Music Man Meltdown

Hey,

Was just at Kanteen. So was Devin. Overheard him talking to Wyatt. They were getting snacks to go watch a movie in the classroom building faculty lounge.

Now's our chance. Meet by the first-floor water fountain in ten?

TO: shinkle@kilteracademy.org;
gryan@kilteracademy.org;
ahansen@kilteracademy.org
FROM: loliver@kilteracademy.org
SUBJECT: RE: Music Man Meltdown

On my way.

—L

TO: shinkle@kilteracademy.org;
loliver@kilteracademy.org;
ahansen@kilteracademy.org
FROM: gryan@kilteracademy.org
SUBJECT: RE: Music Man Meltdown

YAYAYAY!!!! That's PERFECT! Now remember, we have to

TO: shinkle@kilteracademy.org;
loliver@kilteracademy.org;
ahansen@kilteracademy.org
FROM: gryan@kilteracademy.org
SUBJECT: RE: Music Man Meltdown

Oops! Sorry, I was so excited I hit send before I was done! We'll do a quick run-through when we get there. See you in a few!!!!!!! ☺

I check Abe's message again, then my K-Pak clock. He wrote twenty minutes ago. Which means the rest of Capital T is currently in the classroom building. Waiting for me.

I stop walking and listen. Hearing Mystery's footsteps crunching to my right, I change direction and keep going. I'm about to write Lemon back to apologize and let him know I'll be there as soon as I can when a new message pops up.

TO: shinkle@kilteracademy.org
FROM: enorris@kilteracademy.org
SUBJECT: Hi

Dear Seamus,

Hi. How are you? You never wrote back, so I just want to make sure everything is okay. How's school? Capital T? Annika?

I also wanted to give you an update. I'm fine, but things are still a little crazy at home. I really want to return to Kilter, but I'm not sure when I'll get there.

I'll keep you posted. In the meantime, I'd love to know what I'm missing.

Sincerely,

Elinor

She'd love to know what she's missing. She wrote again because I never wrote back. Does that mean she's missing . . . me?

I had stopped walking when I had realized who the note was from. Now a sudden noise makes me look up—and dart behind a tree.

Mystery's stopped walking too. He stands before a small cabin made of crooked logs and crumbling stone. He removes his sneakers, places them by the front door, and goes inside. A light turns on. Smoke spirals out of a crooked, crumbling chimney. Classical music streams through cracks in the thin glass windows.

What is this place? Does Mystery live here? If so, why is he so far away from the rest of the faculty? Does Annika know? If not, can I just tell her about it so she can send the Good Samaritans to check it out?

This last question, at least, I can answer myself. Keeping my K-Pak in hand in case I need immediate emergency assistance, I step out from behind the tree. I crouch down and stay low to the ground as I make my way toward the cabin. I grab some rocks and shove them into my coat pocket. When I near the house, I dash the remaining few feet, round the side of the building, and duck beneath another small window.

"Whoa." The word escapes from my mouth before I can swallow it.

Because while the house's exterior looks like the kind of place Jason, Freddy, or some other horror-movie psycho might call home, its interior looks like the kind of place Cinderella, Sleeping Beauty, or some other princess might hang up her tiara. The walls are pink. The checkered curtains are frilly. The pink-and-white floor tiles are arranged in intricate floral patterns. A small crystal chandelier hangs over a pink dining table. And everywhere—sitting on the pink sofa, perched on shelves, crammed between cabinets and countertops—are stuffed animals and porcelain dolls.

Porcelain dolls, especially old ones like these, with their loose, bobbing eyes and missing lashes, are enough to send me running in the opposite direction. But three more things seal the deal.

1: Green satin ribbons. Looking more closely, I see they're everywhere. Tied around the dolls' necks. Hanging from the chandelier. Looped across the ceiling like birthday party streamers.

2: The sound of a little girl crying.

3: Mystery himself. He emerges from a darkened doorway, nostrils flared and eyes wide but unfocused. His arms are raised overhead. It takes only a split second to realize two more things.

He's holding the ax.

And he's coming right at me.

Chapter 13

DEMERITS: 385
GOLD STARS: 300

"Stop!"

I sit up.

"Drop!"

Jump to my feet.

"Roll!"

Grab Lemon's fist and pry it open. His grip is so tight that the book of matches has folded in half. I yank it out before his fingers snap closed again, then return to my sleeping bag and add it to the growing pile by my pillow. I don't know where he's hiding these fire starters, but I've taken away more than a dozen of them since we went to bed two hours ago.

"Again?" Lemon, now awake, asks.

I pause. "Yes."

"How long?"

I check my K-Pak clock. "Eleven minutes."

He sighs. "You should go."

I look back. "Where?"

"To your room. You'll never get any sleep in here."

After what I saw this afternoon, I may not get any sleep anywhere ever again. But I can't say this out loud.

"I'll get just as much if I leave and there's a fire. No offense."

"No problem."

He sounds sad. I think he might elaborate, but he doesn't. I wait for his breaths to lengthen, which usually happens the instant his eyes shut, but they don't. Not wanting him to stress, I try to change the subject.

"I'm sorry again. For before."

"Seamus."

"I know you said it wasn't a big deal, but it totally was. You guys waited for me. I never came. That's not right."

"You were with Ike. You couldn't get away. It happens."

I rest my K-Pak on my chest, screen side down, so he can't see me frown. I've never liked lying—but I hate lying to Lemon. "Still. I wish you'd gone after Devin anyway. I would've made up the demerits another time, on my own."

"I told you. We were gotten together, and we'll get him back together. That's how an alliance works. All for one or not at all."

"Well, I don't know how much longer Capital T will be in business. Abe was so annoyed he'll probably leave our group and form a new one. And Gabby cut back my yodel part from ten beats to one. Like she thinks that's all I can handle."

I expect Lemon to tell me to chill. That's what he told me earlier when I finally found Capital T in the Kanteen after fleeing Mystery. Of course, he could've meant the instruction more literally, since fear and physical exertion made me overheat until buckets of sweat ran down my face and soaked my clothes.

Although our history teacher might have several decades on his Kilter-centered lessons, thanks to his regular fitness routine the dude can move. By the time he reached the door of the cottage in the woods, I was halfway across the yard. By the time *he* was halfway across the yard, I'd gained only a few feet. In seconds he was able to grab the hood of my coat. It took all my strength to bolt left—and leap over a shallow ditch. With his eyes apparently glued to where the ax blade was about to meet my neck, Mystery didn't notice the hole and fell right in, twisting his knee in the process. As he howled and stumbled, I took advantage of the delay and sprinted the rest of the way to the Kanteen, barely breathing and never looking back.

Lemon didn't seem too upset when I finally found him, Abe, and Gabby, so I figured he didn't think I should be either. But he doesn't tell me to chill now. He doesn't say anything. And unlike my yodel part, his breaths grow longer.

Realizing I've bored him back to sleep, I close my eyes too.

Mystery lunges toward me, ax raised.

Determined to think happy thoughts, which Dad says is the only way to combat terrifying ones every time he goes to the dentist, I open my eyes again, pick up my K-Pak, and start a new message.

TO: enorris@kilteracademy.org
FROM: shinkle@kilteracademy.org
SUBJECT: Hi!

Dear Elinor,

It's so great to hear from you. I'm sorry I didn't write sooner, but I actually wasn't sure if I should. It sounds like you have a lot going on right now, and I didn't want to bother you. Whatever IS going on, I hope it works out soon. More importantly, I hope you're okay.

As for what you're missing at Kilter? For starters, the milkiest, most mouthwatering hot chocolate EVER! I don't know what they put in there, but it's a million times better than the best I've had anywhere else. And the crazy sugar high lasts about twelve hours, so if you have a cup at breakfast, you can barely blink until the crash strikes right before bedtime. Which is pretty useful when you're going to classes, completing assignments, training, and fending off teacher attacks. ☺

I stop typing. Is the smiley face too much? Not enough? Deciding to trust my gut, I leave it and continue.

Everything else is great. Capital T got hit pretty hard by Devin, but we're planning a stellar comeback. I'd tell you all about it, but it'll probably make more sense when you can hear the digital recording Gabby plans to make and sell in the Kommissary.

Classes have been really fun—and pretty interesting, too. For example, did you know that honey mustard has the perfect consistency for finger painting "I'M WATCHING YOU" and other strange messages that'll stick without dripping on kitchen walls? I didn't, at least not until Wyatt demonstrated it for us in art the other day.

And my one-on-one lessons are lots of fun. Ike's a really good guy. We don't talk about much besides weapons and demerits, but I can tell. I don't have an older brother, but if I did, I'd want him to be just like my troublemaking tutor.

Anyway, there's tons more, but I don't want to take up too much of your time. Because the sooner you take care of whatever's going on, the sooner you can come here—and the sooner I get to tell you the rest in person!

From,

Seamus

I reread the note. I'm tempted to mention Mystery without referring to Annika's top-secret task or what I saw in the woods today. But I don't want to taint my happy message. Depending on what's going on, that could scare her off and keep her from writing back. And if she doesn't write back, how will I know she's still okay enough to hold her K-Pak and type?

I hit send.

My K-Pak buzzes.

TO: shinkle@kilteracademy.org
FROM: parsippany@cloudviewschools.net
SUBJECT: Parents, a.k.a. Life's Great Mysteries

Dear Seamus,

Thank you for your note. I'm happy to hear school's going well and that your friends have come around. They make all the difference, don't they? I've found that no matter how fast and furious the curveballs sometimes come at us, hits are always best made with loved ones nearby.

Speaking of curveballs, I've given a lot of thought to your question about parents and what they want. First, I must say you're right to be confused. I'm a grown woman, but my parents still puzzle me more than my childhood Rubik's Cube ever did. One day my mother tells me to stand up straight lest I grow a permanent hunchback, and the next day she tells me to relax my shoulders because living people don't take kindly to corpses.

Ouch. I guess my mom's not the only one with issues.

In any case, mixed messages and disconcerting delivery aside, I think parents want one thing above and beyond anything else. And that's for their kids to be better people than they are. They want them to be happier. Healthier. Smarter. Stronger. They don't always go about it the right way, but that only makes the goal more worthwhile.

She left out sneakier. Trickier. More dangerous. If her theory is correct, that's what Mom wants for me.

I keep reading.

I'm guessing this curiosity didn't come totally out of left field. Did something happen with your parents to prompt the question?

I'm all ears—or eyes, as the case may be.

With kind regards,

Miss Parsippany

Wanting to read the message again, I scroll up. I'm still watching text blur down when my K-Pak buzzes again.

This is a lot of late-night communication. Maybe I'm not the only one Mystery terrified into a permanent waking state today.

TO: shinkle@kilteracademy.org
FROM: enorris@kilteracademy.org
SUBJECT: RE: Hi!

Dear Seamus,

Thanks for writing.

You didn't say anything about Annika. How is she?

Sincerely,

Elinor

"Stop!"

I scroll up.

"Drop!"

Read.

"Roll!"

Scroll again.

The smell of sulfur tickles my nose. Snapped out of my technological trance, I leap to my feet, grab the water bottle from Lemon's nightstand, and dump its contents on the lit match he holds.

"How long?" he asks.

I return to my K-Pak. "Seven minutes."

He gives his wet hand a single shake, then drapes his arm across his forehead.

I slide back into my sleeping bag and lie down. "Something's wrong."

"I know."

"You do?"

"Yes. I can't fall asleep without worrying about the waking nightmare I might create for everyone around me. That's not right."

Oh. "We'll work on that. But I was actually talking about Elinor."

Blankets rustle as he rolls onto his side. "Why? What happened?"

"Nothing. At least not that I know of. But I've sent her a few e-mails since Christmas vacation, and except for her last message, which came really fast, it's taken her forever to write back. And her notes have been off, too. I mean, I guess I don't really have anything to compare them to since we never e-mailed before break, but still. I can tell. They're short. And kind of cold."

"They do call her the Ice Queen," he reminds me.

"But she's only distant to keep from hurting people. By lying to them." Lying is Elinor's troublemaking talent. She told me that on our way to Annika's Apex last semester. "And she wasn't like that with me."

"Would you rather she wrote about all the fun she's having wherever she is? Then you'd have to wonder whether she was telling the truth or trying to hide something."

Interesting point. And one I'm not sure I find reassuring.

"She said she had a family emergency," I add, "but didn't say what kind. Could that be a lie too?"

"It's definitely vague. And people usually shoot for that when they want to skip the details and not seem rude."

Again, not very reassuring.

"But there could be a million reasons why she didn't say more," Lemon says. "And not one of them has to be because she's hurt or mad or sad."

Or in some kind of danger. Which, after going to Mystery's cottage, hearing the little girl crying (who sounded a little like Elinor but who I don't think was Elinor), and seeing all those green satin ribbons (just like the kind Elinor wears in her hair), is what I'm afraid of.

"For example," Lemon continues, "no one—not my parents, little brother, friends, Annika, or anyone else—knows why I first started playing with fire. Whenever I'm asked, I just say because it was fun, and pull out matches for proof. That usually prevents more questions."

"Vague," I say.

"Very. But I don't keep the truth to myself because I'm hurt, mad, or sad. I keep it to myself because . . . I'm embarrassed."

Embarrassed? Lemon?

There's a soft click of a lighter. The room fills with a warm, gold glow. "When I was really little, do you know what I wanted to be?"

Despite his current interests, I'm guessing not a professional arsonist. "A veterinarian?" Because who doesn't want to help hurt animals feel better?

"A firefighter."

I crane my neck to look back. "What happened?"

"I was kicked off my old school's Scrabble team."

"Scrabble? As in the board game?"

"I know I don't use them much, but I kind of have a thing for words. I like them. How they sound. The way you can twist them around. The fact that they can say one thing but mean something totally different."

Did Houdini steal my roommate and replace him with a Lemon look-alike? Because this definitely doesn't sound like the same kid I've been sleeping (or not sleeping) near for the past four months.

"Unfortunately, I'm pretty bad at forming words from seven

random letters. Especially when I have to build them on other words. And worry about points. All in ninety seconds or less, which is how long it takes the sand to get from one end of the timer to the other."

"That's a lot to think about," I agree.

"Too much. Anyway, two years ago our team made it to the regional Wordsmith Wars—no thanks to me. And the first round in, our team lost the regional Wordsmith Wars—thanks to me."

"Bummer."

"It wouldn't have been such a big deal if I didn't like words so much—or if I hadn't been kicked off six other teams that semester. Baseball, soccer, Mathletes, the debate squad, Latin club, bowling. None of them wanted me." Before I can offer sympathy, he adds, "Not that I blame them. The first requirement of any organized school group is showing up. The next is practicing the skills needed to participate. And my afternoon naps usually got in the way of both those things."

Now *this* sounds like the Lemon I know and love.

"But for the Scrabble team," he continues, "I showed up. I practiced. Until they told me I couldn't anymore."

He stops speaking. I wait for him to connect the dots for me.

He doesn't, so I say, "I'm sorry that happened . . . but I don't get it. How did getting kicked off the Scrabble team make you not want to be a firefighter?"

He releases a long, slow breath. "I have to warn you. This wasn't my best behavior."

"Understood."

"The bad news came a few days after the Wordsmith Wars loss. I was in the middle of a rehearsal round and didn't see it coming. I was surprised. Disappointed. Mad. So mad, I grabbed a bunch of tiles from the board and threw them on the floor. My anger must've given me some sort of superhuman strength, because when the tiles hit concrete—we were playing outside on a patio—they sparked. Like miniature fireworks."

I try to picture this emotional outburst but can't. Lemon's usually mellow to the point of comatose.

"And I felt a rush. An excitement that I had created something as powerful as fire with a couple of tiny wooden squares. I couldn't form seven-letter words for three hundred points in a minute and a half . . . but I could do *that*."

An image of Mrs. Lubbard of Hoyt, Kentucky, pops into my head. I have to admit, I experienced a similar feeling when I fired beauty products so successfully she spun and fell off her velvet stool.

"Anyway, I started playing with fire because I stunk at Scrabble and then acted like a brat. Nothing to brag about. So I don't." On the ceiling, his shadow shrugs. "And maybe that's what's going on with Elinor. Maybe she did something she's not proud of, annoyed her parents so much they kept her home, and feels silly talking about it. But no matter what, I wouldn't stress. I'm sure she'll tell you the truth eventually."

Eventually. By then it may be too late.

My K-Pak buzzes.

Lemon's lighter clicks off. "Go ahead."

Hoping Elinor wrote again, I check my messages.

TO: shinkle@kilteracademy.org
FROM: annika@kilteracademy.org
SUBJECT: Breakfast

Hi, Seamus!

Thanks for your latest update. I hope Mr. Tempest didn't scare you too much in the woods. I'm sure there's a logical explanation for what you saw, and I'd love to figure it out together. Let's chat over breakfast tomorrow (or today, depending on when you get this). I'll send a cart at six thirty.

Sweet dreams!

Annika

Happy thoughts. Happy thoughts. Happy thoughts.

Those are failing me right now, so I put down my K-Pak and return to my conversation with Lemon instead.

"Thanks for telling me all that. I really appreciate it, and I promise I won't tell anyone else." I pause. "So what do you think Elinor could've done that she'd feel silly talking about?"

His silence is punctuated by a long, deep inhale and a long, deep exhale. The response is surprising, though not entirely unexpected.

Because in the ten seconds it took to read Annika's message, Lemon fell asleep.

Chapter 14

DEMERITS: 385
GOLD STARS: 300

Hoodlum Hotline, how may I direct your call?"

I pull the phone away from my ear. Look at it.

"Helloooo?" Ms. Marla calls from her end.

"Sorry." I bring back the phone. "But I didn't call you."

"We're talking, aren't we?"

"We are, but I didn't dial. The phone rang. I answered it."

"What do you mean, the phone—wait. Seamus Hinkle? Is that you?"

This sounds like a trick question. "Yes?"

"Well, I'm guessing the only thing you do more often than call me is brush your teeth. You probably picked up the phone without even realizing it."

"No, I really didn't. I was just sitting here, on the couch, waiting for Annika's golf—"

Oops.

"Annika's golf cart?" Ms. Marla asks, not sounding particularly surprised. "The sun's not even up. Where are you and our illustrious Kilter queen off to so early?"

I think fast. "Did I say Annika? I meant Ike. My tutor. He likes practicing when everyone else is asleep and we have the whole campus to ourselves."

"Sure. Right. Interesting." There's a soft yap in the background. Ms. Marla shushes Rodolfo. "Anyhoo, since I have you on the phone, what do you think the chances are that you'll see George today?"

"George?" I ask. "The Good Samaritan?"

"Could there be another?"

I don't know how to answer that. "Do you want, like, a percentage?"

Ms. Marla chuckles like I've made a joke. Then there's a shrill ringing on her end of the phone, and she sighs.

"Shucks," she says. "That's the other line. Listen, if you do see George, would you do me an enormous favor and tell him I said the silly bear ducks at dusk? Pretty please? He'll know what it means. Thanks for calling the Hoodlum Hotline!"

"Wait, I don't get gold stars since you're the one who—"

I stop when I hear the dial tone. I hang up and look at the phone again, like it might contain clues as to what just happened, then turn to put it back on the coffee table.

"Morning."

I jump. Drop the phone. Snatch it from the floor and press the off button before I accidentally call the Hotline for real. I sit back and hope I look pleasantly surprised to see Abe sitting in the armchair across from me.

"Hi." I smile. "You're up early. How'd you sleep?"

"Adequately." His eyes narrow, like now I'm the one asking trick questions. "So. Pre-dawn tutor session, huh?"

"What? Oh—yup."

"Didn't you just train with Ike yesterday?"

It seems so long ago I have to think about it. "I did."

"I meet with my tutor once a week. So do most other Troublemakers."

I'm not sure what Abe's getting at but figure it boils down to the same basic theory: As a murderer, and, therefore, star student,

I'm getting special treatment. When I'm supposed to be one equal part of an alliance.

"He has some projects coming up that may interfere with our training schedule. So he's trying to get in as many sessions as he can while he can."

It's a funny thing about lying: The more you do it, the easier it gets. I tell myself this particular lie is for the greater good of everyone, since I can't be any kind of alliance member if I'm found out and expelled from Kilter—and only hope that doesn't turn out to be yet another stretch of the imagination.

"Whatever." Abe stands up. "We're meeting behind the Kanteen delivery truck at seven forty-five. Try to wrap up your little game of catch by then."

I stand too. "Seven forty-five? This morning? What for?"

His back to me, Abe's head falls forward, then shakes slowly. "Hinkle, Hinkle. Don't you check your K-Mail?"

Yes. About eleven times a minute since becoming such a popular pen pal. Even when I don't hear my K-Pak buzz, just in case it does and I miss it. I checked right before the phone rang, and now go to check again.

"Music Man Meltdown, take two," he continues before I

press the digital envelope. "Devin always runs through his scales after breakfast, inside the Kanteen delivery truck. Something about the acoustics."

I don't know how long I'll be. Or where. Or whether I'll make it at all.

I mean to say these things out loud, but the words get stuck somewhere between my chest and mouth. Then Abe leaves the room, and I hear the soft hum of a golf cart engine grow louder. Not wanting him to see my transportation and grow even more suspicious, I run out the front door and down the walkway. As the golf cart zips away from the curb, I glance back at the house. The door remains closed, the windows empty. Temporarily relieved, I turn forward. The cart picks up speed, and I use all my strength to keep my K-Pak raised without letting it slam into my face.

No new messages. Was Abe stretching the truth himself?

Guessing I have a few seconds to kill, I start my own new message.

TO: enorris@kilteracademy.org
FROM: shinkle@kilteracademy.org
SUBJECT: RE: RE: Hi!

Good morning!

Just wanted to answer your last note. Annika's fine. She seems busier than usual, and maybe a little more stressed, but fine. I'm sure she misses you TONS and can't wait to have you back ASAP!

If you have other questions, or need anything else, or even just feel like saying hi again, please let me know!

Have a great day!

From,

☺ Seamus ☺

Elinor wrote right back when I used one smiley face. Maybe she'll hand deliver her next note if I send two.

I press send. I'm still scrolling through my in-box for Abe's invisible message when the golf cart jerks to a stop in front of Annika's house.

"Morning, Mr. Hinkle."

"The angry deer runs at dawn."

Good Samaritan George's head falls to one side. Sliding out of the cart, I try again.

"The funny fox flies at midnight."

GS George's lips pucker. His eyebrows arch. "The silly bear ducks at dusk?"

"Yes!" I smile. "Ms. Marla asked me to tell you that."

He returns the smile as he lifts his head. Bounces his shoulders up and down. Holds open the front door. "Goody."

I want to ask why she couldn't call him instead of me to relay this message, but don't. Partially because it's none of my business. Partially because it's a little weird to think about GS George and Ms. Marla's relationship, whatever its nature might be. But mostly because the second I step inside, my senses are slammed from every direction. There's loud bluesy, jazzy music. Voices. Warmth from a lit fire in the foyer fireplace. The unmistakable scent of breaded fish frying, which is so strong—and yummy—I can taste it.

"Faculty meeting!" George practically shouts over the din. He motions for me to follow him. "She should be done shortly!"

We hurry down the hallway. The voices grow louder as we near the last room on the left. The door's open. I try not to look inside, but my eyes have other ideas.

"Morning, Seamus!"

My feet stop so fast my torso leans forward. I look at GS George. He shrugs.

"It's okay!" Annika calls out. "Come say hi!"

I do as she says and find all my teachers arranged around a large glass conference table. Well, *almost* all my teachers. Houdini, Wyatt, Fern, Samara, Devin, and Lizzie are sitting in clear, high-backed chairs. The chairs are angled toward Annika, who sits at the head of the table. Open laptops and half-eaten plates of food are on the table before them.

Mystery's sitting in a folding chair in the corner of the room, arms crossed and lips turned down. Instead of a laptop or plate of food, he holds a glass of water.

Everyone but my history teacher smiles and calls out their greetings. I do the same, trying not to look at the digital map of the United States projected from a computer in the center of the table, which is so big it takes up an entire wall. Or at the red, blue, and silver digital dots scattered across the map, some of which blink while others shine steadily. Or at the TROUBLEMAKER TERRITORIES AND EDUCATIONAL EXPANSION header near the top of the map. But once again, my eyes seem to have minds of their own.

"We're just wrapping up," Annika says. "I'll be right with you."

"Okay," I say, forcing my eyes to meet hers. "Great."

I wave once more and follow George to the living room. I sit on the couch and he stands by the doorway, fiddling with his walkie-talkie. I think about last semester, when Lemon took me to a secret phone to call my parents. The phone was in a secret room in a secret basement annex of the classroom building. The room required passwords and handprints to get in. And with its map and laptops, it looked a lot like the conference room here in Annika's house—only with a bunch of other high-tech, unidentifiable electronic equipment.

When Annika and I talk today, I plan to stick with my original question, the one I never got to ask on the helicopter last week, about when Elinor's coming back. But I think I already know what I'll ask after that.

What, exactly, is Kilter up to?

The voices are broken up by laughter. Soon both grow louder as the meeting moves from the conference room to the enormous back patio, passing through the living room on the way. Through the floor-to-ceiling windows I watch Annika point toward the distant horizon. I can't hear what she's saying and wonder if it has anything to do with Annika's Apex, the dilapidated amusement park that, once upon a time, was a fun, happy amusement park. Her father presented it to Annika as a gift for her sixth birthday, but was so busy he only took her there once. It's been falling apart and rusting away ever since—and was partially destroyed by Capital T last semester, as part of the Ultimate Troublemaking Task to make Annika cry. What's left sits on top of a tall, distant mountain, but even from the couch I can see the steep loops of the roller-coaster track.

Remembering the Apex makes me remember my first visit there last semester. Our entire class went for a history lesson led by the Mystery man himself.

Speaking of, I should be keeping better tabs on him here. Especially since the rest of the faculty's outside . . . and he's not.

"Bathroom."

GS George looks up. "Is that another secret message from the exquisite Ms. Marla?"

Okay, definitely no more undercover Cupid for me.

"Sorry, no. I just need to go. To the bathroom."

He hooks his walkie-talkie on his belt and starts toward the hallway.

"It's okay," I say quickly. "I know where it is."

"George?" Annika opens a sliding glass door and pokes her head inside. "Would you please join us for a sec? Some of our faculty members have security questions related to . . . you know."

He looks at me. I nod. Apparently reassured, he goes outside. I wait for the sliding glass door to close before darting down the hallway. I peek into the conference room. The library, den, and first-floor restroom. I peer out the front windows and am glad when the yard is empty and the golf cart is still there.

I'm about to open what looks like a coat closet when there's a thump overhead. From my end of the hallway I can see all the way to the living room windows at the opposite end. Annika, George, and the faculty are still outside. So I head for the wide white staircase.

I'm halfway up when I hear another series of thumps. Remembering Mystery's ax and picturing heads rolling, I run back down to the foyer. A round marble table is in the middle of the room. A glass vase holding white flowers is in the middle of the table. Instead of water, the vase is filled with small silver beads. I reach into the vase and grab a handful. The beads are heavier than they look and remind me of BB gun pellets. I shove them into my jeans pocket, then remove the silver ribbon tied around the vase's base and loop it around my wrist. It's not very stretchy, but if necessary I can still use it to launch beads lacrosse-style.

Sufficiently armed, I run upstairs.

The doors lining both sides of the second-floor hallway are closed, but it still takes all of five seconds to pinpoint Mystery's location. Three for him to drop something else, two for me to reach the door I think muffled the noise, and one to confirm this guess when a thin cloud of dust shoots out from the crack between the door and the floor, turning my brown boots gray.

It takes ten times as long to work up the nerve to turn the knob. When I finally do, words burst from my mouth before I can stop them.

"What are you *doing*?"

Chapter 15

DEMERITS: 385
GOLD STARS: 300

Of course, this is the wrong question. Because I can see what Mystery's doing—he's taking all Annika's old dolls, teddy bears, and other stuffed animals from her bed, bookcase, and toy chest, where they've sat long enough to collect inches of dust, and shoving them into a black trash bag.

What's not as clear is why.

"Those are Annika's things," I say. "From when she was a little girl."

Mystery turns toward me, the sudden movement creating a swirling gray funnel cloud. "How do you know that?"

I don't know that. Not for sure, anyway. I put two and two together the first and only other time I was in here, when Capital T was invited over for a celebratory dinner. I accidentally came upon the bedroom while trying to hide out—and avoid Annika's official announcement of my secret criminal past, or so I thought. The room looked then as it does now, minus the ransacking, and like the young girl who called it home hadn't done so in a very long time. The purple wallpaper was yellowing. The furniture was covered in sheets, sunlight blocked by thick curtains. The only sign anyone besides me had set foot in the room in years was the top of the dresser, which was covered in pictures. The photos of young Annika and her family, as well as a newspaper clipping about Annika's mother passing away when Annika was my age, were clean and clear, like someone had just polished their frames.

But I can't tell Mystery this. So instead I tell him, "You shouldn't be in here."

He smirks and reaches toward the floor. I yank the ribbon from my wrist and reach into my jeans pocket.

Annika will be grateful I stopped him. She'll let me stay at Kilter as long as I want. Maybe she'll ask me to teach a class.

Happy thoughts. Happy thoughts. Happy thoughts.

I don't know whether to be relieved or disappointed when Mystery stands up holding not an ax, but a stuffed monkey. He kisses the toy's cheek. Gives it a squeeze. Takes its tiny hands in his and does a mini spin.

There are tons of things I should be thinking right now, mostly about getting out of there as fast as possible, but the only thing that comes to mind is that the poor primate's already missing one eye and would probably like to keep the other.

Then, as if the silent waltz in his head came to an abrupt end, Mystery stops dancing. Thrusts the monkey under one arm. Snatches the trash bag of toys from the bed and strides toward the door.

Somehow, my feet stand firm. I don't move, even when he stops two inches before me and lowers his face toward mine. When he speaks, his breath smells like black licorice.

"Despite what this school teaches you," he hisses, "there exist in this world things to which children are not entitled."

My eyes burn from not blinking, but I keep them raised to his. Inside my jeans pocket, my fingers tighten around two silver beads.

"My business is mine and mine alone. Do you understand, Mr. Hinkle?"

I swallow. Nod.

"Good boy." He pats my head with his free hand, then brushes past me. Halfway down the hall, he stops and turns around. "Oh, by the way. The next time you decide to stroll through the woods, you might want to better prepare. The K-Pak's an impressive instrument, but it rips like paper under the force of a razor-sharp blade."

He tips an invisible hat toward me and continues on. I finally blink, and the heat in my eyes spreads to the rest of my body. My legs ache to run to Annika so I can tell her everything that just happened . . . but should I really do that right now? After what Mystery said? And with him still on the premises? If he knew I immediately ratted him out, wouldn't that throw a huge wrench into Annika's and my top-secret project? Since he'd probably go to even greater lengths to keep his bizarre behavior under wraps? But isn't this exactly what our top-secret project is *for*? To discover crazy, creepy, made-for-TV-movie kind of stuff about Kilter's history teacher?

TV movies. That reminds me of the last one Mom watched, and that I saw part of while spying from the top of the staircase, since they're supposedly for audiences more mature than me. It was about a kid trapped in a tree house by his crazy uncle, who apparently had him confused with a very tall house pet, for ten years.

I picture Mystery's cottage in the woods. All the kids' stuff inside. The green ribbons. It's so terrible I can barely think about it. . . . But could that be what he's doing? Hiding kids away? Hiding *Elinor* away? As some sort of punishment? Is that what he'll do with me if I get in his way?

I haven't moved an inch when I hear footsteps again. They're coming back up the stairs. Guessing Mystery's returning for another bag of toys, I lunge toward the closed door across the hall from Annika's childhood bedroom. The knob turns easily. I shoot inside and close the door.

I stand there. Not breathing. Just listening.

The footsteps grow louder, come closer. They seem to stop by Annika's childhood bedroom, then continue.

He's looking for me. He won't stop until he finds me. I lock the door slowly, carefully, even though he can chop his way in if he's come back with the ax. I tell myself to never go anywhere without my K-Pak ever again, since it's not doing me any good in my backpack in the living room, where I left it. Then I spin and sprint as fast as my tiptoes will allow.

My destination is the wall of windows overlooking the

backyard. So I can jump and wave until I get Annika's attention. That or, fingers crossed, land on a fat, soft bush after leaping two stories to my freedom.

But I take only two steps. Then I see the large, round bed covered in silver satin. The glass desk. The white leather chair with a sparkly AK—not KA, which is usually how the letters are arranged on buildings, sculptures, and ski parkas throughout campus—embroidered across the back. A flat-screen computer monitor.

Guessing this is Annika's grown-up room, I should be even more inclined to reach the windows and find a way out. But then my eyes catch two familiar words on the computer screen. And I go to the desk instead.

When I get closer, I see the words are actually names.

Mine. And Elinor's.

I glance behind me. The door's still closed and locked. I listen. The hallway's silent. I turn back to the computer and skim the e-mail on the screen.

TO: shinkle@kilteracademy.org
FROM: enorris@kilteracademy.org
SUBJECT: RE: RE: RE: Hi!

Dear Seamus,

Any idea why Annika might be stressed? Maybe because she's trying to be the best director she can be and run the best academy possible in hopes of producing the kind of strong, smart, skilled young adults our world could use so many more of? That's a lot of responsibility—and pressure. It could make a person tense every now and then.

As for her missing me? I doubt it. She might be my aunt, but she can be a real

The note stops there. I scroll down, but the rest of the message box is empty.

This sounds like a reply to the note I sent Elinor on my way here. But how is it on Annika's computer? And why is it half written?

A gray square rimmed in silver digital flowers grows in the center of the screen. Its note covers Elinor's.

NEW MESSAGE: SEAMUS HINKLE

I stare at the bright white words. New message? To me? From me? Is GS George snooping through my backpack downstairs? And playing with my K-Mail?

The gray box fades. Elinor's note narrows and moves to the right side of the screen. A new sidebar appears on the left side of the screen. It has three boxes with three labels.

KILTER, A.

HINKLE, S.

NORRIS, E.

The middle box is blinking. My eyes shift from the screen to the clear mouse next to the keyboard.

I could definitely get kicked out for tampering with the director's K-Mail.

Then again, I could also be promoted to assistant director.

I take the mouse. Guide the cursor to my name. Click.

"What the . . . ?" I breathe.

The sidebar and Elinor's half-written note fade as my in-box appears. And my sent-message folder. And my trash. And every other item and option I see whenever I load my K-Mail on my K-Pak. The new message is from the Kommissary. I ignore it and click on my sent messages. The entire list pops up, with every note I've sent Lemon, Abe, Gabby, Elinor, Annika, and Miss Parsippany. There's even the one I sent Dad last semester. I click the trash folder next and see dozens of notes about Kilter sporting events and menu changes.

I exit my message system and click on Elinor's. I feel a pinch of guilt in my stomach as her in-box loads, but something stronger tells me to keep going.

She doesn't have many messages. In fact, most of the ones in her in-box are from me. Since she's not here, she's probably been removed from the master class list so doesn't receive those notes sent to all students.

There's a thump in the hallway. At least I think there is. It's hard to tell with my pulse hammering in my ears. Either way, time's not on my side. So I exit Elinor's message system and aim the cursor toward Annika's box. Before I can click again, another gray square appears.

MESSAGE MOVE FROM KILTER, A. MOBILE TO MASTER TRASH SUCCESSFUL

A white garbage can at the bottom of the screen flashes. I click on it instead.

My pulse grows faster. Louder. It sounds—and feels—like one of those ancient steam locomotives is chugging back and forth between my temples. Against the glass mouse, my fingers become slick with sweat. I force myself to focus and open the new deleted message. According to the time stamp, it was sent five minutes ago.

TO: shinkle@kilteracademy.org; loliver@kilteracademy.org; gryan@kilteracademy.org
FROM: ahansen@kilteracademy.org
SUBJECT: Music Man Meltdown Rescheduled. Again.

Hey,

Since Hinkle's busy schedule kept him from our second retaliation attempt, and since Lemon's still so gung ho on doing this thing as a complete alliance, I'm suggesting a third option. Why don't we meet at the gazebo after first period today? Devin has choir rehearsal there second period. It'll be trickier since it's so exposed, but I think we can still get him.

Later.

—A

I close that note and open the next in the list. According to the time stamp, it was sent this morning. Before Abe's and my awkward exchange.

Only I never got it.

TO: shinkle@kilteracademy.org;
loliver@kilteracademy.org;
gryan@kilteracademy.org
FROM: ahansen@kilteracademy.org
SUBJECT: Music Man Meltdown, Take Two

Hey,

Great idea. Did some sleuthing (you're welcome) and found out Devin runs through his scales every morning inside the Kanteen delivery truck. Something about stellar acoustics. Want to unleash our yodel on him? This morning at 7:45?

Abe-man out.

I close that note. Skim the list and choose another note toward the bottom. It was sent three weeks ago, right after school started

.

TO: shinkle@kilteracademy.org
FROM: enorris@kilteracademy.org
SUBJECT: Hi

Dear Seamus,

Thank you so much for writing. I can't tell you how happy I was to get your note. My arm's almost healed and the doctors say scarring should be minimal. They also said it would've been nonexistent if I'd gotten medical attention sooner, but that's okay. It's still good news.

In less good news, I'm sorry to say I won't be returning to Kilter this semester. Annika decided I didn't really want to be there and kicked me out. I have to return my K-Pak but wanted to make sure I wrote you before I did. I know we weren't always best friends last semester, but you were nicer to me than anyone's ever been. I'll be grateful forever, and I'll never forget it.

And since we probably won't see each other again, I can say something now I'd be too nervous to say in person.

I miss you. And I wish you were here. Because my new school's okay, but it'll definitely take some getting used to.

I guess they don't call it Blackhole, Arizona, for nothing.

Good luck with everything. I know you'll be an amazing Troublemaker.

—Elinor

As I stare at the screen, Annika's voice shoots through my head.

I don't care where, when, or how. We will bury *that place. And be done with her, once and for all!*

I close the note. The trash can. The sidebar. Until the original message is the only thing on the computer screen.

Then I go back downstairs. My teachers are gone. GS George and Annika are waiting for me in the living room.

"There he is!" Annika beams. "I'm so sorry I kept you waiting, Seamus. To make up for it, what do you say we save the update and start with your question first?"

"I say that's a great idea."

"Fantastic!" She sinks to a velvet couch and pats the seat next to her. "Do you know what you'd like to ask?"

"Yes." I take my backpack from the floor and hitch it onto my shoulders. "I don't feel well. Can I leave?"

Chapter 16

DEMERITS: 385
GOLD STARS: 300

Annika's surprised by my request but lets me go. I tell her I'll check in later, then take the golf cart back to the main part of campus. After e-mailing Wyatt, Samara, and Lizzie to say I'm sick, which isn't a lie because my stomach's been turning since discovering Annika's K-Mail kleptomania, I skip my afternoon classes to think. Plan. Prepare.

After dinner that night, I'm as ready as I'm going to be. For Phase One, anyway.

Of Operation Evacuate Elinor.

“Operation what?” Lemon asks.

“Evacuate who?” Gabby asks.

“You’re kidding, right?” Abe asks.

They’ve just gotten home from the Kanteen. I’ve just asked them to join me at the kitchen table and introduced the mission. Now I repeat it. Slowly.

“Operation. Evacuate. Elinor.” I look at Abe. “I wish I were.”

“Evacuate her from where?” Lemon asks.

“Another school,” I say.

“Why?” Gabby asks.

“Because she doesn’t want to be there.”

“How do you know?” Lemon asks.

“She wrote me.”

“And asked you to come get her?” Gabby asks.

I pause. “Not exactly.”

That’s all Abe needs to hear. He sighs and shoves back the chair.

“Abraham—”

“No.” He cuts off Lemon. “Hinkle’s too busy and important to even e-mail and say he can’t make it to an alliance mission—four times—and now he expects us to just drop everything and help him save his girlfriend?”

"She's not my girlfriend."

"Because he's lonely or lovesick or whatever?"

"I'm not lonely." I don't deny the second ailment because who knows? Maybe that's why my stomach feels like I've been riding the roller coaster at Annika's Apex all day.

"Well, I'm sorry." Abe stands and pushes in the chair so hard it knocks into the table. "Oh, wait. No, I'm not. I'm busy too. And I don't have time for this."

He turns to leave.

"Annika hacked my e-mail." I rehearsed these words before the bathroom mirror, but they still sound strange. Abe must think so too because he stops. I quickly continue. "That's why I didn't know about the second Music Meltdown plan this morning or about the other two plans you tried to make when I didn't show. I never got your messages. Because Annika deleted them from my account."

"And why would she do that?" Abe asks, like he's an adult and I'm the five-year-old he keeps trying to make understand that monsters have better things to do than hang out in the narrow space between my bed and the floor.

"I don't think she wanted me to go with you guys. At least not today."

"Why not?" Gabby asks.

"Because I think she wanted me with her."

Lemon's head tilts to the right. "Why?"

One of the first things I decided when trying to make sense of everything I learned this afternoon was that, no matter what, I wouldn't tell anyone about Annika's top-secret Mystery project. She made it clear that doing so would definitely get me expelled, and I don't want to risk that—especially now. Even more importantly, I don't want to risk it happening to my friends.

I feel good about that decision. What I don't feel as good about is the little white lie I tell instead.

"She just got in a prototype for the Kilter Painter 10,000," I say.

"Like the paintball gun you used last semester?" Lemon asks.

"Yes, except way more powerful. She wanted me to try it out to make sure the Kommissary should stock it."

"Why didn't she ask Ike to try it?" Abe asks, his back still to us. "He's a senior. He knows more."

"He was busy." One by one, the lies just roll off my tongue. "Anyway, while I was at her house—"

"You were at her house?" Abe fires a look at me over his shoulder. "Why couldn't you try the rifle on campus?"

"In case it backfired, or was too dangerous. Anyway, while I was there I went upstairs to use the bathroom. And while I was upstairs, I passed by Annika's bedroom. Her door was open. I peeked in before I knew it was her room and saw her computer. On the screen was a half-written K-Mail message. To me." I pause. "From Elinor."

"And?" Abe prompts after another pause.

"And *she* was Elinor. Or pretending to be, anyway."

"How do you know?" Lemon asks.

"If she accessed your account, maybe she accessed Elinor's, too," Gabby says. "And was reading a message Elinor was in the middle of writing."

"She did access Elinor's account," I say. "But she was definitely the one doing the writing."

I explain everything else I saw. The three in-boxes. The alert that popped up when Annika, using her K-Pak, moved Abe's message from my in-box to her master trash. The other deleted, intercepted messages. Elinor's note from three weeks ago.

"Weird," Gabby says when I'm done.

Abe doesn't say anything, but he does turn back around.

"There were no other student accounts on her computer?" Lemon asks.

"Not that I saw," I say.

"But why the focus on you and Elinor?" Gabby asks.

"I don't know about Elinor," Lemon says, "but like it or not, Seamus is a standout student. I'm sure Annika wants to make sure his attention stays on Kilter—and only Kilter."

I actually haven't figured that part out yet, but it's better he suggests this theory than me.

"That's pretty shady," Gabby says.

"It is," Abe agrees, "but so what? If the school director wants you to be as successful as possible, why is that such a bad thing?"

"No student's success should hurt another student," I say. "Remember the Ultimate Troublemaking Task last semester? When Elinor was burned? And you guys snuck her off the mountain for help because Annika was too busy celebrating our victory to bother?"

Gabby and Abe nod. Lemon's gaze lowers to his hands.

"Well, that would've been terrible if Annika was only the school director. But she's not. She's also Elinor's aunt."

They exchange puzzled looks.

"I learned that accidentally, when I found Elinor looking at an old photo album." There's a bit more to it than that, including a secret trip to Good Samaritan Headquarters and a certain Wanted poster featuring Nadia Kilter—Annika's sister and Elinor's mother. But not sharing this is simply omitting, not lying. "Can you imagine? If something like that happened to us, and our moms, dads, aunts, uncles, or whoever, didn't automatically freak out and drop everything to take care of us?"

I give that a minute to sink in. When it does, Gabby speaks first.

"No," she says quietly. "I can't."

I wait for Lemon and Abe to respond. They don't, so I continue.

"Here's the thing. Lemon might be right. Annika seems to have certain expectations of me that she wants met, no matter what. But with Elinor, I think there's something else going on. Something bad. In her note from three weeks ago, Elinor said Annika didn't want her back at Kilter. And I'd bet all my credits that Annika was the one who not only kept her away from here, but decided where she should go instead."

"Did Elinor say what was wrong with her new school?" Lemon asks.

"Not really. Just that it'd take some getting used to. And that she wished she wasn't there by herself." That last part's not the whole truth either, but for my current purposes, it's enough.

Abe half sighs, half groans.

"But she didn't have to say more than that," I add. "I know you guys didn't get to know her very well last semester. No one did, not even me. Because that's how Elinor is. Shy. Private. Which is why I think something had to be really wrong to make her admit even that much."

"Seamus has a point," Lemon says.

"I repeat," Abe says. "So. *What?*"

"So we should help her."

"Because Hinkle has a hunch?"

"No." Lemon's voice is low but firm. "Because *she* helped *us*."

Abe starts to protest. Lemon continues before he can.

"When we went up to the Apex for the Ultimate Trouble-making Task last semester, Seamus was in solitary confinement. Between you, me, and Gabby, we had a book of matches, a can of spray paint, and a canister of gasoline. There was no way we were going to burn down the amusement park and make Annika cry, especially in the middle of a blizzard. The only reason we did was because Seamus helped. And the only reason he was able to help was because he left solitary confinement and immediately drove up the mountain—with Elinor."

"She came and got me," I add. "I never would've escaped on my own."

Abe folds his arms over his chest. Looks down at his feet.

"You're proud of Capital T," Lemon continues, his voice gentler. "You take being a member very seriously. We all do. But we haven't been totally successful on our own."

Abe sighs. Pulls out the chair. Sits.

"Fine. What do we do?"

"We go get her," I say.

"Where?" Lemon asks.

I practice saying the words in my head. Besides admitting to Annika's special treatment, this was the other part of Phase One I've been dreading the most.

"Blackhole, Arizona."

"Arizona?" Lemon asks.

"As in, like, a million miles from here?" Gabby asks.

I look at Abe, already wincing. He looks at me. Then he laughs. And laughs . . . and laughs . . . and laughs. When the hysterics die down to chuckles, Lemon poses a perfectly reasonable question.

"How do we get there?"

"Leave that up to me. I have a plan." I don't know how effective it'll be, but they don't need to know that.

"When do we go?" Gabby asks.

"Tomorrow night. While everyone's asleep."

This tickles Abe's funny bone again. While he cracks up, Lemon asks what they should do to prepare.

"Go to the Kommissary. Buy whatever you think you might need for an intense, potentially dangerous mission. Then just act like it's any other day and everything's normal. Whatever you do, don't mention one word about it in K-Mail. The last thing we need is for Annika to read something that makes her even more paranoid than she already is."

Lemon nods. Gabby takes a notebook and pen from her backpack and starts writing. Abe giggles a few seconds more before asking a question of his own.

"You're not serious. . . . Are you?"

I glance at Lemon and catch his eye. Does *he* think I'm joking? Lemon shakes his head. We both look at Abe.

"Let me get this straight," Abe says, no longer amused. "You want us to sneak off campus? In the middle of the night? To go to another state on the other side of the country?"

I mentally review the checklist, then say, "Yes."

Abe's head shoots forward. His eyes bulge from their sockets. When no one says anything else, he sits back and shrugs. "Nope. No way. Not going to happen."

"But—"

"I understand everything you just said," Abe says, interrupting Lemon. "I agree we couldn't have won the Ultimate Troublemaking Task without Elinor, and I appreciate her help. But if we're caught doing what Hinkle's suggesting, we're done. Kicked out of Kilter. For good. I'm appreciative . . . but I'm not stupid."

Now, this reaction I expected.

"Kilter's a school for Troublemakers," I remind him. "Where bad behavior is not only encouraged, but rewarded."

His face relaxes slightly.

"I bet no other students have ever tried to pull off something like this. If we're caught, we might get docked a few days of troublemaking. That would be unfortunate, but not the end of the world." I hesitate. "But if we're not? If we see it through to the end?" I think I'll have to force a smile, but I don't. It comes naturally. "Capital T will be forever known as the best bad kids in Kilter history."

"And probably earn enough demerits to buy the entire Kommissary," Gabby adds.

Maybe it's the promise of eternal fame. Maybe it's the idea of owning any troublemaking item he could ever want. It's probably not the desire to return a favor or be a good friend, but that's okay.

Something convinces Abe to sit back. Sigh heavily. And say:

"Whatever. I'm in."

Chapter 17

DEMERITS: 385
GOLD STARS: 300

After a long, sleepless night, Phase Two of Operation Evacuate Elinor begins the next morning.

> **TO:** ike@kilteracademy.org
> **FROM:** shinkle@kilteracademy.org
> **SUBJECT:** Tin Man
>
> Hi, Ike!
>
> So I know it's short notice, but would you be up

for a training session before classes start today? I'm feeling a little rusty.

Let me know! Thanks!

—Seamus

His response comes while I'm getting dressed.

TO: shinkle@kilteracademy.org
FROM: ike@kilteracademy.org
SUBJECT: RE: Tin Man

Hey, Seamus,

You got it. See you at the gazebo at seven.

—Ike

I finish getting ready. Fling forks at the bread bin until a direct hit pops it open, then grab a muffin. Remind my alliance-mates, who are silently eating breakfast, to act like today's no different from any other day. And leave the house.

I'm halfway to the gazebo when my K-Pak buzzes. Worried someone's having doubts about participating—and wanting to catch their note saying so before Annika does—I yank the mini computer from my backpack and read as I walk.

Fortunately, the note's not from Lemon, Abe, or Gabby. Unfortunately, it's from Annika herself.

TO: shinkle@kilteracademy.org
FROM: annika@kilteracademy.org
SUBJECT: How are you??

Dear Seamus,

I'm sorry you left so suddenly yesterday. I hope you're feeling better today!

You probably haven't been able to monitor Mr. Tempest too closely while under the weather, but I thought I'd check in anyway. Do you have any updates?

Get lots of rest! And be sure to have a big bowl of fish stick chowder for lunch today. When it comes to killing a cold, it kicks chicken soup's you-know-what. And I've already asked the Kanteen chefs to make a special batch just for you.

xo,

Annika

I start to put my K-Pak away without answering, but then think better of it and take my own advice.

> **TO:** annika@kilteracademy.org
> **FROM:** shinkle@kilteracademy.org
> **SUBJECT:** RE: How are you??
>
> Hi Annika,
>
> Thanks for checking in! I'm sorry I had to leave so suddenly yesterday too. I rested all day and am feeling a little better this morning.
>
> As for Mr. Tempest, everything seems to be business as usual. I'll keep you posted.
>
> Can't wait to try the chowder! It sounds delicious!
>
> Thanks again!
>
> —Seamus

I press send. The digital envelope swishes around the K-Pak screen—and shoots past my right ear. Or at least, it sounds like it does. I'm about to look behind me, just in case, when something buzzes by my left ear.

"Morning!"

I follow the greeting. Through the early-morning fog, I see Ike standing in the gazebo entrance. I wave and jog toward him.

"Hi," I say as I get closer. "Thanks for meeting on such short notice."

"No problem." He waits for me to reach the bottom step, then holds out one hand.

I stare at the device in his open palm. "What is that?"

"The Kilter Icickler. It turns water into frozen daggers with the push of one button and fires them with the push of another."

Once again, I asked the wrong question. I try a better one. "Where did you get it?"

"Where I—and you, and every other Troublemaker—gets anything. The Kommissary."

A hot, fast heat blooms in my belly and spreads to my fingers and toes. Does he know about Mom and her addiction to the Hoodlum Home Shopping Network? Are they in cahoots, which is what Dad asks whenever a neighborhood dog digs in his flower beds the same night deer swing by for a snapdragon snack? Or is Ike's introduction of a weapon I already own simply a coincidence?

I don't have time to worry about another conspiracy theory.

So I shrug off my coat, wipe my brow, and take the Icickler.

"Ten demerits for pants, twenty for coats, thirty for cold-weather accessories." Ike lifts his chin toward a group of Trouble-makers gathered on the other side of the lawn. They're too far away for me to see their parka patches, but their faces are tilted skyward and hazy stars, hearts, and other shapes float above them. So I assume the older Biohazards are taking advantage of the cold to practice turning breath clouds into geometric shapes.

I raise my arm. Aim the Icickler. Register Ike's instructions.

"Wait." I lower my arm. "You don't want me to actually hit them, do you?"

"Of course not." Leaning against a gazebo post, he points to a cluster of trees just behind my targets. "Think thumbtacks and corkboard."

Easier said than done. If you get hit with a thumbtack, you might lose a droplet of blood. If you get hit with a Kilter-made icicle, you might lose a limb.

You can rock this, Hinkle.

Houdini's voice zips through my head. He still sounds more confident than I feel, but the clock's ticking. So I raise my arm again. Aim. Fire.

I get a hit on the first try. And the second. And the third, fourth, and fifth. Soon the entire Biohazard group is stuck to three wide tree trunks, their clothes—and bodies—held in place by cold spikes. One girl cries out in surprise, but no one screams in pain. They twist and turn and crane their necks, trying to break free and figure out what just happened at the same time.

"Rusty, huh?" Ike asks.

Maybe I shouldn't have been so good so fast. I don't want to make Ike even more suspicious than he might be by the time we're done. Then again, this could be the perfect time to accomplish what I really wanted to in this morning's training session.

"Ever feel that way?" I ask. "A little out of it? Not quite good enough?"

He turns toward me. Despite the rising sun, his face darkens. The corners of his mouth droop. He looks like he did at the track the other day . . . just as I hoped he would.

"Sometimes," he says.

He retreats into the gazebo. I follow.

"It's a lot of pressure," I say. "Going to classes. Completing assignments. Learning new skills. Trying to get in as much trouble as possible without hurting anyone. Especially when not doing any of those things well enough can get you sent home."

"It can be." Ike leans against a gazebo post, gazes out toward the mountains.

"Want to know what my biggest fear is?" I lean against the post next to his.

"Going to sleep Seamus and waking up a pile of gray ash?"

"Surprisingly, no." I smile at the Lemon reference. "It's disappointing people. Teachers. Parents." I pause. "Annika."

I'm actually not sure where this falls on my lengthy list of fears, but giving it the top spot now has the desired effect. The invisible dark cloud hanging over Ike's face expands. I continue.

"I have an idea. A way to get ahead."

He looks up from his boots. "Aren't you already ahead? You just earned a ton of demerits in two minutes."

"I'm not sure." Demerits-wise, this is the truth. "But if I pull off what I want to, I don't think I'll ever have to worry about disappointing anyone again."

This is a stretch, but it makes Ike's eyebrows lift.

"It's complicated, though," I say.

"What is it?"

Now I look at my boots. "I can't say."

"Oh."

I look up again. "But I could still use your help."

He shifts so his shoulder presses against the gazebo post and he faces me. "I'm listening."

I glance behind me. Past him. Outside the gazebo. Besides the Biohazards, who are still wriggling against the trees, we're the only ones out this early.

I lean toward Ike and lower my voice anyway. "To do what I need to, I have to leave campus. Tonight."

"For how long?"

"That's the thing. I'm not sure. It could be a few hours. It could be a few days."

"You want me to cover for you."

After asking about his post-Kilter plans seemed to stress him out, I'd assumed Ike was uncertain about his future. Based on my real-world mission with Houdini and my helicopter ride with Annika, I'd also assumed there were Kilter-related opportunities he hadn't yet been chosen to participate in. And that he was feeling rusty, out of it, and not quite good enough as a result. But given how quickly he got where I was going, I, for one, am impressed.

"Yes," I say. "Please. If it's not too much trouble."

He gazes toward the mountains again. "Maybe it'll be just enough."

In that case, "Can you cover for Lemon, Abe, and Gabby, too?" I'd assured them we wouldn't be gone long, so we hadn't discussed whether they should talk to their tutors. But it doesn't hurt to overprepare.

Ike thinks about it, then says, "Okay."

There's a soft crunching sound behind us. I look over my shoulder and see a tall, thin figure hurrying across the frozen lawn. His hands are in the pockets of his black wool coat. He's stooped forward against the cold and doesn't seem to notice the pom-pom of his black knit hat bopping his forehead with every other step. He keeps his eyes to the ground as he makes his way toward the Kanteen.

I turn back. "One more thing."

"Shoot," Ike says.

"Could you keep an eye on the instructors? And let me know if any of them act any stranger than usual?"

"Sure. But why?"

Because one of them is an ax-wielding, stuffed-animal-stealing

Kilter history buff who may be trying to go down in world history as the scariest teacher ever by hiding children in a secret cottage in the woods. Which is something I'll have to deal with the second I get back.

I shrug. "Just 'cause."

"You're keeping a lot of secrets."

"I know. I'm sorry."

"Don't be. That's what real Troublemakers do." He claps me on the back. "Good luck. Be in touch."

With that, he crosses the gazebo, jumps over the steps to the ground, and jogs across the lawn.

"Morning."

I spin around. GS George is standing on the other side of the gazebo railing, walkie-talkie in one hand, MY CORNISH REX THINKS I'M THE CAT'S PAJAMAS travel mug in the other.

"Hi," I say. "What's a Cornish rex?"

His eyes light up. He rests his walkie-talkie and coffee on the railing, takes his K-Pak from his fanny pack, and holds it up so I can see the screen.

"The picture on the mug doesn't do it justice. This one's much better."

According to the picture that's GS George's K-Pak's backdrop, a Cornish rex is a long, skinny, ratlike kitty. Some might even call it the feline equivalent of a hairless Chihuahua.

If that's not a sign, I don't know what is.

"What's the word?" GS George swaps his K-Pak for the travel mug. Nods to the Biohazards still stuck to trees like magnets to a refrigerator.

"Not sure," I say casually. "Some human glue experiment, I think. They were like that when I got here."

He looks at me. Arches one eyebrow. I want to minimize the lies as much as possible, so rather than offering up another that may or may not convince him I had nothing to do with the spectacle across the yard, I try to distract him with a more important one.

"The hairless Chihuahua wants a snuggle buddy."

GS George's other eyebrow shoots skyward.

"I talked to Ms. Marla this morning. She asked me to tell you that."

Both eyebrows drop. He scratches his head with one mittened hand.

"That one's not code. There's another hairless Chihuahua. A girl, named Rosita. Ms. Marla found her on a website for needy pets. She said it's high time Rodolfo had a friend."

"*Everyone* should have a friend," GS George agrees.

"Right." I take a deep breath. Continue. "Anyway, I was thinking . . . Valentine's Day's coming up."

He sips. Grins. Wiggles his hips, which wiggles his shoulders. "Don't I know it."

Now my eyebrows drop. Do all adults possess this capacity for corny?

"I don't have a girlfriend." Images of Elinor fill my head before I've even finished the sentence. "But if I did, I bet she'd love a new puppy more than flowers or chocolates."

"Really? What about those coconut-filled ones?"

I look at him. He looks at me.

"Oh! You think I should get a friend for Rodolfo. For Ms. Marla. For Valentine's Day." He raises his K-Pak, starts typing. "That's a great idea. I bet there's a shelter around here that—"

"I think you should get her the friend she already picked out. Online."

"Oh." He lowers the K-Pak slightly, then raises it again. "Okeydoke. You can get anything online these days, can't you? My good buddy, GS Carl? He bought a jar of mayonnaise once owned by the guy who played Batman on TV nearly fifty years ago. It was on some auction site. Can you imagine?"

Finding a fifty-year-old jar of mayo online? Yes. Actually buying it? Not so much.

"There's just one problem," I say.

"What's that?"

"Someone else wants the same dog. If you don't get her as soon as possible, you might not get her at all." My pulse grows louder in my ears. I hurry up with the rest before I lose my nerve. "And you have to go there in person. To meet Rosita. And the company owners. They need to make sure you're a good fit. If I were you, I'd leave after work today."

GS George stands up straight. Puffs out his chest. "I'll do it. I'll go tonight."

I exhale. Smile. "Awesome. She's going to be so excited, you have no idea."

"And if Ms. Marla's excited, I'm—" He stops. "Wait a minute. Where am I going?"

My lips, still reaching toward my ears, freeze. When I answer, GS George shakes his head.

"What's that?" he asks.

I bite my bottom lip. Try again.

"Arizona."

"Arizona? As in next stop, California?"

I nod.

His face falls. "Well, thanks for the tip, but Rosita will have to be some other pup's pal. There's simply no way I can get all the way there and all the way back in time for my six o'clock shift tomorrow morning."

Frowning, he puts his K-Pak in his fanny pack. When he reaches for his travel mug, I put one hand on his arm.

"Of course there is."

Chapter 18

DEMERITS: 465
GOLD STARS: 300

WELCOME, SEAMUS HINKLE! YOU HAVE 0 CREDITS!

I stare at the flashing print pad. I emptied my credit account when I bought supplies earlier, but the zero's still weird to see. Telling myself I'll easily earn more, I remove my hand and push through the turnstile. Lemon, Abe, and Gabby do the same. We split up inside the Kommissary. I head for the marksman aisle and pretend to browse. Two minutes later, there's a loud pop at the front of the store. Over the shrieks and groans that follow, I can barely make out Gabby's voice.

"Oh my goodness! I'm *so* sorry! I'll get some paper towels!"

Footsteps dash down the aisle to my right. Two more pairs clomp down the one to my left. I replace the darts I'd picked up and run. I meet up with Capital T at the back of the store and lead them to the unmarked door.

"Spitball?" Abe asks as we enter the stairwell.

"Booger Bomb," Gabby says. It's too dark to see the twinkle in her eyes, but I can hear it in her voice. "Right in the face. Poor Martin might want to be more careful when putting certain items on display. After that faulty firing, he'll be blinded by slime for at least ten minutes."

Ten minutes. It's not much time, but it'll have to be enough.

We start down the stairs. I can't find a light switch, so we use our K-Paks to illuminate the way. No one speaks. The only sound is the tapping of our shoes climbing concrete steps—and the thumping of my heart, which is so loud I'm sure they hear it too. I'm relieved when they don't ask where we're going or if I know how to get there. I didn't tell them anything about our transportation in the likely event it didn't pan out, and answering those questions now will only make them worry. And I want them to think happy thoughts until other thoughts make that impossible.

After three wrong turns that lead to dead ends, we find the elevator and file inside. I press the UP button. We watch the silver lightning bolt move above the door.

"That's why you wanted us to wear black," Lemon says. "So we blend in with the dark."

"What do you—?" Abe stops. "Oh no. I can't . . . I don't . . . I can't . . ."

He's just realized we're shooting above campus in a glass chute. And we've just realized our resident tough guy has a severe fear of heights. As he gasps for breath, buries his face in his hands, and leans against a clear wall, Gabby puts one arm around his shoulders and smiles at the scenery below.

Soon the elevator stops. The doors open. I force the lump in my throat back toward my chest. Step onto the glass platform.

And run for the helicopter.

Afraid of losing my balance to the whipping wind and toppling to the ground, I don't look back until I reach the other side. Lemon's right behind me. Gabby's a few feet behind him. Abe's on his hands and knees by the elevator.

"Wait here!" I call out over the whirring helicopter blades.

I keep my eyes locked on Abe as I sprint down the platform.

It takes some gentle prodding, but he finally moves away from the elevator. He doesn't get up from his hands and knees, and halfway across he actually lowers to his belly and slides like a slug, but it doesn't matter. We reach the other side just as the helicopter begins to lift off.

"Step as lightly as you can!" I instruct as quietly as I can, which isn't very quietly at all. "Bobbing's okay. Full tilting isn't!"

Lemon and Gabby nod. Abe looks up and clutches his stomach. I grab the silver door handle and pull. The door opens easily. The gap between the platform and the helicopter's legs widens as Gabby, then Lemon, then Abe climb inside. By the time it's my turn, the chopper's so far off the ground I have to grab one leg and lift myself up.

Lemon helps hoist me into the cabin. I close the door right before the helicopter lunges left. Abe drops onto one of the leather couches. I motion for Lemon and Gabby to do the same, then tiptoe toward the front of the aircraft.

The silver curtain dividing the cockpit from the cabin is pulled tight. Hooking my pointer finger around one side, I tug until I can see GS George. He's sitting in the pilot's seat and looking straight ahead. His Cornish rex travel mug is in one cup holder, his K-Pak in the other. Show tunes blare from small speakers attached to the top of the windshield; GS George sings along and taps his fingers on top of the steering lever. A computer screen in the center of the console displays a map of the United States. A crooked white line marks our route. Tucked in the bottom right corner of the screen is a photo of Ms. Marla and Rodolfo. Its edges are worn, like it's been pocketed and unpocketed many times before.

Satisfied, I release the curtain and join Lemon on the couch. Abe and Gabby sit on the other couch, facing us.

"What now?" Gabby asks after a moment.

"Now," I say, "we wait."

The Kilter Kopter travels at warp speed, but still. Arizona's two thousand miles away. I have no idea how long the trip will take, but we must have some time to kill.

I expect more questions, but either my alliance-mates are confident that my plan extends beyond this flight, which would be a generous assumption, or they're too nervous (Abe), excited (Gabby), or ambivalent (Lemon) for small talk. Abe keeps his head between his knees for a while but eventually sits up, takes a drawing pad from his messenger bag, and starts sketching. Gabby takes a pair of binoculars from her backpack and examines the artwork displayed around the cabin's interior. Lemon shifts down the couch, stretches out, and closes his eyes.

I remove my K-Pak from my backpack and hold my breath as my K-Mail loads. When there are no new messages, I exhale. I open old messages and stare at them without reading. Then I put aside my K-Pak and sort through the supplies I brought. After a while I open my notebook and try to sort out my thoughts on what we've done and what's to come. When an hour passes and the only thing on the page is a bunch of doodles that would look like random circles to the naked eye but that I know are pennies, I pick up my K-Pak again. Open an old message. Press reply. And start typing.

TO: parsippany@cloudviewschools.net
FROM: shinkle@kilteracademy.org
SUBJECT: RE: Parents, a.k.a. Life's Great Mysteries

Dear Miss Parsippany,

Thanks so much for your last note. I'm really sorry your mother nags you about your posture. That's actually one thing my mom's never commented on. Probably because I'm so short I look the same standing up straight as I do stooping forward. Maybe try lying down whenever she comes into the room? If she can't see your spine, she can't judge it, right?

As for why I asked about what parents really want from their kids, let's just say mine threw me a pretty major curveball a few weeks ago. It came so hard, so fast, I didn't know whether to catch, duck, or run. I ended up running, but I'll have to turn around eventually. And I'm still not sure what will happen when I do.

I stop typing. Think. When I start writing again, I imagine not just Miss Parsippany reading this next part, but Mom and Annika, too.

I like what you said about parents wanting their kids to be better people than they are. It's a great theory, and in many ways, it makes a lot of sense. But it also makes me wonder something else.

What if the person your parents want you to be . . . isn't the person YOU want to be? What do

> you do then? I've been thinking about that a lot lately, and here's what I've come up with:
>
> Nothing. Because I have no clue.
>
> Anyway, thanks again for all your input. Not many adults would take the time to e-mail a kid they barely know. But I'm really glad you do.
>
> Have a great day!
>
> —Seamus

With access to my K-Mail account, chances are good Annika really will read this. That being the case, I want the message to be perfect. So I scroll to the top to reread. I haven't gotten past the first paragraph when the helicopter drops suddenly. The unexpected movement makes Abe gasp, Gabby squeal, Lemon roll off the couch—and me press the send icon.

"Are we there?" Lemon asks, climbing back up on the couch.

Turning off my K-Pak, I shift to my knees and look out the window. I don't know what I expect to see. Maybe houses. Streets. Cars. Far away but still visible thanks to lamps and headlights. But all there is up above, down below, and all around us, is blackness.

"I don't think so," I say. "It hasn't been that long. And—"

The chopper drops again. It tilts and swerves. It swoops down, nose first, until gravity's pull is so strong we have to grab on to the couches, coffee table, and anything else that's bolted to the floor to keep from flying past the silver curtain and breaking through the cockpit windshield.

"Maybe you should check on GS Georgie," Gabby says, sounding nervous for the first time tonight, "and make sure everything's okay."

I frown. I wanted to wait to reveal his stowaways until we were far enough from Kilter that turning around without going to Arizona first wouldn't make sense. And at this point, I don't know where we are or even how long we've been airborne.

But then Lemon says, "Probably not a bad idea." So I untangle myself from the coffee table legs and crawl toward the front of the chopper.

I stop before the silver curtain and tug it to one side again. I can't see much so close to the floor, but I *can* see the bottom half of the computer screen. The map's still up. A red dot flashes near Blackhole, Arizona. A white arrow, which I assume is the helicopter, bounces around off-course an inch or so past our destination. The speakers have fallen silent, and I hear GS George muse softly.

"Where on earth . . . ?"

I climb to my knees, then my feet. Open the curtain until I can stand between it and the wall, then speak.

"Knock-knock."

GS George's hands fly from the steering lever to his chest. The chopper plummets. My alliance-mates cry out. I fall into the copilot's seat.

"Seamus Hinkle!" GS George stares at me, bug-eyed, like I'm a risen Wright brother. "What are you doing here?"

Gripping the armrests, I nod to the steering lever. His head snaps to the left, then down. It takes him a second to register the device. When he does, he grabs it with both hands and yanks back. The helicopter's nose lifts. The aircraft straightens.

"Sorry," I say. "I didn't mean to startle you."

"Could've fooled me. And that you did, I guess." He shoots me a sideways glance. "I repeat. *What* are you doing here?"

"I thought you might need some help. Or want some company. Or both."

"And your amigos back there?"

"They just felt like going for a ride." This is my attempt to lighten the mood. It fails. Big time.

"Do you have any idea how much trouble you could get in for a stunt like this?" GS George demands, the words shooting from his mouth like frozen daggers from the Icickler. "Never mind you. What about *me*? Do you know how much trouble *I* could get in? Not just for stealing the fancy school helicopter, but for doing so with four students on board? I could get fired. *Fired.* Then where would I be? Back home. In New Jersey. Hundreds of miles from the lovely Ms. Marla, who I'd never see again and who'd immediately be courted by an army of handsome Good Samaritans who'd go to any lengths necessary to win her heart. While I'm at the Paramus Park Mall. Staring at the puppies through the pet shop window. Drowning my sorrows in enormous sugar-covered pretzels."

This is a very vivid, very sad scenario. He needs to snap out of it, or we're all doomed.

"There's no Rosita."

He looks at me.

"I made her up."

He blinks.

"My friends and I really need to get to Arizona. Like, right away. Scooters and golf carts are too slow. We would've been caught before we even reached the state line. Flying was the only option—but none of us knows how to operate an aircraft."

He swallows. "So the hairless Chihuahua wants a snuggle buddy. . . . That was just some story? Some *lie*?"

I look at my lap. I knew I'd feel terrible whenever he found this out, but the burning in my stomach hurts even more than I imagined. I tell myself he'll understand once he knows the whole truth, that he'll even be proud to have been a part of the adventure. And if he's not, I'll make it up to him somehow.

Then I add fuel to the fire.

"It was an emergency."

"What kind of emergency?" he asks.

"I can't say. Not yet." I sit up, turn toward him. "But please. We're so close. If you just take us there and bring us back, it'll all make sense."

He holds my gaze for a long moment, and I think he's actually considering it. But then he faces forward. Keeps one hand on the steering lever and reaches for his K-Pak with the other.

"Uh-uh. Not a chance, mister. I have too much on the line.

I'm e-mailing Annika, we're turning this ship around, and we're going back to Kilter. Where I may or may not still have a job, and you'll be docked more troublemaking days than any Troublemaker before. That is, if you're not expel—"

Expelled. That's what GS George would've said if the helicopter didn't suddenly hit a rough patch of air, making him lose his grip on the steering lever. The chopper bounces around like a plastic ball in one of Dad's old Bingo cages. Soon it tips forward, forms a ninety-degree angle to the Earth, and plunges straight down.

In my head, I see Elinor.

Through the windshield, I see blackness.

Then cactus.

Then dirt.

Chapter 19

DEMERITS: 465
GOLD STARS: 300

Dear Mom. I'm sorry I wasn't the son you *wanted. I'm sorry I wasn't more like Bartholomew John. I'm sorry we didn't have more time together to try to work things out. But please know I love—*

The mental e-mail vanishes. I assume this is because my head has disconnected from the rest of my body, a result of the helicopter slamming into Earth like a misguided meteor. But then I realize I'm thinking about why the mental e-mail has vanished, which means my head must be okay.

"Awesome!" a female voice exclaims.

"Is this a dream?" a male voice wonders aloud.

"I think I'm going to hurl," a second male voice grumbles.

I open my eyes, one at a time. The first thing that comes into focus is a terrifying creature with an arched back, fangs, and long, skinny tail that could double as a whip. I start to scream—but then notice the black liquid sliding down the animal's side.

"Seamus? Are you okay?"

I sit up straight. Retrieve the Cornish rex travel mug from the floor, and replace it in the cup holder. Look at GS George, who leans toward me and puts one hand on my arm.

"I think so," I say. "What just happened?"

"Unplanned landing."

My head, definitely still on top of my neck, turns. The view through the windshield, which somehow survived impact without a single crack, is illuminated by the helicopter's front light. I see brown land. Black sky. Swirling dust. Rolling balls of twigs.

Is this what the Earth's core looks like? Because after our supersonic, ninety-degree descent, that's where we should be.

"The chopper switched into emergency autopilot," GS George

explains, apparently seeing the confusion on my face. "My guess is it leveled off half a second away from turning night into day with a big red fireball."

"Wow," I say, still staring through the dirty windshield.

"Indubitably," GS George agrees.

"Are *you* okay?" I ask, turning back.

"Fit as a fiddle. Why don't you go check on our passengers in the back while I reboot the system? We should be flying again in no time."

I nod and climb out of the seat, too rattled to argue immediate departure. Once upright I give my legs a second to steady, then push through the silver curtain and enter the cabin.

"Hey," I say. "You guys all right?"

"Yup." Lemon sits on one couch and rubs the back of his neck.

"Oh my goodness." Gabby stands on her knees next to Lemon and looks out the window. Then she jumps up, hurdles the coffee table, and lands on her knees facing the window behind the other couch. "We almost crashed. We *totally* almost crashed! Do you think this counts as a near-death experience? I've always wondered what it would feel like to have one of those. And now

I know. It. Feels. *Awesome.* Wait till everyone back at school hears about this. They're. Going. To. *Die.* Just like we almost did!"

As she peers outside, I peer past her. To the figure curled up on the couch with his legs to his chest, his forehead to his knees, and his arms wrapped tightly around his shins.

"Abe?" I start toward him. "Are you okay?"

He says something, but the words are lost in the space between his quads and torso. I sit carefully on the edge of the coffee table facing him.

"Abe?" I try again, gently.

"I want to go home," he mumbles.

"We will," I say. "GS George is going to have the helicopter up and running in no time. We'll be back at Kilter before—"

"Not Kilter." Abe sniffs. "*Home.* With my parents. And my bed. And my Boppy."

I swivel on the table and catch Lemon's eye. He shrugs.

"Your Boppy?" I ask.

"My blankie. That my nana made for me when I was a baby. It's the only thing that helps whenever I'm sad or scared or—"

The helicopter shakes suddenly. Like a turtle in a shell, Abe's head lowers behind his knees. Gabby drops to her bottom and presses her palms to the couch. I can't tell what Lemon does because I'm gripping the edge of the coffee table with both hands and am afraid to turn around. The motion lasts several seconds, then stops.

"That was weird," I say, exhaling. "I wonder if—"

There's a loud thud. It makes the table vibrate beneath me. A second, louder thud makes the cabin wobble. A third reaches sonic-boom status and sends the entire helicopter, and its contents, tilting to one side. As gravity pulls Lemon and me to the couch with Abe and Gabby, the thudding turns to a steady, deafening drumming. We watch—eyes wide, mouths open, and hands over our ears—as the opposite wall begins to crumple toward us.

"Get out!"

GS George stands in the cockpit doorway, gripping the thin partition to keep from falling over. Given the way his lips stretch and neck vein bulges, he must be screaming. But I hardly hear him.

When we don't move, he hobbles toward us. He reaches Lemon first and tugs on his jacket collar. Then he grabs Gabby's binocular strap. The brim of Abe's baseball hat. My ear. He pulls until we start pulling ourselves up and over the cushion's edge.

As we shuffle along the front of the couch on our hands and knees, he hobbles to the helicopter door, leans against it, and yanks the handle. The door gives. GS George, apparently anticipating working a little harder, falls through the opening.

My heart stops. Because of me, we all almost died. No thanks to me, we survived. And now the poor man who lives for his cat and loves singing show tunes, who was just trying to do something nice for his girlfriend—

GS George's head pops through the open doorway.

My heart resumes beating.

He helps Lemon down, then Abe. Gabby has one foot out the door when she stops.

"Wait!" she cries out over the pounding. "My stuffed unicorn! It's in my backpack!"

"Leave it!" GS George shouts. "There's no time!"

"But I see it!" Gabby tries to lift herself back in. "It'll just take a second!"

GS George grabs her ankle. His eyes protrude and his nostrils flare. To be honest, he looks a little crazy.

"The chopper's going to *blow*!" he screams.

And now I understand why.

Gabby leaps out. I do too. Once my feet hit dirt, GS George turns and starts running after the others. I'm about to follow, but then a fresh wave of drumming tilts the helicopter further. I'm still standing where I landed, so as the aircraft lowers, my head ends up back inside the cabin. Looking down the length of the interior, I see Gabby's backpack. A white felt horn pokes through an opening in the zipper. The bag's about five feet away, its strap caught around a fallen silver coatrack.

I quickly assess the situation. The air's warm, but not hot. I don't see flames, and I certainly don't hear them over the noise, which I assume is the helicopter's engine preparing to combust. I don't smell smoke either. The opposite wall's still crumpling, probably melting from heat I don't yet feel, but it's pretty far away.

So I press my hands to the wall on either side of the doorway. Push with every iota of strength my linguine-like arms can muster. And lift myself up and inside.

The helicopter holds steady as I scurry down the front of the couch. I can just reach the stuffed animal's horn without coming off the sofa. Trying to take the whole bag might jiggle the coatrack and send things flying, which could make the helicopter fall completely on its side—with me stuck in the cabin.

Instead I grab the horn between my pointer finger and thumb, hold my breath, and gently pull. It takes a little wiggling and a lot of patience, but eventually the unicorn drops from the bag and into my arms. I zip it inside my coat, then shimmy backward as fast as my hands and knees will move.

I'm halfway to freedom when I spot a stick figure screaming for help. He could also be laughing. It's hard to tell when the face in question consists of three dots and one line. The important thing is that he's screaming or laughing from the pages of Abe's drawing pad, which is wedged between an end table and a magazine rack.

I shift my position slightly, reach forward, and tug it toward me, inch by inch. It slides out fairly easily—until the spiral binding catches. The space between the end table and magazine rack is too narrow for it to pass through. Holding my breath again, I give the pad one last, quick yank.

The spiral binding bends. The pad slips out.

The helicopter drops.

I stay perfectly still for a few seconds. When there's no more movement, I look between my legs, toward the door. The ground's closer, but I'm guessing there's still two feet or so between it and the aircraft. For someone who's barely cracked five feet, that's plenty of room.

There's still no sign of smoke or flames, so right now my biggest concern is getting out before the chopper lands completely on its side, blocking my only exit. Following close behind is my concern that I've saved something of Gabby's and something of Abe's, but nothing of Lemon's.

I scan the cabin. The first thing I see is my best friend's favorite matchstick-shaped lighter. I change direction and lean forward until my belly hits the floor. The lighter's stuck in the other couch, between the cushion and the frame, which is likely where Lemon put it, out of habit, before taking a nap. He always slips fire-starting supplies between the mattress and box spring before going to bed each night. I know, because I always take them out so he can't reach for them in his sleep.

Fortunately, the thickest part of the lighter, the matchstick tip, is sticking out. I strain until my right shoulder feels like it's going to pop out of my socket, and am just able to take the tip between my pointer and middle fingers.

I tug. The lighter slides out.

I shove it in my coat pocket and shimmy backward.

The helicopter drops.

This movement is harder, sharper. It makes pillows fly from the couch. Paintings fall from the wall. Water bottles and juice boxes tumble from an open refrigerator near the cockpit's silver curtain.

I cover my head with both hands. This sends me off balance—and sliding back. Fast. *Too* fast. My legs shoot through the open door. I reach out one arm and flail my hand at something, anything. My fingers graze something cool and hard, and tighten instantly.

"Seamus!" GS George shouts off in the distance.

I look down. The gap between the ground and the helicopter's side is narrowing. But I can't go. Not yet.

I force my left arm parallel to my right. My fingers intertwine around the coffee table leg. A groan spurts from my pressed lips as I pull my body up. My weight shifts the table, which is good and bad.

Bad because something that was lodged between the coffee table and the couch breaks free, falls—and slams into my ribs.

And good because that something is my K-Pak.

I shove the mini computer down the front of my coat. Then I reach my right hand toward the back of an armchair. The left toward the open refrigerator door. The right toward the cockpit partition. The left toward a dangling seat belt. I move slowly, carefully, as if hanging from monkey bars set over a pit of flames. Which, let's face it, is pretty much what I'm doing.

The pounding grows louder. The crumpling wall closer. My palms sweatier.

But finally I see it. I see *them*. Ms. Marla and Rodolfo.

I inhale until lung hits bruised rib. Stretch one arm forward. Lunge.

I snatch the photo from the scrambled computer screen on the first try. This is good, since one try is all I have time for.

The helicopter drops again. Through the windshield, I see a gray lizard skitter across the ground.

It's inches away.

"Seamus!"

That was Lemon. I had no idea his voice could reach such volumes.

"Sorry, Mr. Rex," I whisper to the scary cat-rat glaring at me from the out-of-reach cup holder.

Then I slip the photo inside my coat-sleeve cuff. And move.

The next two minutes are a blur. All I can think is that for the first time, I'm glad I'm short. Because if I were any taller, I wouldn't be able to squirm out of the eight-inch gap between the helicopter and ground a millisecond before the two crash together. Or run as fast. Or duck under cactus arms without having to shift direction and lose time.

Or hide behind the crooked, rusty DESERT FLOWER FILL 'N' FUEL sign.

At minute three, though, things start to clear up.

Starting with the air. When the helicopter collapses, the propeller arms, which are still moving slowly, snap off, one by one. The dust settles. Soon I have an unobstructed view of the damaged aircraft half a mile away. It's in bad shape, but it's not on fire. It groans and wheezes, but it doesn't explode.

A quick glance behind me shows GS George and the rest of Capital T hiding behind old gas pumps. An ice cooler. A mountain of shredded rubber tires. I try to catch GS George's eye to see if he has any idea what's happening, but he doesn't look away from the helicopter. It's like he's mesmerized. Hypnotized.

When I turn back, I see why.

The deafening drumming? That wasn't the chopper engine getting ready to combust.

That was people. Kids. They're running around like numbers without decimal points, as Dad would say, so it's hard to know exactly how many there are. I count at least ten. They all yell. Laugh. Beat their fists against metal. Break windows. Climb in and out of the chopper cabin.

All of them, that is, except one. Who stands off to the side and occasionally chimes in with a halfhearted whoop or holler, but mostly stares at the ground.

Fiddling with her long red braid.

Chapter 20

DEMERITS: 465
GOLD STARS: 300

Elin—"

A hand clamps over my mouth. It smells like pencil lead, so I assume it's Abe's. I try to wriggle free, but not for long. Because as we watch, a tall, wide figure scales the fallen helicopter. At the top, which is really the beaten-in side, he pounds his chest with both fists. Howls. Grunts. The other kids form a loose circle around the chopper and do the same. Then the leader, who's so big he makes Bartholomew John look like a munchkin, releases one final *ah-WOOO*, pumps his fists in the air, and jumps to the ground. They turn and run, abandoning the helicopter and leaving a thick brown cloud in their wake.

"Animals," Abe says, releasing my mouth.

"Elinor." I spin around and face GS George and Capital T, who come out of their hiding spots. "She was there. I saw her. We have to go before they—"

"Do to us what they just did to that fine piece of machinery?" GS George finishes. "You're right. We do."

He pushes past us and starts jogging.

"Don't move!" he calls over his shoulder. "I'll see if I can salvage her!"

By "her" I think he means Elinor and by "salvage" I think he means save. My heart lifts. But then he reaches the helicopter, pats its side, and gives one of the broken blades a peck, like the chopper's a sick Cornish rex in need of some TLC. As he enters the cockpit through the hole left by the shattered windshield, I realize he intends to fix our ride so we can leave ASAP. And my heart sinks.

I turn to my alliance-mates. "We can't go. Not yet."

"Um, did you see the same thing we did?" Abe asks. "Those kids—if you can call them that—were out of control."

"All the more reason to rescue Elinor," I say.

"But how?" Gabby asks. "We don't know where we are, who they are, or where they went. All we know is that they can kill a helicopter with their fists. I'm all for a fun troublemaking adventure, but that's enough to get me on the first flight out of here."

I try to answer her questions. "We're in Arizona. I saw that on the cockpit computer map before we lost control and started falling. We must be near, if not in, Blackhole because those kids, who are probably Elinor's new classmates, reached us really fast. And they must've run back to their school, because besides this ancient rest stop, there doesn't seem to be anything else around for hundreds of miles."

"Wrong," Abe says.

I look at him. He bends down and picks up a faded, rusty sign.

1 MILE TO MAIN STREET!

STROLL & SHOP THE BEST STRETCH IN THE WEST!

TRY OUR WORLD-FAMOUS PRICKLY PEAR PUDDING!

MINUTES AWAY FROM HISTORIC ROUTE 666!

"Isn't it Route sixty-six?" I ask.

"Isn't six-six-six a bad number?" Gabby asks. "Like if you dialed it on a phone, you'd reach the devil?"

I don't want to think about this. Fortunately, Lemon distracts us with another question.

"Which way?" He nods to the red arrow at the bottom of the sign. It points to the right, but since the sign was on the ground it's hard to know where it originally stood.

Before we can guess, fast footsteps sound behind us. I spin around and see GS George running.

"Bad news," he gasps, out of breath, when he reaches the gas station. "It's broken. They stripped the engine. And dismantled the electrical system. And took the computer. I can't fix it. Not by myself."

Two thoughts come to mind immediately.

The first is that if GS George can't fix the helicopter, then we can't leave. And if we can't leave, we can try rescuing Elinor.

The second is more of a question.

If we can't leave . . . what good is rescuing Elinor?

"We'll get help." I point to the sign. "There's a town. Towns have cars. Cars need mechanics. I'm sure we can find someone who'll come take a look at the helicopter."

"And how will we *explain* the helicopter?" Abe asks. "Carrying a bunch of kids and crashing in the middle of the desert? Without alerting everyone in the town and inviting unwanted attention?"

I frown. Abe seemed to return to his normal self once he was back on solid ground. He has a point. . . . But I still think I like him better scared.

"It's worth a shot," Lemon says. "What other choice do we have?"

We fall silent as we think about it. Then GS George sighs, unzips his fanny pack, and removes his K-Pak.

"What are you doing?" I ask.

"Writing Annika."

"What? Why?"

"So she can send someone to get us."

"But what about your job?" I ask. "I thought you were afraid of losing it?"

"I'd rather be out of work than dead in a dust bowl."

He starts typing. I want to convince him to give our mission more time, but my head's spinning too fast. I can't find the words.

So I use a visual instead.

"Ms. Marla!" Beaming, GS George lowers the K-Pak and takes the photo I hold toward him. "Rodolfo! When I didn't see this in the chopper just now, I didn't think I'd ever see it again." He looks at me. "When did you get it? How?"

"When I was getting these." I unbutton my coat, remove the stuffed unicorn and drawing pad, and hand them to Gabby and Abe. I take the matchstick-shaped lighter from my pocket and give it to Lemon. "And very carefully."

"You thought the helicopter was about to explode," Gabby says, squeezing her stuffed animal, "and you still went back for these? For us?"

I shrug. "You came all this way. I had to try."

Gabby grins. Abe takes a pencil from behind his ear, scribbles something on a blank piece of paper, and turns the pad around so I can see the smiley face with spiky hair. Lemon reaches over and taps me on the shoulder with his (unlit) lighter.

"Thanks," he says.

"You're welcome."

They're so appreciative I almost forget my selfish reason for kicking off the gift-giving with GS George's picture. But then our pilot tucks the photo into the front pocket of his fanny pack and clears his throat.

"Elinor," he says, "as in Annika's niece?"

Oops. I didn't mean to say her name in front of him. I didn't want him to know the emergency that brought us here because

I thought it would make him even more determined to take us back. After all, if Annika had wanted Elinor rescued, she would've instructed GS George to go get her. At the very least, I thought it'd make him contact Annika to see what she wanted him to do with us before we had a chance to do anything ourselves.

But I guess the rat-cat's out of the bag.

"Yes," I say.

"She must be something special for you to go to all this trouble."

I look down.

"All righty." He claps once, snapping my head back up. "Here's what we're going to do. I'm going to e-mail my good buddy, GS Carl. He's a techno whiz and knows the ins and outs of that machine back there better than the machines that made it. Without giving anything away, I'll see if he can help me figure out how to get it running again. While I'm doing that, you four are free to do what you'd like. Chase tumbleweeds. Eat prickly pear pudding. Find your friend. Whatever. If I don't know what you're up to, I can't worry about whether I should report you. Fair?"

"Definitely." I smile.

"Good." He checks his watch. "It's ten p.m. Mountain Standard Time. You have an hour."

"An *hour*?" Abe scoffs. "Town's a mile away. We don't even know if that's where the school is."

"Should I make it half an hour?" GS George asks. "Troublemakers usually work best under pressure."

"We'll take the hour," I say quickly. "Thank you. Really."

He tips his invisible hat and shuffles backward. "Meet back at the chopper. Don't be late. I won't wait."

He turns and starts running. Gabby hurries after him.

"Where are you going?" I shout.

"To get my backpack! We need supplies!"

This GS George responds to. "Don't bother!" he hollers without turning around. "They took it all! Backpacks, K-Paks, juice boxes . . . There's nothing left!"

Gabby slows to a stop.

"That's strange," Lemon says.

"And mean." I shake my head. "What kind of kids would hijack a grounded helicopter in the middle of nowhere, scare off its stranded passengers, and steal everything inside? We're training to become professional Troublemakers, and even we wouldn't—"

Lemon stops me by pressing the tip of his lighter to my arm. "Not that," he says. *"That."*

I hear it before I see it. A steady, constant crunching. A gentle rumbling. A soft squealing that makes me think of Wheezing Willie back home. Of course, Willie gets his name from wheezing, not squealing, but the sound that pierces my ears every time he hits the brakes is the same.

As the rumbling grows louder, I understand why.

It's a school bus. Or what looks like it used to be a school bus. It's brown instead of yellow. Its windows are blacked out. The headlights are broken. The name of the district it once belonged to is scratched off the side, revealing dull gray metal beneath even duller paint. Every now and then it squeals and slows down to allow for passing lizards, scorpions, and furry black spiders as big as my head.

"Gabby!" Abe hisses.

She's still standing where she stopped when GS George said there were no supplies left, and now spins around. Spotting the vehicle lumbering toward us, she crouches down and darts back to the rest stop.

"I didn't know this was a road," she whispers, joining us behind the DESERT FLOWER FILL 'N' FUEL sign.

Me neither. Because there's no pavement. There are no lines to differentiate it from the surrounding dirt. There aren't even tire tracks suggesting it's an unmarked route only local residents know to travel.

Still, the strange brown bus is headed somewhere. And right now, with the clock ticking and no other clues, following it is our best bet.

"Let's go," Lemon says, reading my mind.

We bolt out from behind the sign. As we run we stay low to the ground several yards behind the bus, partially to avoid being seen but also to keep from choking on the sprawling dust cloud the bus's tires create. The sky darkens the farther we go, but I don't turn on my K-Pak and Lemon doesn't flick on his lighter. This also helps keep us from being spotted—and makes it impossible to see the desert creatures all around us. There's not much that could stop me right now, but if anything can, it's coming face-to-face with an oversize tarantula.

After what feels like hours but is probably only five minutes, we pass the first sign since leaving the rest stop.

NOW ENTERING BLACKHOLE, ARIZONA!

POPULATION: 1,032 (crossed out), 811 (crossed out), 560 (crossed out), 278 (crossed out), 99

COME ON IN! STAY A WHILE!

The next sign appears almost immediately. It's bigger than the first. A single flickering lightbulb at its base shines on a peeling picture of a pretty neighborhood filled with orange houses.

RUSTIC ROSE ESTATES

YOUR PERSONAL OASIS

NEW HOMES AVAILABLE! CALL 555-SAY-AHHH

FOR MORE INFORMATION

I've just finished reading when my right foot drops. The rest of my body follows. I sail through the air before my foot hits the ground again. Then I half bounce, half roll down a long, steep incline until I'm stopped by a knobby cactus trunk. I pull my lips between my teeth to keep from crying out in pain. . . . But nothing hurts. Looking down, I see a dozen desert needles sticking out of my coat sleeve. The parka's thick padding saved me from becoming a human pincushion.

I scramble to my feet. Scattered around me, my alliance-mates do the same.

"Aliens," Abe whispers as we draw closer together.

"Oooh," Gabby breathes, looking to the sky. "Where?"

"Not up there." Abe lifts his chin and moves it in a wide, slow circle. "Out *there*."

Following his chin, I see houses. Cars. Buildings. More cacti. The streetlights are dim, so I can't make out details, but there are also no UFOs hovering overhead or green glow-in-the-dark figures roaming around. Overall, it looks like a fairly normal town.

"You think our hijackers are aliens?" I ask.

"No. But I think their spaceship crashed here a long, long time ago."

"It is a pretty big crater," Lemon says.

"In the middle of nowhere," Abe says. "Where normal people would never want to live."

And then I realize what they're talking about. I look above and beyond the houses, cars, buildings, and cacti to the tall, steep slopes surrounding them. The entire town is located at the bottom of an enormous dirt ditch.

I guess they don't call it Blackhole for nothing.

"This way." Lemon stoops forward and starts jogging.

The weird brown bus has slowed down, and we catch up quickly. This time we cover our mouths and stay closer. Unlike the surrounding desert, there are roads here, but they're not paved, and the vehicle's dust cloud keeps us hidden as we make our way through town. It also keeps us from seeing what we're passing, so we don't know exactly where we are until the bus squeals to a final stop.

"Get out!" a low voice barks nearby.

Our shield thins, grows transparent. Spotting an empty alleyway between two boarded-up buildings, I wave to Capital T and run. We press against a stone wall and watch as dozens of boys and girls gather around the bus. They wear ripped, stained pants. Sweatshirts with holes that expose dirty, scuffed skin. Boots without laces. Their hair is greasy and tangled, like it hasn't been washed or combed in months. They chant. Cheer. Thrust their fists in the air.

"Now!" the same low voice demands.

The bus door shrieks open. The vehicle bobs as people hurry down the steps. Unlike the kids waiting to greet them, they wear sharp, dark suits. Crisp, clean khakis. Matching argyle sweaters and socks. Pretty dresses. Spotless sneakers, shiny loafers, and high heels. They carry briefcases and purses, which are yanked from their grasp the second they clear the last bus step.

"Single file! Keep it moving!"

The passengers, who are clearly adults, form a long line down a dirty sidewalk. Their line's kept straight by a huge beast of a boy who taps their calves with a baseball bat. He has two feet on everyone else, so I assume he's the same kid who scaled the helicopter and beat his chest earlier.

Up until now, the new arrivals have been kept in the dark by the dirty tube socks knotted between their foreheads and noses. At the boy-beast's instruction, they remove the blindfolds. Their eyes blink, then widen, as they look around.

The bus bobs again. This time, no one gets off. Someone climbs on the hood, then the roof. She's older, probably around the same age as my parents, and wears a long dress that looks like it's been sewn together with scraps of old quilts and curtains. She wears ripped black stockings and no shoes. Her long brown hair is pulled back in a messy ponytail. She holds a clipboard in one hand and a megaphone in the other.

I've never met her, but I recognize her immediately.

She's Nadia Kilter, a.k.a. Annika's sister.

And Elinor's mother.

When she lifts the megaphone, I cringe. The adults cower. The kids clap and stomp their feet until dirt flies.

"Welcome," she bellows, "to IncrimiNation!"

Chapter 21

DEMERITS: 465
GOLD STARS: 300

Incrimi*what*?" Gabby whispers.

Abe gives her a quick nudge with his elbow. Noticing a shredded banner hanging over the street, its rope ties hanging onto crooked lampposts by threads, I point.

Judging by the scribbles, lines, and original type, here's what the banner once said:

BEHOLD BLACKHOLE'S BUSINESS DISTRICT!

CELEBRATING 20 YEARS OF UNPARALLELED CUSTOMER SERVICE

HOW MAY WE HELP *YOU*?

STOP BY THE GENERAL STORE AND RECEIVE

A COMPLIMENTARY SOUVENIR!

And here's what it says now:

BEHOLD INCRIMINATION!

CELEBRATING AN ETERNITY OF AWESOME ADULT CORRECTION

HOW MAY WE FIX *YOU*?

STOP BY THE GENERAL STORE AND RECEIVE A LESSON

YOU'LL NEVER FORGET!

Gabby squints as she reads the sign. "I don't get it. Is this place some kind of—?"

She's cut off by a series of loud, sharp pops. My alliance-mates cover their heads and duck. Having fired enough weapons to know what real danger sounds like, I take another step closer to the wall's edge for a better look.

"As you begin your stay," Nadia shouts into the megaphone, "I'd like to share with you a tip my parents offered me more times than I'd like to remember!"

The kids scream their approval. The adults, still reeling from the firecrackers thrown at their feet, spin and hop.

"Don't mess with the bull . . . because you'll get the horns!"

More firecrackers are launched. The adults jump and knock into each other. A few of them drop to the ground. The ones still standing help the fallen back up. The kids scream louder, only now they're not just cheering. They're chanting. It takes them a while to sync up, but when they do, I make out two words being repeated over and over again.

Shepherd . . . Bull! Shepherd . . . Bull! Shepherd . . . Bull!

I scan the crowd for a bearded guy holding a staff and surrounded by sheep, and an enormous, snorting beast pawing the dirt with heavy hooves. While I'm doing this, the same child-giant who scaled the helicopter joins Nadia on the roof of the bus. His weight's so great and the bus is so beaten up, two tires blow from the pressure. The vehicle tilts toward the adults. They cower. One woman in a frilly green skirt, black sweater, and pearls, falls to her knees and cries.

Someone dashes forward and gives the hysterical lady a handkerchief. I can't see the kid's face.

But I can see her long red braid.

"There she is," I say quietly to Lemon, who's recovered from his fear of gunfire and crouches next to me. Hearing ticking overhead, I glance up and see a clock on top of an iron post. The post is bent and the timepiece cracked, but, somehow, its second hand's still clicking.

10:23. If we're going to get back to GS George before liftoff, we need to make a move. Like, now.

Or, better yet, thirty seconds ago. Before Elinor tried to dry that woman's eyes. And was seen by Nadia. Who now leaps from the top of the bus, Spidey-style, grabs Elinor's braid, and pulls so hard, so fast, her daughter's heels drag in the dirt.

I start to bolt from the hiding space. Lemon grabs my coat and tugs me back.

"We'll follow," he says. "But let's give them a small head start."

He's right, of course. The closer we are the likelier we are to be caught. But how come the right thing to do is rarely the easiest? This seems like a good question for Miss Parsippany. Maybe I'll ask it in my next note.

It takes all the mental and physical strength I can manage not to immediately run after Elinor and her mother, but I do as Lemon says. In the meantime, Shepherd Bull, who appears to be the leader of this messy misfit army, tucks his massive body into a cannonball and throws himself from the bus. His feet shoot out just before slamming into the ground. He selects a dozen kids from the gathered group and barks orders. Still in line, the adults turn to the right—away from us, thankfully—and place their hands on the shoulders of the person ahead of them, like this scene's a party and they're about to conga. Then they shuffle down the sidewalk while their kid keepers bounce and leap around them, shouting and cackling.

Finally, at 10:26, the entire crew rounds a corner and disappears.

"Let's go." I step one foot out of the alleyway—and am tugged back again.

"What's our plan?" Abe asks.

"Um, to rescue Elinor?" I say.

He rolls his eyes. "How? We're just going to waltz in, say hi, take her by the hand, and excuse ourselves? Something tells me that's not going to fly here."

I glance at the clock. 10:27.

"We don't have time for plans. They probably wouldn't do much good anyway since we have no idea what else we'll find when we find Elinor. We just have to do whatever it takes to get her out of here."

"But did you see those crazies?" Gabby asks. "All muscley and dirty and out of control? Armed with baseball bats, firecrackers—and who knows what else? Without my backpack, my only weapon's a stuffed unicorn. Its cuteness quotient's unmatched, but this group would totally rip it to shreds long before that magic's put in motion."

"And . . . I have a drawing pad." Abe lifts his shoulders and tilts his head to one side.

"Well, I have a lighter." Lemon holds it up for proof. "And as we all know, I'm not afraid to use it."

"I have my K-Pak," I add, realizing how silly that sounds. What am I supposed to do if we get into trouble? E-mail GS George? The Hoodlum Hotline? The Kommissary Krew? A lot of good that'll do if we're tossed into another black hole and buried alive. "And if you see anything along the way that might be useful, grab it."

"Okay," Abe says, sounding doubtful. "But here's the thing. When I agreed to this little project, I thought we'd take a trip, see some sights, get your girl, maybe swing by the Grand Canyon on the way back—"

"Oooh, good idea!" Gabby squeals softly.

"—and be done with it." Abe pauses, looks around. "I didn't

realize I was agreeing to this, whatever this is. And dealing with them, whoever *they* are."

"Me neither. But forget about them. *We* are Capital T." I look at them, one by one by one. "We're the best of the best, remember? And we can rock this."

I sound more confident than I feel. I'm guessing they look as confident as they feel—which isn't very. But then Gabby hugs her stuffed unicorn. Abe pats his drawing pad. Lemon flicks on his lighter. And when I turn toward the alleyway entrance, they do too.

I glance at the clock once more.

10:30.

I'm the only one who saw Elinor dragged off, so I take the lead and we head in that direction. We're alone on Main Street now, but voices are all around us. They seem to come from inside buildings and nearby roads. They're loud. Excited. They make me wonder when these kids go to sleep. We don't have curfews at Kilter, but since twelve hours of troublemaking can be exhausting and we have to be up early for classes, we're usually in bed at a reasonable hour.

Picking up the pace, we pass abandoned cars. Jump over broken glass. Weave through discarded telephones, cash registers, and cardboard boxes that litter Main Street's sidewalks like leaves after a crazy summer storm. Peer into stores and cafés, which look like they were broken into long ago, their owners and patrons permanently run out of Blackhole. The shelves are empty. Dishes shattered. Furniture toppled.

It's a ghost town. Like the ones you see in movies.

Only here, given the way they're howling, the ghosts are very much alive.

Besides us, the only sign of life currently on Main Street comes at the very end. Two businesses, one on each corner, appear to be open. As we scurry closer, I see the first is the General Store. My brain tells my torso to lower and my feet to sprint by the illuminated window, but only my torso listens. Lemon, Abe, and Gabby slow to a walk too, so they must see the same thing I do.

There are more adults. But they're not the ones who just got off the bus. They still wear suits, khakis, and dresses, but the pleats are gone, the fabric faded and torn. They're all barefoot. The men have mustaches and scraggly beards. The women's hair stands around their heads, forming what I imagine would be lovely homes for some wayward desert birds. Unlike the kids running through the aisles, they move slowly. Awkwardly. Like they haven't sat down in weeks.

"What did I say?" one kid yells so loudly I hear him like he's standing right in front of me. He looks about my age, maybe a year or two older. "Use. Your. *Words!*"

The man he addresses winces as he tries to stand up straight. He takes a box from the shelf, which, unlike those in the other stores we passed, is fully stocked. His mustache moves, so I assume he's speaking, but I can't make out a single syllable.

"What's that?" The kid cups one dirty hand to an even dirtier ear. "You want me to buy you a limited-edition sandstone coaster set? Even though it's not your birthday? And I just bought you those jarred chili peppers last week? I. Don't. *Think so!*"

The man's mustache moves faster. The kid shakes his head.

"Drop and give me twenty!"

The man's suit sleeves, which were made for a much larger figure, hang from his thin arms. I doubt he has the strength to do one push-up, let alone twenty. But it's soon clear the kid wasn't talking calisthenics. Because the man gets on his hands and knees, lowers his head to the kid's boots like a dog to a water bowl, and puckers up.

"Ew," Gabby says as the man kisses one filthy shoe, then the other.

"Absolutely not!" another voice yells. This one's female. It belongs to a tall girl holding a sombrero-shaped statue in one hand and a donkey-shaped statue in the other. Black and white dust sprinkles the floor around her, so I assume the statues are salt and pepper shakers. "Did you make the bed the way I told you? Or put away your clean clothes?"

She's shrieking at a woman who's wearing what was probably once a bright yellow sundress. The woman's lips move. The girl steps toward her. Glares. Raises both arms overhead. The woman crumbles like a cookie to the floor.

"You don't *have* clean clothes? What an ungrateful little—"

Another tug on my coat pulls me away from the window. This is good and bad. Good because we have to keep moving. But bad because these kids are definitely playing several cards short of a full deck. And the more we see, the more I want to help the adults.

As we hurry away, we hear more shouting across the street. I glance over my shoulder. A strange scene is visible through the smudged window of the Prickly Pear Café. More scruffy adults sit at tables, their heads lowered and shoulders slumped. More kids stand over them and yell, ordering the diners to eat their vegetables or starve.

"Now where?" Abe asks.

I turn back. We've reached an intersection. Across the street is a large dirt square. It's empty except for a set of swings without seats and an upside-down slide. To the right and left are houses. I check the roads for fresh footprints, but there are so many it's impossible to tell which, if any, are new.

But then I see it. Lying in the middle of the road to our left.

A single green ribbon.

"This way." I run, snatching up the hair tie along the way.

The road leads to the entrance to Rustic Rose Estates. That's what the sign says, though the houses inside the complex look better suited to Rundown Rows Estates. They're pretty big and at one point were probably the nicest homes in all of Blackhole, but now graffiti covers their exterior walls. Doors are off hinges. Roof tiles litter yards. Garbage is strewn about. Forgotten cars are dented, their tires flat and windshields shattered.

"They all look exactly the same," Gabby says. "How do we know which one she's in?"

It's a good question. And at first, I don't have a good answer. But then the front door of a house halfway down the block squeals open. It slams into the side of the house, sending stucco flying. Nadia Kilter flies down the steps and jumps into a battered pickup truck parked in the driveway. Through the hole where the driver's side window used to be I see her bend down. A few seconds later, there's a sharp scratching noise. It's followed by a loud rumbling as the engine starts.

"She just hot-wired the car," Abe says. "Like on TV. Probably because the little mongrels swallowed the keys."

"Awesome," Gabby says.

The rumbling grows to a roar. The pickup fires backward from the driveway, turns so fast its tires spin through dirt before gaining traction, and heads for the entrance. We dart and duck behind the closest hiding spot: a six-foot-tall iron coyote sculpture in someone's front yard. I hold my breath as the truck nears, but it zooms by without slowing down. As soon as it leaves the neighborhood, we start running again.

When we reach the house, we move without speaking. Lemon, Abe, and Gabby crouch below windows and peer inside the house. I go to the front door, which is still open after being thrown into the exterior wall.

"Seamus!" a voice hisses.

I jump. Look to the right. Lemon's standing by a cracked wooden gate several feet away. He waves for me to follow. I do the same to Abe and Gabby, who are behind me. We all dash through the gate and into the backyard.

Where I don't know what Lemon wants us to see. The backyard resembles the front yard. It's grassless and empty. The only difference is an inground pool, which doesn't look like it's ever held swimmers—or water, for that matter. Lemon, however, seems to think the crumbling stone edges and deep, unlined ditch make for prime doggy-paddle conditions.

"Hope you brought a bathing suit," he says. "Or better yet, a wet suit. Made of metal. And a helmet. The old-fashioned kind. That's so big and heavy it looks like it could double as a submarine."

Despite his Scrabble affection, these are a lot of words for him to say all at once. This suggests he's nervous, which is reason enough to be concerned. But then I hear scratching. Skittering. Clicking. Whimpering. All coming from the direction of the pool.

I look at Lemon.

"We'll be right behind you," he says with a nod.

I book it toward the ditch. A dull light shines out from underneath the sagging diving board. The rest of the yard is dark, and I'm glad. The house behind us is silent, but there's no telling if Elinor's roommates are lurking around, waiting for the perfect chance to attack.

Five seconds later, they're the least of my worries. Because when I reach the pool, I see that it's not empty after all. Filling the bottom, zigzagging across the sides, crawling all over each other . . . are scorpions. Tarantulas. Lizards. Beetles. Centipedes. It's like the bus that dropped off the adults drove back out into the desert, picked up every critter and creature in its path until the vehicle was stuffed, and dumped them all in here. Until the wriggling mass was two feet deep.

A red inner tube sits in the middle of the madness like a tiny desert island. And straddling the hole with one foot on either side, fighting for her balance as the creatures close in . . . is Elinor.

Chapter 22

DEMERITS: 465
GOLD STARS: 300

I start to call her name. But then something slides over my right sock and shimmies up my calf. A hundred tiny legs tickle my skin. I close my eyes. Bite my tongue to keep from screaming. Lift my foot, bring it back, and fling it forward. The insect sails through the air and dives headfirst (or tail first, it's impossible tell) into the pool.

"Hello?"

My eyes snap open.

"Mother? Is that you?"

Elinor's voice wavers. She sniffs. She clearly doesn't see us, and I understand why.

She can't look up. She's too busy watching the critters, too focused on nudging them off the tube while trying to keep her balance—and avoid being eaten alive.

"I'm so sorry," Elinor cries softly. "It won't happen again. I promise."

Promise. There's that word again.

Annika's voice fills my head. I shake it out.

I open my mouth to say hi, then think better of it. At the very least, Elinor's rattled. At most, she's terrified. Either way, she's not expecting to see us there. And I don't want that shock to make her lose her concentration and send her flying into the fray.

I turn toward Capital T and press my pointer finger to my lips. They look confused but stay quiet. Stepping away from the pool, I take my K-Pak from inside my coat, turn it on, and shine it around the yard. There's a turned-over picnic table, a pile of rocks, and about a million dried exoskeletons left over from desert critters shedding skin.

I'm thinking we may have to look indoors for something to fish her out with when I spot a long, fat rattlesnake coiled up on the cracked patio. It appears to be sleeping, but still. It's a *rattlesnake.* As in the vicious, venom-shooting king of the desert. It makes the creepy-crawlies in the pool suddenly seem as threatening as fluffy puppies.

I grab Lemon's arm. He holds up one hand, which apparently means he'll take care of it, and shuffles toward the beast.

"What's he doing?" Gabby whispers as he gets closer and squats down.

"I don't know," I whisper back as he takes his lighter from his coat pocket and flicks it on.

"Crazy as a loon." Abe shakes his head. "I knew it."

I'd argue, but then Lemon leans forward. Waves the small flame before the beast's face. And laughs.

"Wait," I hiss, hurrying toward him. "What are you—?"

I'm too late. He already has the snake by the mouth and is dragging it across the patio. Toward us.

Gabby squeals. Abe leaps behind the toppled picnic table. I somehow stand my ground long enough for Lemon to reach me and hold up the rattler's head.

Which is unlike any snake I've ever seen in any zoo or rattler picture I've ever seen online. Because it doesn't have beady eyes or fangs. It doesn't have a triangular neck or pointy tongue. What it does have . . . is a rubber nozzle.

"A garden hose?" I ask.

"Looks like," Lemon says.

I shrug. "That'll do."

I slide my K-Pak down the front of my coat. I take the nozzle, turn, and walk, dragging the hose behind me. It grows lighter as I near the pool, and I know without looking back that my alliance-mates have picked up the slack—literally. Staying in the shadows as much as possible, I tug until I hold several feet of hose. Then I raise it overhead, swing it around until the nozzle whistles through the air, and let it soar.

Now that the rattlesnake's just a hollow rubber tube, the creatures in the pool have regained their original scary status. Still, I feel kind of bad. Because unlike animal actors in movies, I'm pretty sure some of these are harmed during production—since there's a bunch of crinkling and crackling when the hose finally lands. Stepping forward, I make a mental note to go to the pet store whenever I return to Cloudview and give some tame, friendly insect or amphibian a nice, double-walled, padlocked home.

I watch Elinor. She sees the hose but isn't sure what to make of it. Wanting to encourage her without terrifying her even more, I take the hose and gently wiggle it back and forth. My hope is that she assumes it's a peace offering from her mom.

It works. She carefully lowers to her hands and knees and waits until she's balanced in the lower position. Then she reaches one hand forward and grabs the nozzle, first with one hand, then both.

"One, two, three . . . pull!" I shout over my shoulder.

We engage in the strangest tug-of-war ever fought, and I revise my mental note. Because as the tube slides slowly through the pool, the cracking, creaking, and squeaking is deafening. I'll probably have to beg Mother Nature's forgiveness by adopting a hundred creepy-crawlies. Maybe I can tug on GS George's heartstrings, since he's such a pet enthusiast, and convince him to take in some.

That reminds me. When I pull back again, I peer down the opening near my coat collar. I can just see the clock at the top of my K-Pak screen, which must've automatically adjusted to Mountain Standard Time.

10:46.

I look up. Still on the tube, Elinor reaches the diving board. She wobbles to her feet and stretches both arms overhead. She grabs the board's edge with her fingertips and moans softly as she pulls herself up. I fight the overwhelming urge to run over and help, since I don't want her losing her grip and falling back into the pool.

I exhale once she's safely on the ground, and wait for her to get her bearings. She shakes out her legs, then, staying several inches away from the pool, leans forward and peers inside. She hugs her arms around her torso, shudders, and starts toward the house.

"Hi, Elinor."

She stops. Her back's to us.

I glance at Lemon. He shrugs.

She turns. Slowly. Her eyes—her pretty, warm, copper-colored eyes—travel from Abe. To Gabby. To Lemon. To me.

"Seamus?"

I smile. Wave.

"What are you doing here?"

The corners of my mouth begin to droop. I force them back up. "Rescuing you!"

Her pretty, warm, copper-colored eyes widen. I think I see a hint of a smile on her lips, but it's too dark to be sure and the hint's gone as soon as it appears. And there's no mistaking the frown that follows. It takes up half her face.

She looks behind her and steps toward us at the same time. "*Rescuing* me?" she asks loudly. "From what? Heaven on earth?" She pauses and listens before sprinting the remaining distance. When she speaks again, she whispers. "Seamus, what . . . ? How . . . ?"

"I can explain," I say quickly, "but not now. There's no time."

I reach for her hand. Not to be mushy, but because there's a chance shock and confusion might root her feet to the dirt. And with minutes to go before GS George leaves, we need to run like our lives depend on it.

And in this place, they probably do.

"You shouldn't be here, Seamus," Elinor says sadly, sliding her hand from mine. "You shouldn't have come."

I start to disagree. But then there's a tug on my coat again. Thinking it's Lemon hurrying us along, I shoot him a pleading look over my shoulder.

But it's not Lemon.

It's the child-giant.

Shepherd Bull.

Chapter 23

DEMERITS: 465
GOLD STARS: 300

Little lady's right," growls Mr. Bull, who's probably our age but is so big—and intimidating—the adult title seems appropriate. He raises a shovel with one hand, smacks the blade into his other. Again. And again. And again. "You shouldn't be here."

My gaze fixes on the shovel blade. Its tip is caked in a dark red substance, but I can't tell if that's rust . . . or blood.

"Sorry." I swallow. Breathe. "We were just leav—"

He laughs. The sound is like nothing I've ever heard. It begins with a boom that shakes the ground beneath my feet, then grows louder, higher. Until it reminds me of a singing chipmunk. Under other circumstances, such a girly laugh might shrink such a big guy. Under these, it just makes him scarier.

"Who are you?" he demands.

"Wouldn't you like to know?" Abe scoffs.

My head shoots toward my arrogant alliance-mate. It's nice he's so proud of Capital T, but now's not really the time to fan our feathers.

"Actually, no." Mr. Bull says. "I wouldn't. Matter of fact, I couldn't care less."

He opens his mouth. I can see his teeth. They're cracked. Chipped. Filled with the remains of his dinner. I brace for screaming, but it doesn't come.

Instead he burps. Whistles. Burps some more. Clucks his tongue four times. Coughs. Spits.

The instant saliva hits dirt, eight kids step out from the darkness behind him. They're miniature versions of him, but they still tower over me. They hold baseball bats. Tennis racquets. Rakes. Screwdrivers. Hammers. Forks.

"Listen," I say. "You seem like a reasonable guy. I'm sure we can—"

He burps again. The baby bulls rush past him and swarm

around us like flies to roadkill. They don't pulverize us, which is what I expect, but they do move so fast there's no time to think—or retaliate. My one attempt at self-defense is trying to snatch a racquet from the shortest kid in the group, but rather than getting a weapon, I get a swift smack upside the head.

The next thing I know, I'm lifted up and hoisted onto something. I can't tell what because I can't see. I think the blindness must be a side effect of my concussion, but then I smell sweat. Mud. Maybe even mold. Like my nose is shoved inside an old sneaker. And I realize I'm blindfolded. By tube socks. My hand automatically reaches for my face but doesn't get far. Because my wrists are tied together behind my back.

Happy thoughts, happy thoughts, happy thoughts.

Whatever I'm sitting on dips once. Twice. Three times. Four times.

"Lemon?" I whisper.

"No talking!" Mr. Bull roars.

My seat dips again. An engine starts.

As we begin moving, I hear two light taps. They sound like knuckles against metal. Certain this is my best friend communicating without words, the way he so often does, I breathe a silent sigh of relief. As long as Capital T's together, we can get through anything.

I keep telling myself this. It's the only way to prevent panicking about Elinor. The time. GS George. The Kilter helicopter.

Our ride doesn't last long and soon I'm being dragged, lifted, and led. I pay attention to my still-functioning senses for clues, but all I smell is sweat. All I hear is the shuffle of feet. All I feel is the occasional shove against my back.

Finally, a door opens. I'm given one last push, which sends me flying to my knees. The pain is so great my hands and feet tingle, but I manage to keep my mouth shut and not cry out.

"Nadia will be right with you," Mr. Bull grunts.

The door closes.

My pulse pounds in my ears. I count twenty heartbeats, then quietly test my voice.

"Lemon?" Pause. "Abe?" Pause. "Gabby?"

Pause.

"I'm here."

Beneath my blindfold, my eyebrows scrunch together. "Elinor?"

"I think they're gone," she says. "We're alone."

"Um, not quite," Abe adds quickly. Probably because in his mind, the idea of overhearing potentially mushy chitchat is worse than the idea of being overheard by our captors.

"I can't *see*," Gabby whines. "This is way worse than the time Mystery blinded me with pepper spray!"

Mystery. It's crazy, but compared to this, being kidnapped by him and locked up in the cottage in the woods would be like participating in a fun game or sport. At least then I'd know my playing field.

"And that *stench*!" Gabby groans. "I think I'm going to throw up."

"Oh no," Abe says. "Please don't. If you do, I will, and then—"

"Hang on," Lemon says. "Nobody move."

I follow his instructions. Soon my still-functioning senses pick up a soft click. A pocket of heat. The smell of butane, then something burning.

The pressure around my wrists disappearing.

My hands are free. I rip the tube socks from my head.

It takes a second for my eyes to adjust to the bright light. Once they do, they find Lemon. His blindfold's also gone. The left corner of his mouth lifts in a half smile as he holds up his lighter and a fistful of seared string.

"Thanks." I grin.

"Anytime."

As he works on releasing the others, I look around. We're sitting on the floor in some sort of closet, although this one's three times the size of my mom's walk-in back home. And there are no clothes, shoes, or purses. And low benches frame the space. And whoever was here before us carved messages into the walls for those who came after.

BEHAVING'S FOR BABIES

ACT UP OR GET OUT

KIDS RULE

ADULTS DROOL

"You shouldn't have come."

My eyes meet Elinor's. "So you said."

"I'm serious, Seamus. This place . . . It's dangerous."

"So is Kilter to the average kid," I remind her. "But we're not average. We're Troublemakers. And there's nothing these oversize bullies can throw at us that we can't handle."

"Really?" Abe asks, shaking out his freed hands. "Is that why we're locked up? In this"—he scans the closet—"whatever this is?"

"It's a sauna," Elinor explains. "In the former Blackhole Beauty Salon and Spa. When students misbehave—or don't misbehave enough—Nadia locks them up in places that only adults normally enjoy in the real world."

"Students?" Gabby asks. "IncrimiNation's a school?"

Elinor hesitates, then nods. She turns back to me. "How did you know I was here?"

"You mentioned Blackhole in your note. Lucky for us, the town's not that big."

She frowns. "If you really think Troublemakers can hold their own against IncrimiNators, why'd you come? Why'd you think I needed to be rescued?"

I look at my knees, which are pulled to my chest, and try to think of the best way to answer. When I look up again, Lemon, Abe, and Gabby are staring at me. They avert their gazes, move to the far end of the sauna, and pretend not to listen.

I face Elinor, take a deep breath, and begin.

"Because of the same note. The one you sent a few weeks ago." I leave out the part about reading it only days earlier. There will be time for the whole story later—I hope. "I thought you needed me. I mean—not me, specifically," I add quickly, my cheeks warming. "But someone. To help. Because you sounded lonely. Unhappy. Scared."

Her face softens slightly. When she speaks again, her voice is sad. "Nadia Kilter's my mother."

Gasps fill the far end of the sauna.

"I know," I say, ignoring them. My hands are between my torso and legs. I cross my fingers that she doesn't ask how. "And?"

"And I appreciate your caring enough to come all this way." She turns and says in Capital T's direction, "Really, I do. Thank you." She turns back to me. "But kids belong with their parents. I belong here."

I could respond with a few things. Like when kids are at Kilter, they're not with their parents. And when kids are at IncrimiNation, they're not with their parents (present company excluded). And when parents are mean, angry, aggressive adults who don't care whether the kids they're responsible for bathe, eat right, and take a few hours each night to stop destroying things and get some sleep, a little time apart can be good. Healthy. Necessary.

They're valid points. But I go with the only one that matters.

"You just said this place is dangerous. For that reason alone, you belong anywhere *but* here."

Finally, a smile. Her copper eyes have been cool, but now they warm. Brighten.

At the far end of the sauna, there's a soft *thwat.*

"Hear that?" Gabby whispers, presumably to Abe. "That's what a *gentleman* sounds like."

"Thank you," Elinor says. "But I couldn't leave even if I wanted to. There's nowhere else for me to go."

"Sure there is. You can go back to Kilter."

She pulls her legs in tighter, rests her chin on her knees. "No. I can't. Annika kicked me out. She was mean and cold when she did it, just like she always is to me, but this time I don't blame her. She gave me three semesters to improve, to show I have what it takes to succeed there. I took the same classes three times, and I still couldn't steal a pack of gum or fake a bodily noise or draw a scary picture. There's no way I'd ever become a professional Troublemaker. I'm just not good enough at being bad."

Again, I have multiple responses to choose from. Like if she doesn't think she can be a professional Troublemaker, why does she think she can be a professional criminal—or whatever else IncrimiNation trains its students to become? Doesn't the latter require worse behavior? Also, she revealed at the end of last semester that her troublemaking talent was lying. How do I know that's not what she's doing right now?

Before I can pick one, Lemon speaks up.

"We have our own rooms now. Seamus has been sleeping on the floor of mine since the beginning of the semester."

Elinor frowns. Like me, she must be wondering what this has to do with our current conversation.

"Why?" she asks.

"Because I'm too good at starting fires. I can't control myself. So Seamus stays with me to make sure I don't burn Kilter to the ground in my sleep. More than anything, that's what I want—what I *need*—to learn at Kilter. How to keep the flames in check so I don't hurt someone again."

Again?

No one else seems to have caught this, because Elinor nods. Abe and Gabby exchange looks.

"I'm a nerd," Gabby says quickly, loudly, like this is a confession she's been dying to share.

"Really?" Abe asks. "I had no idea."

"I know. I hide it really well. But at my school back home, I get straight A-plusses. Not As. *A-plusses.* I never need extra credit, but I do it whenever it's offered. I finish my chores before they're given to me. I read instead of watching TV. I go to bed early and get up early to make my parents breakfast. I eat all my vegetables, all the time. I've never had a cavity. I volunteer at the local library, nursing home, and animal shelter. For my birthday every year, I ask people to donate to their favorite charities rather than buy me gifts. On Halloween, I don't go trick-or-treating. I stay home and hand out rice cakes."

"Rice cakes?" Elinor asks.

"Rice cakes." Gabby sighs. "Being good is like this terrible, awful, incurable disease I was born with and can't get rid of."

"And you're sharing this fascinating info because . . . ?" Abe asks.

"Because the way you steer clear of someone who's coughing up a lung? Or sneezing nonstop? That's what kids do with me. What they *did* with me." She shakes her head. "Last year, I started watching the popular kids. They were usually the ones doing ridiculous things like tooting with their armpits in the middle of class. So I taught myself some of their tricks. Which got me sent to Kilter. Where, for the first time ever, I have real friends."

I still don't understand the impromptu sharing session, but it's kind of nice. Even Abe stays quiet at this last part. For a few seconds, anyway.

"My dad plays football. Professionally. If you ever meet him, he'll tell you he always wanted a son with a wicked throwing arm who could follow in his footsteps. That's what he tells everyone—our neighbors, my teachers, store cashiers." Abe quietly taps one finger on the drawing pad in his lap. "Unfortunately, he got a son with a drawing arm instead. I tried making him happy, but if I even look at a football my bicep shrinks. Give me pastels or watercolors, though, and I'm like Popeye after a can of spinach."

Sitting next to him, Gabby raises one hand to pat him on the back. Then she seems to think better of it and lowers her hand. "You're an amazing artist. I'm sure he's superproud of you."

"Thanks, but no. He's not. That's why I'm at Kilter. My mom signed me up because of the public graffiti and endless wall murals at home, but when I was there over break, she said I'd learned my lesson and that I didn't have to go back if I didn't want to. But I did want to. I thought it was the only place that could teach me things—tough, nonfootball things—that Dad might approve of."

This is all news to me. Funny how you can spend so much time with people and still not know who they really are. Maybe I'll bring this up with Miss Parsippany in my next note. If there *is* a next note.

Which reminds me.

Heart racing, I unzip my coat and take out my K-Pak. There's no reception in here, but the clock still works.

11:19.

My heart sinks. But before it can reach my toes, I have a genuine happy thought.

GS George left—but only nineteen minutes ago. He couldn't have gotten far. He has his K-Pak, so if we can just get out of here and go somewhere with reception, I can e-mail and beg him to turn back around. If Annika's checking her messages in the middle of the night (which wouldn't surprise me), this could risk alerting her to what's going on, but at this point, that risk is worth taking.

"Guys," I say, raising my eyes from the screen, "we really have to—" I stop. They're all watching me. "What?"

"You're up," Abe says.

"Up? What do you mean?"

"We all shared our stories," Gabby says. "About being mostly good kids who don't really belong at Kilter. Now it's your turn."

My heart resumes its descent. The blood in my head follows.

"Um . . . well—"

I'm saved by a bell. Literally. The shrill ringing starts overhead but fills the sauna instantly. It's so loud my hands shoot to my ears. My eyes squeeze shut. It finally ends five excruciating seconds later, and I breathe a sigh of relief.

When I inhale again, something seems off. The air's different. Warmer. Moister.

When I open my eyes, I can barely see Elinor through the thick white haze.

"Steam," she says. "Mother's coming."

She jumps to her feet. Lunges across the sauna. Steps onto a bench and hops until her fingertips hit the ceiling. A small piece of wood pops up; she shoves it aside and faces us.

"Go."

"Go?" I stand too. "Where?"

She points to the square hole above her. "That's an attic. It runs the length of the building. The main entrance is above the nail salon. It should be unlocked, and the salon should be empty. You can get out that way."

"How do you know?" Gabby asks.

"I've spent a lot of time in here," Elinor says.

"Why would Nadia—your mother—put you in here with us if you knew how to get out?" Abe asks.

"She doesn't know I know. I always explore and come back before she finds me missing."

Gabby raises her eyebrows. "You don't give yourself enough credit." She motions for Abe to stand. "Knee, please."

This request would normally invite a string of sarcastic responses before Abe eventually, reluctantly, possibly obliged. But steam is swirling. The temperature's rising. Outside the sauna door, footsteps are nearing. So he doesn't bat an eye before putting one foot on the bench. When his thigh is perpendicular to the seat, Gabby steps onto his knee, grabs the sides of the ceiling hole, and pulls herself up. Then she reaches one arm down to help Abe. Then Lemon.

This is all happening too fast. I turn to Elinor.

"Why don't we just stay here? And explain who we are and where we go to school? I mean, Nadia is Annika's sister. Once we apologize for trespassing and maybe even blame the whole thing on a troublemaking assignment, I'm sure she'll let us go."

Elinor slowly shakes her head. Her copper eyes fill with tears. "Oh, Seamus," she says softly. "You don't—"

She's cut off by a loud bang. My head snaps toward the sauna door, which I expect to be off its hinges. It's not, but it is shaking.

"Go." Elinor puts one hand on my coat sleeve. "Now. Please."

"Eli-*Snore*!" a deep female voice sings on the other side of the door. "I'm simply *dying* to meet your friends. Shepherd's already told me so many wonderful things about them!"

There's a click, like the sound a key makes turning a lock.

Elinor's fingers tighten around my arm. "I'll be okay. I promise."

No wonder Annika doesn't like that word. In a situation like this, it doesn't carry much weight.

"But—"

She grabs the front of my coat. Pulls me toward her until we're so close I can see my reflection in her watery eyes.

"Listen to me," she whispers. "If you don't leave now, you never will. Mother will throw you in a deep ditch where bugs bigger than your head will be your only company and food source. That's where you'll stay. Forever. Or at least until *you* become *their* food source." She bites her lip. Puts her arms around my shoulders. Hugs me tightly and demands near my ear, "And then what will I do when I *really* need you?"

Gabby's right. Elinor definitely doesn't give herself enough credit. Because up until these words leave her mouth, I'm confident nothing she says will convince me to go anywhere without her. But this does.

There's another click. The doorknob begins to turn.

Elinor pulls away. There are a million things I want to say, but we only have time for one.

"Be careful."

She nods. I hold my eyes to hers a second more, then bolt to the bench, jump on, and grab Lemon's hand. I've just pulled my feet into the attic and slid the ceiling tile back in place when the door below is thrown open.

"Greetings, my little desert dev—" Nadia's booming voice falls silent. "What is this? Where are they?" Heavy footsteps pound the floor. "What did you do?"

"Nothing." Elinor's voice trembles. "I don't know what you're talking about."

"Of course you don't. Why should today be different from any other day?" It sounds like Nadia starts back across the sauna. Then the footsteps stop. The floorboards creak. The footsteps turn and stomp back toward Elinor. "Four blindfolds, no captives. Care to guess again, daughter dearest?"

The tube socks! I swallow a groan. We must've left them wherever we took them off. I look at Lemon, who's crouched next to me and in front of Abe and Gabby, listening. In the light of my K-Pak, I see him frown.

"No? Have it your way. You always do!" There's more stomping. The door opens. "Wait here. I just have to instruct your pool attendants to add two additional feet of beetles and spiders. Maybe I'll even ask them to toss in a cobra for kicks."

The door slams.

"Um, guys?" Abe asks. "We gotta go."

"He's right," Gabby says. "I'm really sorry, Seamus."

The attic is more like a crawl space with a dim light at one end. They start shuffling toward the light on their hands and knees.

"You all right?" Lemon asks.

I lift my chin, then let it drop. It's all I can manage.

He starts shuffling too. My brain orders my body to follow, but once again, my body has a mind of its own.

I move closer to the loose ceiling tile. Lift it up and move it aside. Lower my head into the sauna and finally share the huge secret I've been guarding even more carefully than my last huge secret.

"She's alive."

Elinor's sitting on a bench. Her head lifts. Her eyes, now overflowing with tears, find mine.

"What?"

"My substitute teacher. Miss Parsippany. She isn't dead. I didn't kill her." I try out the next words in my head before saying them out loud. "I'm not a murderer. So if anyone doesn't belong at Kilter . . . it's me."

Click. The lock turns. The door inches open.

Elinor looks at it, then at me.

I hold out my hand.

"*Five* cobras?" Nadia asks, apparently talking to someone just outside the sauna. "Fabulous! Maybe daughter dearest will finally learn something!"

Elinor jumps up. Dashes across the sauna. Takes my hand. Between the two us, we lift her up and replace the ceiling tile with exactly one second to spare.

In which time she brushes her eyes, smiles, and calls me the nicest thing anyone ever has.

"Liar."

Chapter 24

DEMERITS: 465
GOLD STARS: 300

As we crawl I tell Elinor about GS George. The helicopter her classmates helped destroy. The time deadline. My plan to write our pilot and beg for his return. The chances of this happening growing smaller with each passing second.

She listens carefully. Then, once we reach the end of the attic, drop into the lobby, and leave the salon as easily as Houdini left Shell's Belles weeks earlier, she takes the lead.

"Are we sure this is such a good idea?" Abe whispers to Lemon and me as we run. "Following the director's daughter? What if she's taking us to the lion's den to make her mom happy?"

"If she wanted to make her mom happy," I whisper back, "she wouldn't have just helped us escape from the sauna."

Abe doesn't look convinced. But he keeps running.

We sprint through town, passing an abandoned Laundromat. Gas station. Bakery. Post office. We stay low to the ground and away from flickering streetlights. Several IncrimiNators are out and about, and my heart feels like it'll burst through my chest every time we near one. But then Elinor clucks her tongue or whistles, they mimic her greeting, and we cross the street before they can get a good look at us.

Until we round a corner. And stop ten feet short of Shepherd Bull and his gang of grunge. They're holding shovels, rakes, and other assorted weapons, which makes me think they were scouring the town for sauna escape artists—before they got distracted. By the window display in what used to be the Blackhole Toy Shop. Now they face the three adults popping in and out of wooden crates covered in ripped tinfoil like sad, tired jack-in-the-boxes. As the adults force smiles and sway back and forth, the kids heckle and howl.

I lean toward Elinor to ask if there's a detour to wherever

we're going. The gang of grunge is taking up all of the sidewalk and most of the street, so it'd be hard to get by unnoticed. I've just opened my mouth when she takes my arm. Squeezes. And rips my coat sleeve.

"Okay," I whisper. "We are in the desert. I guess I didn't need—"

I'm stopped by the handful of dirt she flings at my chest. I step back and look down like I've been shot, then raise my eyes to hers.

"Sorry," she says softly, quickly. "But you look too good."

I look too good? In front of her? Impossible.

"You, too." She throws a handful of dirt at Lemon. "And you, and you."

I try not to be disappointed as she shares the sentiment and soil with the rest of Capital T. Abe's face turns neon-red the instant he's hit. Before suspicion and anger cause a loud verbal explosion that could invite attention and kill us all, Elinor presses one finger to her lips, then points behind us.

To what was once the Blackhole School for Gifted Youth. And is now, according to the spray-painted correction, the Black-hole School for Doomed Adults.

"Shortcut," she whispers.

"You want us to go in there?" Gabby asks.

"It's crawling with people," Lemon says, peering through the dusty window.

"Lion's den." Abe shakes his head. "I knew it."

For a second, I actually wonder if he might be right. I understand wanting to make your parents happy, and Elinor helping us escape only so she could be the one to recapture us and save the day would certainly please Nadia. But then there's a loud whoop behind us. I spin around and see another armed gang of grunge heading our way. They seem to be looking past us, at Mr. Bull and company, but they'll spot us soon.

Which means the only way out of the lion's den . . . is through it.

I grab my other coat sleeve and pull. The material rips and feathers fly out. I bend down, scoop up as much dirt as my hands can hold, and throw it at my legs, stomach, and back. I pat my dirty palms to my neck and face. Untie my shoelaces. Mess up my already messy hair some more. At first Lemon, Abe, and Gabby look at me like the desert dust has gone to my head, but when there's another, louder whoop behind us, they all jump and do the same. Abe even drops to the ground and rolls around like a pig in mud.

By the time we enter the Blackhole School for Doomed Adults, we look like we belong.

Almost.

"What's *wrong* with them?" Gabby shouts.

I shake my head. Because I have no idea. The hallway's packed with kids. They run, scream, laugh, and bounce off of the walls—and one another. As we elbow our way through the crowd, one teenage boy uses another as a springboard to launch himself over our heads. When he passes above us, I notice his eyes are dark, unfocused. Then he slams into a locker, denting it, and falls to the floor with an excited shriek.

"Too much sugar, freedom, and power!" Elinor yells. "Dangerous combination!"

The effects of which I'd like to get away from immediately. Unfortunately, that's impossible. The hallway's so crammed we have no choice but to go with the slow flow. To keep from panicking, I distract myself by peeking into classrooms—and at the IncrimiNation curriculum.

First up is language arts. At least that's what the sign outside the door says. But the students inside aren't learning pig Latin, pig French, or how to speak granny-style, the way we do at Kilter.

They're bending over adults, who are kneeling on the floor and scrubbing tiles with toothbrushes. When we're right in front of the open door, I see that the adults aren't just cleaning the floor. They're scrubbing words into the gray grime. They make full sentences, like BECAUSE MY SON SAID SO, THAT'S WHY. And MY DAUGHTER'S THE BOSS. And AS LONG AS I LIVE UNDER MY CHILDREN'S ROOF, I'LL DO AS THEY SAY.

The kids dictate, the adults write. Some scrub the same sentence a dozen times. An older female teenager—I assume the teacher—walks around the room, surveying the progress and barking orders. She's wearing ripped shorts, a stained T-shirt, and no shoes. From here I can see the dark lines of dirt under her toenails. Houdini doesn't exactly dress to impress, but this girl's outfit makes his pajamas look like a three-piece suit.

Speaking of Houdini, the next class we pass is math. At Kilter, math is all about stealing personal belongings. Here, it's all about playing video games. A dozen old TVs are scattered throughout the room. Two players sit before each: one kid, one adult. Only they're not working as teams. They're playing against each other. The kids clearly have the edge, while the adults struggle to keep up. Every time a kid's game character causes an adult's to step on a land mine, fall out of a plane, or somehow end his or her turn, the kid cackles in delight, forces the adult to guzzle a gallon of root beer, and restarts the game.

"Points!" Elinor shouts near my ear. "They have half an hour to get a thousand each. If they don't, they're grounded!"

The adults look so miserable trying to avoid being grounded, I can't imagine what that punishment might involve. Before I can ask Elinor, we reach the biology classroom—where rather than tooting with their armpits or hocking fake loogies, students are making fists, pounding them into walls and other hard surfaces, and simultaneously bulging their eyes and lunging forward. All to make the adults cringe and cower, which they do. The teacher, a tall, skinny boy, occasionally demonstrates other scare tactics, like leaping on top of desks and jumping up and down until the floor shakes.

"Monsters!" Gabby declares, shoving forward.

Next up is gym. It's in what probably used to be a normal gymnasium, complete with bleachers and basketball hoops. But no one's cheering or shooting. Once again, kids are yelling. And adults are running a very strange obstacle course.

"Sixty seconds!" Elinor shouts. "That's how long they have

to make their beds, pretend to shower, floss, iron, put clothes on over the ones they're already wearing, make a nutritious breakfast, pretend to eat it, wash and dry dishes, take the trash to one side of the room, and book it back all the way to the other side to catch the invisible school bus!"

"And if the invisible school bus leaves without them?" I ask.

"They try again—but with fifty seconds on the clock! If they fail a second time, they're grounded!"

As I watch two tired, dizzy adults run into each other and collapse between the fake bed and shower stall, I wonder if being grounded is really that bad. At least it'd give them a break from this.

We continue down the hall. I try to process everything we've just seen.

"So IncrimiNation teaches kids how to control adults?" I yell.

"Sort of!" Elinor yells back. "It also—"

She's cut off by the loud, long honk of a bullhorn.

"Greetings, my precious pupils!" Nadia sings from the opposite end of the hallway. "Sorry to disrupt your lessons, but it seems we have a small security breach!"

Elinor takes my hand. We've been moving through the crowd in a crooked line, so after I recover from the pleasant shock of her fingers in mine, I reach behind me and take Gabby's hand. She reaches behind her for Abe's, who pulls back but gives in when Gabby locks her eyes on his. He doesn't take Lemon's hand, but he does look over his shoulder to make sure our fire starter's still with us.

Then, like an impenetrable wall of Trouble, we push through the rest of the pack, reach the back door, and burst outside.

"This way!" Elinor releases my hand and runs.

We follow. As we hurry down a dark street, I try to e-mail GS George twice. But looking at the K-Pak screen throws off my feet, which automatically stumble over rocks and litter. So I wait until we stop.

At the Blackhole Fun Spot. Where, according to the rusty sign dangling over the entrance, a superfun, amazing time awaits the entire family.

"False advertising," Lemon says.

He's probably right. Because superfun, amazing times usually include smiling. Giggling. Laughing. But all I hear is moaning. Crying. Weeping.

"The arcade." Elinor points to the large building to our right. "That's the adults' sauna."

Despite the circumstances—and what I just witnessed in the IncrimiNation math class—this makes me smile. The closest Mom's come to a video game is the doorway of my bedroom. That's as far as she's willing to go to tell me it's time to turn it off and go to bed—a request that takes all of five seconds but still makes her cringe and cover her ears. Imagining her in a room filled with dozens of loud, beeping, ringing, dinging pinball and other assorted machines, especially after what she did, isn't exactly unpleasant.

"HALT!"

We're about to pass through a turnstile. At the command behind us, we freeze.

We don't have to look to see who's there.

Their stench gives them away.

Chapter 25

DEMERITS: 465
GOLD STARS: 300

Did he just say what I think he did?" Abe asks.

"Do you think he just said 'halt'?" Gabby asks. "Rhymes with salt? Malt? Faul—"

Abe looks at her.

"Yes," she says. "He did."

"Might us well give up now!" Mr. Bull bellows. "Save your energy! That bottomless pit you're headed for is *deep*!"

"Abe." I glance behind me. A large herd of messy misfits is running toward us, swinging sports equipment and lawn tools overhead. The dust cloud they kick up is so big, the road and buildings behind them disappear. "Forget it. It's not worth it."

"No way. This is ridiculous. They kill our helicopter. Then they kidnap us. And now they think they can—"

He stops. At first I think this is because Lemon takes him by the hood of his coat and tries to yank him through the turnstile. But then I notice his leg's stuck. And I realize it's because he almost lost a limb to one half of a pair of ancient hedge trimmers. The blade's wedged into the turnstile stand, two inches from his left shin.

"This way!" Elinor shouts. "Hurry!"

We do as she says. Or Lemon, Abe, and Gabby do. I'm last in line and the turnstile arm decides to lock when it's my turn. I shove it with both hands. Lean all my weight into it. Once. Twice. Three times. I throw another look over my shoulder, make accidental eye contact with a female IncrimiNator who then hurls an enormous bag of fertilizer my way, and duck under the arm. The delay costs me ten seconds—plus another three when the heavy sack hits the ground where I just stood.

In my last glance back, I note the unopened bag's weight.

Fifty pounds.

That would've hurt.

"Seamus!"

Darting in the direction of Elinor's voice, I pass through a small concrete courtyard filled with faceless clown statues, cracked penguin sculptures, and other former photo ops. The first door I reach is hanging by a hinge. Its glass is broken. Its sign is faded, but the words are still legible.

NOW ENTERING THE TRACK OF TERROR!

DRIVE CAREFULLY . . .

. . . OR DIE TRYING!

"There's one!" a male voice shouts.

I don't have to turn around to know the IncrimiNators have entered the courtyard. I smell them before I hear them.

I'm about to shoot through the doorway when my eyes catch something reflected in a shard of broken glass by my feet. It's a word. And after many trips to the old Cloudview Putt 'n' Play arcade with Dad, it's one I'm familiar with.

Skee-Ball.

As has been happening more and more lately, my mind quiets while my body shifts into autopilot. With the IncrimiNators quickly gaining ground, I turn and lunge toward a cardboard box.

Holding my breath, I rip open the flaps and find exactly what I'm hoping for.

A dozen heavy wooden balls. Perfect for rolling up a long, lit ramp and into a small hole.

Or for stalling your enemy.

I grab one ball, then another and another. I chuck, toss, and drop them. I'm careful not to throw too hard or aim higher than ankle height. These kids might be dangerous, but *I'm* not. I don't want to hurt anyone—and I don't have to. The balls collide with feet, making kids teeter, then topple. Most take down others while fighting to stay upright. I smile as more fall, thinking of how proud Ike would be to see this. When I'm down to the last two balls, I fire them at the two biggest feet of the bunch.

They belong to the child giant. Who stumbles. Flails his arms. Howls. And collapses backward, knocking out five IncrimiNators around him, who knock out at least twenty more around them. Soon the entire group is on its collective rear end.

"Bull's-eye," I whisper.

And then I run.

I find Elinor and Capital T at the Track of Terror. Or, more accurately, *on* the Track of Terror. In Go Karts. Wearing helmets and goggles.

"That's yours!" Elinor shouts over the buzz of motors.

I follow her nod to a brown toy car. "Where are we going?" I shout back.

"Who cares?" Abe yells. "Hop in, Hinkle!"

The only car I've ever driven was a virtual one, but I do as I'm told. My helmet and goggles are on the seat; I put them on and buckle up. I start to reach for the steering wheel when I remember one very important thing.

GS George. What good is getting out of here if he doesn't come back for us? After all, these aren't Kilter golf carts. There's no way they'll make it two thousand miles. At least not without encountering some serious obstacles along the way.

I hold up one finger to tell Elinor and my alliance-mates I'll just be a second. Then I take out my K-Pak, turn it on, and start typing. For speed's sake, I ignore every capitalization and punctuation rule I've ever learned.

TO: GSGEORGE@KILTERACADEMY.ORG
FROM: SHINKLE@KILTERACADEMY.ORG
SUBJECT: PLEASE COME BACK

HI GEORGE SORRY WE ARE LATE BUT HAVE ELINOR AND READY TO GO CAN YOU PLEASE PLEASE PLEASE COME BACK FOR US PLEASE MATTER OF LIFE AND DEATH STILL IN BLACKHOLE BUT SOON WILL BE JUST OUTSIDE LOOK FOR FLARE

PLEASE

THANK YOU

SEAMUS

I hit send, shove the K-Pak inside my coat, and press the green button next to the steering wheel. The Go Kart shakes and shudders, but eventually starts up. I thrust my right foot forward. It doesn't hit anything, so I try the left one. That doesn't hit anything either, so I shift in my seat and peer around the steering wheel. I see the pedals, which is good and bad.

Good because there *are* pedals.

Bad because I'm too short to reach them.

I slide forward until the steering wheel digs into my stomach. Stretch my foot and point my toes. It's no use.

Ahead of me, Elinor, Lemon, Abe, and Gabby line up in their

Go Karts. Behind me, the IncrimiNators grow closer.

I take out my K-Pak again. It's about five inches long. If I rest the top of it on the gas pedal, I should be able to tap its bottom with my foot. Then when I need to slow down I can just—

"Get in!"

I look up. Elinor left the line and is now parked next to me.

"I just remembered that one doesn't work! It starts fine, but it doesn't run! So get in mine!"

I wait for my body to switch back into autopilot so I can hop out of my Go Kart and into hers. Unfortunately, my head gets in the way. But who can blame it? For one thing, each Go Kart has only one seat. For another, with the dim track light shining above us and a light breeze making her hair float around her face, Elinor's never looked prettier. For another—

"Also, I think that one was custom built!"

"What?" I ask, even though I heard her perfectly.

"Your Go Kart! It's extra long! Probably because it's Shepherd Bull's!"

I check the fronts and backs of our toy cars. They line up evenly, which makes me want to slide down my seat until my head hits the pedals.

She knows I can't reach. And she's just being nice to try to save me from being even more embarrassed than I already am.

A roar sounds near the Track of Terror entrance. I jump—then use the momentum to launch out of my seat and into the small space between Elinor's headrest and the side of the car.

"Liar," I say.

"Thank you." She grins and punches the gas.

As far as speed goes, the Go Kart has nothing on Annika's golf cart. But for a rusty toy car, it has impressive pep. We breeze easily past Lemon, Abe, and Gabby. Elinor waves for them to follow. They do. As we race toward a gap in the track wall, I grip the headrest with one hand and the side of the car with the other. The ground's inches away, so if I fell off, I'd probably survive. . . . But why take a chance?

"Um, Elinor?" I ask as we near the hole in the wall, which seems to shrink the closer we get. "That doesn't look . . . Are you sure it's . . . I think it might be too—"

Narrow. That's what I would've said if I didn't lunge toward her and close my eyes instead.

"Wa*hoooooo*!"

I open my eyes. Sit up. Look over my shoulder.

We made it through. So did Abe, who's driving right behind us, pumping one fist in the air. Gabby follows with a squeal. Her hands clap as fast as a hummingbird's wings, then grab the steering wheel when the car hits a rock and swerves. I watch Lemon approach on the other side, and shake my head as he shoots forward. His car must be wider than the rest. There's no way he'll clear it. The sides will hit. He'll get stuck. The Incrimi-Nators will—

Not get him. Because he slips right through.

I smile. He presses his right pointer and middle fingers together, brings them to his forehead, and gives me a mini salute.

The Track of Terror must sit on the outskirts of Blackhole, because we reach the crater's edge in no time. I'm thinking our toy cars have zero chance of making it up the ninety-degree dirt wall when Elinor turns left and drives on a parallel path. I check our tail every five seconds, but no one's chasing us. Maybe these are the only Go Karts that still work.

"Pout!"

I turn back from my last check. "Pout?"

"Yes! Or frown, yell, rock back and forth, or punch my arm. Whatever makes you look really mad!"

The Go Kart slows slightly. I look up and see flashing lights. They're attached to an iron gate that sits to the right of an old crooked phone booth.

"Tell the others!" Elinor shouts. "Hurry!"

Abe's behind us. I wave for him to come closer before shouting Elinor's instructions as quietly as possible. He turns and shares them with Gabby, who shares them with Lemon. I feel bad when they all grimace and glare, but then I realize they're not unhappy with the orders. They're just following them.

By the time I face forward again, we're pulling up to the gate. A small sign's nailed to the top.

DARK HOLLOW CAVERN. ADMITTANCE BY NK PERMISSION ONLY.

ALL TRESPASSERS WILL BE PUNISHED. SEVERELY.

NK. Nadia Kilter.

The phone booth door screeches open. A kid steps out. He looks older than we are, maybe about Ike's age. He's wearing ripped black pants, a torn black T-shirt, and a baseball hat with DHC SECURITY scribbled across the front in black marker.

"What's up?" He nods to me. "Who's he?"

It takes me a second, but I frown. Rock back and forth. Ball my hands into fists and thump them against my legs. I feel ridiculous, but my performance must be convincing because he turns his attention to Elinor.

Who whistles. Grinds her teeth. Yawns. Spits. Whistles again. If it's possible to sound annoyed while making a bunch of random noises, she does.

The security guard nods. Grunts. Shakes his head.

And opens the gate.

We shoot through the entrance and into the cavern.

"What'd you tell him?" I yell once we're out of hearing range.

"That you all snuck bread and water to the adults! And Mother wanted me to escort you to Rock Bottom!"

"What's that?"

She glances at me. "You don't want to know. Trust me!"

I do. And it's a good thing, too. Because Dark Hollow Cavern lives up to its name. It's blacker than night inside. The Go Kart has headlights, but the dim yellow beams reach only two feet ahead. And it's definitely hollow, although the tunnel's height and width varies with every twist and turn. Glow-in-the-dark arrows indicate when to duck or move to one side, but you can't see them until the rock that's about to decapitate you is inches away. Despite these driving hazards, Elinor zips through the dark labyrinth, making me feel like a marble in a pinball machine.

Eventually, we zoom through another opening. This one leads out of the crater and into the wide-open desert.

I look over my shoulder. Abe, Gabby, and Lemon are right behind us. I grin and wave, then swivel around and check my K-Pak. There are no messages, but GS George probably turned back toward Blackhole the second he got my note. And it's probably impossible to man the controls and e-mail at the same time.

"There's an abandoned tire factory not too far from here!" Elinor shouts over the sound of tires crunching across dirt. "We can hide there until our ride comes!"

"Great!" For the first time since climbing in her car, I relax my grip on the headrest. "That was way easier than I thought it'd be!"

Then, as if they were just waiting for our defenses to lower, the army of misfits appears. This time I hear them before I smell them. They're screaming. Barking. Pounding something that, when I turn around, I see is the resurrected brown school bus. They hang out the windows, hammering the sides of the bus with brooms, shovels, hockey sticks, and fists. Some wave brown IncrimiNation flags. A few ride on the roof, jumping up and down and banging their chests.

And leading the pack from the driver's seat . . . is Mr. Bull.

I turn to Elinor. "Where'd they come from?"

"No idea!" She tightens her fingers around the steering wheel. Punches the gas. "There must be another way out I don't know about!"

Something hits my left arm. I grab it, thinking I've been shot, but my hand comes away dusty—not bloody. I look up and see Lemon driving next to us. His speeding tires must've sent dirt flying.

"What do we do?" he yells. Or rather, asks loudly. Because he's Lemon.

"We can't outrun them!" Abe shouts, pulling up next to Elinor's side of the car. "The bus might be old, but it can move!"

"Maybe we should split up!" Gabby calls out behind us. "To confuse them!"

"No way!" I call back. "Capital T sticks together!"

"Well, we need a plan!" Abe insists. "Because they clearly have one!"

Best-case scenario, their plan is to rekidnap us. Worst-case, it's to kill us. Either way, it's happening soon. Because the screaming and pounding is growing louder.

"How far to the factory?" I ask Elinor.

She glances over her shoulder. "Too far!"

"But what if we get there even a second before they do? Could we run and hide inside?"

She shakes her head. "If I know about it, Shepherd Bull definitely knows about it. He probably has every room and hallway memorized! They'd find us in no time!"

"What about—?"

Our Go Kart lunges sharply forward. I slip from my seat and thrust my hands against the tiny dashboard to keep from flying out.

"You okay?" I ask Elinor.

She slides back in the seat. Brushes her hair from her face. Nods. Floors the gas.

"Sorry!" Gabby yells. "They just hit me! And I hit you!"

I look back—then up. The front of the bus is about a foot from Gabby's rear bumper. Through the broken windshield, I see Mr. Bull laughing.

"We have to fight back!" I yell.

"How?" Abe demands. "We don't have any weapons!"

We're quiet for a second. Then Gabby shouts, "Sure we do!"

After which, a strange thing happens. The way my body's

been switching to autopilot lately anytime it's engaged in conflict? That's exactly what Capital T does.

First Gabby motions for Abe to pull his Go Kart next to hers. When he does, she kisses her stuffed unicorn, lodges it between the steering wheel shaft and the gas pedal so that the motor revs nonstop, and hops out of her toy car and onto Abe's. Her unmanned Go Kart flies to the right, making Shepherd Bull ease up on the gas and a half-dozen IncrimiNators leap to the ground and run after it. Next she waits for the front of the bus to come close again, then climbs on top and crawls up the hood to the broken windshield.

"What's she doing?" Elinor yells.

Something completely crazy and definitely dangerous—that still makes me smile. Mostly because I know she's having fun doing it. "Staring him down!"

Gabby's blocking my view, so I can't see Mr. Bull's expression. But it must work because several seconds later, the bus slows. Gabby scrambles to the front of the hood, waits for Abe to draw closer, and drops onto the back of his Go Kart. Abe speeds up, leaving the bus in his dust. Once they're far enough away, he motions for Gabby to take the steering wheel and for Lemon to drive next to him. Then, while the child giant shakes off his hypnosis, Abe pulls out his drawing pad, rips out page after page after page, and starts folding.

"What's he doing?" Elinor yells.

"Not sure!" I yell.

Abe says something to Lemon I don't quite catch. Lemon nods, reaches into his coat pocket, and removes his lighter. He holds it toward Abe. A flame appears. Abe holds a piece of paper over it. The paper catches.

Abe cups one hand around it and thrusts it at me.

I take it. When I do, I realize it's a paper airplane. One of dozens he's made in a matter of seconds.

I look at Elinor. "Can you drive parallel to the bus?"

I cup my hand around the flame to protect it from the wind. She swerves to the left and eases up on the gas until we're even with the back of the bus. Abe and Gabby drive next to us. Lemon drives on the other side of them.

The IncrimiNators are so busy screaming and beating their transportation they don't realize right away that we've moved. I take advantage of this head start and stand on my knees. Assess the situation. Eye potential targets. Just like I didn't want to hurt the misfits with Skee-Balls, I don't want to hurt them with fire. . . . But I do want to get them off the bus.

"The flags!" Elinor yells.

My head snaps toward her, then to the row of broken windows lining the side of the bus. Five kids fling around brown Incrimi-Nator flags. Unlike everything else associated with this dirty, strange place, the flags are shiny. Clean. Pristine.

"They're the only things Mother insists we take care of!" Elinor adds. "If anything happens to them, we're thrown in the pit for a week!"

Point taken. As the heat of the burning paper airplane nears my pointer finger and thumb, I pull back my arm. Aim. And fire.

I get a direct hit. Abe holds another paper airplane toward Lemon, who lights it. Abe gives me the flaming flyer. Elinor hits the gas until we're even with the next flag. I get that one too. And the next one and the next one and the next one. When we run out of targets on this side, we loop around to the other side and start again.

The reactions are even better than I could've hoped. As soon as the kids see flames, they shriek. They wave the flags, smack them against the side of the bus, pull them inside, and beat them against seats. The IncrimiNators who aren't holding flags drop their garden tools and sports equipment to help others extinguish. The material must be flammable, because the flames grow taller. The smoke thicker. Soon the IncrimiNators start giving up. Desperate for fresh air, some climb out of the windows and pull themselves up onto the roof. Others dangle from the windows until their arms grow tired. Then they let go, dropping to and rolling across the ground.

To his credit, Mr. Bull holds on a while. He keeps driving even when he starts coughing. But then his coughing turns to hacking. Then choking. Eventually he throws open the door and flings himself down the steps while the vehicle's still in motion. He lands face-first on the ground, flops over onto his back, and gasps for air. Any IncrimiNators still on board join him.

The bus rolls several more yards. Then it bumps into a cactus. And stops.

To *our* credit, we don't celebrate. Not right away. We wait until we've put about a mile between us and the fallen IncrimiNators. And the fire inside the bus reaches the gas tank, the bus explodes, and the black sky turns gold. And a loud whooshing starts in the distance, then comes closer.

We even wait until a scraped, dented, wobbly helicopter appears. And GS George sends down a chain ladder. And we scramble up and inside.

Only then, falling onto the couches, do we finally release a collective sigh.

"That's some flare," our pilot calls from the cockpit as we swoop away from the burning bus.

"Go big or go home!" Abe calls back.

Completely exhausted yet somehow more awake than I've ever been, I smile at him. Lemon. Gabby.

Elinor.

"Let's go home," I say. "To Kilter."

Chapter 26

DEMERITS: 2500
GOLD STARS: 300

You knock."

"No, you knock."

"I can't knock. I don't know what's behind that door. The second we step inside, everything could change. We might get expelled. As in kicked out. Then I'll have to go back to straight A-plusses and extra credit and giving out rice cakes on Halloween and—"

Lemon holds up one hand. Gabby stops rambling. Abe looks relieved. Lemon curls his fingers to his palm, presses his thumb to his pointer finger, and reaches forward. He taps the door once, then turns the knob, and pushes.

"SURPRISE!"

Abe, Gabby, Elinor, and I jump. Lemon slides his hands into his coat pockets.

"If this is what getting expelled looks like," Abe whispers, "we should do it more often."

I know what he means. Instead of landing on the Kommissary roof when we got back to Kilter, we landed in Annika's backyard. GS George told us en route that while we were rescuing Elinor he e-mailed his boss and informed her of our whereabouts because there was no use trying to hide it. The helicopter still flew, but it was so banged up she'd know it had been somewhere it shouldn't have been. And since, until last night, she was the only one who used the chopper, that would mean it had been stolen. GS George thought coming clean was the only chance he had of saving his job.

Annika's response contained a single order: to bring us to the conference room in her house the second we got back. That was all she said, so I figured she was furious. I expected to find her waiting inside the conference room with our packed suitcases. And possibly our parents, come to bring us home. *Home* home. Not Kilter home.

As it turns out, Annika is waiting in the conference room. But she's not with our suitcases and parents. She's with Houdini. Wyatt. Fern. Samara. Lizzie. Devin. Mr. Tempest. Ike. With the exception of Mystery, who stands at the back of the group picking his teeth, they all clap and cheer after yelling their initial greeting. Silver streamers hang from the ceiling. Bunches of silver balloons bob throughout the room. The long table's sprinkled with silver glitter and covered in platters of fish sticks and my alliance-mates' favorite snacks. Champagne flutes surround big glass bowls filled with hot chocolate and sparkling apple cider.

It's a party. Though for what, I'm not sure.

"*Look* at them!" Annika sings, hurrying toward us with arms outstretched. "Back from the battlefield and cuter than ever!"

She gives each of us a quick, tight hug. Even Elinor, who catches my eye when it's her turn. Then Annika takes a champagne flute from the table, fills it with sparkling cider, and turns toward us.

"No one in Kilter Academy's illustrious history has ever done what you four did last night. There are too many achievements to recount them all now, but among the most notable are stealing a school helicopter in the middle of the night. Convincing a Good Samaritan to act as pilot. Traveling across the country.

Rescuing a classmate from a difficult, somewhat dangerous situation. Returning here safely—and before breakfast." She pauses. Smiles. "After you successfully completed the Ultimate Troublemaking Task last semester, I knew you were talented. But I didn't realize until this morning that you were extraordinary."

Abe and Gabby grin. Lemon lets one corner of his mouth lift. Elinor frowns. Still unsure of the situation, I shoot for a neutral expression.

Annika raises her glass. Our teachers quickly take theirs from the table, fill them, and join the toast.

"To the most promising Troublemakers we've ever had the privilege of training!" Annika declares. "Thank you for making our jobs so enjoyable."

The faculty bursts into a chorus of "Hear, hear!"

"You must be starving," Annika says once they've sipped and quieted down. "Please help yourselves."

Abe and Gabby rush to the table. Lemon saunters after them, Elinor trails him, and I follow her. I'm so busy processing everything I can't tell if I'm hungry, but I take a plate and fill it with fish sticks anyway.

"Nice work, Hinkle." Houdini claps me on the back.

"Thanks." I force a smile.

Other teachers offer congratulations. Some let Capital T and Elinor get food, then form a loose circle around them and start firing questions. Abe and Gabby seem more than happy to do most of the answering. Fern, the gym teacher, gently pulls Elinor to the side and asks how she is, if there's anything she needs. Before I can hear Elinor's response, there's a tap on my shoulder.

I turn around. "Ike. Hi." When I smile this time, I mean it.

"Hey. Can I talk to you for a second?"

We go to a corner of the room.

"First," he says quietly, "wow. I don't even know what else to say about what you just did. I'm beyond impressed—and I want to hear all about it at our next session."

"You got it. And thanks for agreeing to help. I wouldn't have felt okay going if you didn't have our backs."

"No problem." He takes out his K-Pak. "And speaking of help . . . Know how you said to watch the faculty? And let you know if anything seemed strange?"

Out of the corner of my eye, I see Mystery use one hand to swipe glitter across the table and into the palm of his other hand. He dumps the sparkles into his coat pocket, then swipes some more.

"Yes," I say.

"Well, you left at night and weren't gone that long, so most of our teachers slept the whole time. Nothing strange there. But I got hungry while keeping tabs, so I stopped by the Kanteen for a late-night snack. And who was there loading up on candy at the ice cream bar?"

"Mr. Tempest?"

"The one and only. I wouldn't have thought anything of it except he wasn't making a sundae. He wasn't even filling his pockets with sweet treats for later, the way some kids do. He was filling bags—big ones. Like a backpack. A duffel bag. A suitcase on wheels."

"That's a lot of candy."

"That's what I thought. Which is why I followed him. Here."

He holds out his K-Pak so I can see the screen. There's a photo. Of a pink house. With purple shutters. White window boxes filled with yellow flowers. A white bench swing filled with dolls and stuffed animals. And lining the roof, eaves, door, and chimney—candy. Gumdrops. Licorice. Peppermints. Lollipops. In every color of the rainbow.

"Did Hansel and Gretel answer when you rang the bell?" I ask.

"I didn't want to get that close. Because the house—which is more like a cottage—is in the middle of nowhere. In the woods."

And then I see it. Thanks to the colorful additions and some new construction, they look nothing alike. . . . But the house in the picture is the same one I followed Mystery to. The one where I was almost axed to death.

"Weird, right?" Ike asks.

"Very."

Before I can add anything else, I catch something Abe says to some of our teachers.

"But this place? IncrimiNation? Oh, man. Talk about insane. For example—"

He's cut off by a sharp clanking.

"One more thing!" Annika declares, tapping her glass with a fork to get everyone's attention. "After everything they just accomplished, we can't let our Troublemakers return to their house empty-handed. They'll each receive more demerits than any student ever has for a single task . . . *and* one of these!"

The wall screen that displayed a map of the United States the last time I was here illuminates behind her. A picture of a super-sleek silver golf cart appears.

"That's the Kilter Kart 5000," Abe says, eyes wide.

"Indeed it is," Annika says. "Would you like a closer look?"

He nods. So do Gabby and Lemon.

"Great. They're in the driveway. GS George will take you."

"Now?" Gabby asks.

"Now," Annika says.

They drop their plates and bolt toward the door. Our teachers, including Mystery, follow. Ike does too. I start after them but am stopped by another tap on the shoulder.

"I'd love a moment," Annika says. "If you don't mind."

Besides us, Elinor's the only other person in the room. She's standing by the door. Our eyes meet. As if wanting to prevent some secret silent communication, Annika steps between us.

"Elinor, please ask Fern to take you to the administration building for paperwork. I'll meet you there in a bit."

Elinor looks at me. I nod. She leaves.

Annika closes the door and faces me. The smile she's worn since our arrival disappears.

"Seamus, Seamus, Seamus."

Happy thoughts, happy thoughts, happy thoughts.

"You've put me in an interesting position."

Normally, I'd automatically apologize. But for perhaps the first time ever, I'm not sorry for doing something that displeased an adult.

"Do you know why?" Annika asks.

"Because I stole a helicopter? And convinced GS George to fly across the country? And everything else you just mentioned?"

"Not quite. I called those achievements, and most of them were."

"Which ones weren't?"

"Not ones. One." She pulls out a clear high-backed chair at one end of the table. Sits. "You kidnapped Elinor."

"Not kidnapped. Rescued."

"Why split hairs? The important thing is that she was sent away. By me. And you brought her back. Without asking permission or even why she was shipped off in the first place. You're an extraordinary Troublemaker, Seamus. . . . But you don't know everything. Not by a long shot. And you'd be wise not to act like you do."

"Maybe I'd know more if I hacked into other people's K-Mail accounts."

Then, realizing my autopilot just kicked in yet again, I clamp one hand over my mouth. Annika stares at me.

"How do you know about that?" she asks quietly.

Keeping my hand over my mouth, I shake my head.

She narrows her eyes. Studies me for several seconds. Points to the high-backed chair at the opposite end of the table. I cross the room and sit down.

"You don't trust me."

I release my mouth. "It's not that I—"

"It wasn't a question. I see it in your eyes." She sits back, clasps her hands in her lap. "What do you say we clear the air?"

I pause. "What do you mean?"

"I mean you're uncertain—probably of Kilter, definitely of me. So ask me anything you want. Right now. No extra assignments required."

This sounds like a trick. But at this point, what do I have to lose?

I sit back, clasp my hands in my lap. "Why did you hack my K-Mail? And Elinor's?"

"By leaps and bounds you're the most promising student I've ever seen. As director, it's my responsibility to make sure you stay focused and on the right path. So you can reach your maximum potential. In order to do that, I need to know about potential distractions. Since Elinor's chief among those, I need to stay on top of her, too."

"Is that why you sent her away? Because you thought she was distracting me?"

"Partially."

"Why else?"

"She failed assignments, refused to try, and rarely engaged in any part of the Kilter curriculum. I would've expunged any other student who behaved the same way much sooner. Also, her mother runs IncrimiNation, which, as you learned, is the devil's satellite den. I thought spending time there would help her better appreciate her time here."

"Why'd she come to Kilter in the first place?"

"Because her mother didn't want her." She lets this sink in. Which it does. Like a boulder to my stomach. "Despite what you may think, my heart's not completely made of stone. I took pity on her and brought her here."

One thought and one image come to mind. The thought is that Annika's cool tone doesn't match her supposedly warm heart. The image is of Elinor alone on Parents' Day last semester.

"Then why are you so mean to her?" I ask.

Annika blinks. "Mean?"

"You hardly talked to her last semester. When you did, you yelled. And then when she was hurt during the Ultimate Trouble-making Task, you didn't even seem to care."

"If someone doesn't appreciate my generosity enough to do the minimum that's expected in return, I'm not about to bend over backwards until she does." Annika shrugs. "As for her injury, I'd seen worse. And no one—not you, me, Elinor, or anyone else—can learn how to deal with pain until they've experienced it firsthand. In that respect, I did her a favor."

I don't know what to say to that. So I shift gears instead.

"What does IncrimiNation do?" I know what I saw, but I want to hear what she says.

"According to my sister, it creates Troublemakers. According to me, it creates juvenile delinquents with atrocious personal hygiene."

"Why don't you and Nadia work together?"

"Clearly, we have very different educational philosophies. Plus, we don't get along. We never have."

The questions dip and swirl through my head like lightning bugs in a jar. With so many to choose from, it's hard to ask them in an orderly fashion. What matters, though, is that they're asked at all. So I try not to think too hard, and just keep going.

"Did you ask me to follow Mr. Tempest to keep me busy? And distract me from other distractions?"

"No. I really wanted help monitoring him. Though distraction from distraction was a nice bonus."

"How come my real-world combat mission was so different from Lemon's, Abe's, and Gabby's?"

"Because your alliance-mates are good on their own, but they're only great when working with you. I though you could handle more faster. And I was right."

"What I did then, helping that little girl who was locked up by her mom—is that what we're training for? To be able to make trouble that will help other kids with mean parents?"

Annika reaches for a champagne flute, takes a long sip, and smacks her lips. "Yes."

"Is that why you want to expand the program? To train more Troublemakers who can help more kids?"

She takes another sip. "Yes."

"And you think because I'm so talented, or whatever, that I can eventually be extra helpful?"

"I don't think. I know. With one thousand percent certainty."

I consider this. It doesn't sound too bad. In fact, after what happened with my mom, it's almost admirable.

Which reminds me.

"How does someone outside of Kilter get Kilter weapons?"

"They don't."

"Yes, they do. My mom did."

Her head tilts. The glass starts to slip from her grasp. She catches it and puts it on the table. "Pardon?"

"When I was home. Over Christmas. My mom gave me tons of weapons—like the Icickler, Knight-Vision Goggles, and Kringle Stars—and had tons more hidden in the attic."

I wouldn't believe it if I didn't see it, but the blood actually leaves Annika's face. Her skin turns as white as snow.

"Seamus, I assure you I have no idea how your mother acquired those weapons. And I *will* get to the bottom of it."

Huh. This sounds like potential bad news for Mom. And for some reason, that makes me wish I'd picked a different lightning bug.

"Now may I ask you a few questions?"

If it means changing the subject. "Sure."

Annika sits up. Rests her elbows on the table. Leans toward me. "Do you want to be here?"

"At Kilter?"

She nods.

"Yes." Autopilot.

"What kind of insurance do you need?" I must look confused because she adds, "More fish sticks? Your own house? Kommissary loan privileges?"

Ah. She wants to know what she can bribe me with that will keep me from changing my mind and jumping ship. I've never given it thought, but several things come to mind immediately.

"I want GS George to keep his job."

"Done."

"And Elinor to be allowed to stay and be treated fairly."

"Fine."

"And Ike to have any troublemaking position he wants when he graduates."

"Okay."

"And Ms. Marla to have an unlimited supply of free pet food for Rodolfo."

"Strange, but doable."

"And you to give up access to every K-Mail account but your own."

She hesitates, then takes her K-Pak from the table and starts typing. "As long as we keep one another in the loop, I shouldn't need access to anyone else's K-Mail. So, sure. And done." She puts down her K-Pak. "Anything else?"

Yes. I need her not to change her mind and throw me out once she learns I'm not who she thinks I am.

The autopilot keeps this last one quiet. Before I can decide whether to force it, Annika says, "Well, I need insurance too. Not much, but some."

"Like what?"

"The faculty and staff don't know about IncrimiNation. Just like I want you to stay focused, I want the same for them. They're excellent teachers, and we can't afford to lose them should curiosity encourage the pursuit of other opportunities. Can you keep what you just witnessed to yourself? And make sure your friends do the same?"

I can't imagine Houdini, Fern, Samara, or any of my other teachers willingly signing up for a career in such chaos, but I agree anyway. Besides, right now I don't really want to talk about what I just witnessed.

"Fantastic." Annika smiles. Holds out one hand. "Do we have a deal?"

I look at her hand. Think about it. I'm still twiddling my thumbs when there's a knock on the door.

"Ah, Annika?" GS George calls out. "We have a bit of a . . . situation? Outside? With one of the Kilter Karts? It's kind of stuck at a hundred miles per hour—with Abe inside."

Annika jumps up. "Don't go anywhere."

"I won't. Promise."

There's that word again.

Annika leaves. My K-Pak buzzes. I take the mini computer from my backpack and open the new message.

TO: parsippany@cloudviewschools.net
FROM: shinkle@kilteracademy.org
SUBJECT: You, the Person

Dear Seamus,

What do you do when the person your parents want you to be isn't who YOU want to be? That's an excellent question. When you find out the answer, let me know.

In the meantime, it might help to remember that our parents were once kids themselves. Whenever

I'm unhappy with my mom or dad, I always picture them half as tall with freckles, braces, and only their stuffed animals for company. And that makes it much easier to get past any anger, hurt, or frustration I might be feeling. At least for a little while.

That said, DO you know the person you want to be? If so, do you have any tips for figuring it out? Because I'm thirty years old . . . and I'm still not sure.

I look forward to hearing from you soon.

With kind regards,

Miss Parsippany

I close the note. Put my K-Pak in my backpack. Take it out when it buzzes again.

No new messages. I exit K-Mail, then open it again. Still nothing.

That's strange. I definitely heard buzzing.

Autopilot raises my eyes to the far end of the table . . . where Annika's K-Pak sits unattended.

I shouldn't look. I *know* I shouldn't look. But she just said she took away her access to other accounts. Was she lying? In the midst of clearing the air?

If this is going to work, I have to know. So I stand up. Tiptoe down the side of the table. And press the flashing digital envelope on Annika's K-Pak screen.

As it turns out, Miss Parsippany's note didn't reach Annika's computer.

But another one did.

TO: annika@kilteracademy.org
FROM: taxmannumerouno@taxmannumerouno.com
SUBJECT: My Son, Seamus Hinkle

Dear Ms. Kilter,

Hello. How are you? I hope the spring semester is off to a lovely start.

I hope you don't mind my writing. To be honest, I've been going back and forth about whether I should ever since my son, Seamus Hinkle, returned to Kilter last month. In the end, I decided I must. It's in everyone's best interests, but especially Seamus's.

You see, you kindly accepted my son late last semester upon learning he accidentally (supposedly) killed his substitute teacher with an apple in the school cafeteria. I was so elated by this acceptance, I sent him off without waiting for official confirmation of his teacher's passing. Since then, I've learned that, unfortunately, the teacher survived. Which means, unfortunately, that Seamus is not a murderer.

If I know my son, and I think I do, he's already shared this information with you. It didn't sit well with him when he learned the truth himself while home for the holidays, and I'm sure he wouldn't feel right continuing at Kilter under false pretenses. That'd be like cheating on a final exam, which, also unfortunately, isn't something Seamus would do.

I expect this news will likely affect your estimation of my son's Troublemaking qualifications. I understand, but I ask—no, I beg—you to keep in mind all of his recent accomplishments. Seamus might not be a natural-born Troublemaker, but he's a fast learner. And I know he has what it takes to succeed at Kilter.

Also, he can't come home. For lots of reasons,

> but mostly because we've given away his room. To another talented young man named Bartholomew John Baker. Perhaps you've heard of him?
>
> Thank you in advance for your time and consideration.
>
> With great respect and admiration,
>
> Judith Hinkle

I look up. White spots swirl across my vision. I close my eyes. Open them. Close them. The spots multiply. I try to replace them with images of Mom, Dad, and Annika as kids, but instead I see Lemon. Abe. Gabby. Elinor. Even little Molly Lubbard of Hoyt, Kentucky.

Who do I want to be? The jury's still out on that one. But I have a pretty good idea of who I *don't* want to be.

The kind of person who lets any bully, young or old, walk all over him, pick him up, and throw him back down for someone else to do the same.

Which is why I close Mom's e-mail. Delete it from Annika's K-Mail account.

And join my friends outside.